SUSAN PENHALIGON is
known for her film and televisio
Pru in *A Bouquet of Barbed Wi*
Fine Romance. During 2006 sh
Hope in *Emmerdale*.

Her TV appearances include *Doctor Who*, *Upstairs Downstairs*, *Remmington Steele*, a BBC production of *Dracula* and a part in Inspector Wycliffe filmed in her beloved Cornwall. She played a leading role in Stan Barstow's *A Kind of Loving* and the lead in Fay Weldon's series *Heart of the Country* for BBC 2 and most recently has appeared in *Casualty*, *Doctors* and *A Touch of Frost*.

Her films include the cult thriller, *Patrick* and Paul Verhoven's *Survival Run*. She starred in *The Land that Time Forgot* and was the heroine in the film of the Mills and Boon story *Leopard in the Snow*.

She has worked many times in the theatre. In the West End she has appeared in *Three Sisters*, *Dangerous Corner*, *Of Mice and Men*, *The Mysterious Mr Love* and Tom Stoppard's *The Real Thing*.

Her many tours include *The Constant Wife* by Somerset Maugham and *Lord Arthur Savile's Crime* by Oscar Wilde. At the West Yorkshire Playhouse she appeared in Arthur Miller's *Broken Glass* and at the Manchester Royal Exchange Theatre she was in *Time and the Conways* by JB Priestley, *The Cherry Orchard* and *Lower Depths* by Gorky.

She is proud to come from a Cornish family and her formative years were spent living in St Ives among the St Ives colony of artists. She feels the combination of her Celtic roots and the freedom of a bohemian childhood has greatly influenced her life and work. She lives happily on a house boat on the Thames in London and has one son Truan Munro who is a film director.

This is her first novel.

ISBN 978 185022 222 4

Published by Truran, Croft Prince, Mount Hawke,
Truro, Cornwall TR4 8EE
www.truranbooks.co.uk

Truran is an imprint of Truran Books Ltd

First published 2008 © Susan Penhaligon

Cover image © Carte de Visite
by Polkinghorne of Camborne, circa 1870.
From the Quick Album: Penlee House Gallery and
Museum Collection, Penzance

Printed in Cornwall by Rowe the Printers, Hayle

For the Love of Angel

For Andrea

Before

She remembered when it all began. The first sight of him. His tall figure stood out from the usual Cornishman in Boscawan Street. His smile and black moustache. From their first meeting they knew they wanted each other. The difficulty was sneaking time with him. He was easy to spot being a foreigner. His flamboyant dress and high heeled boots marked him out for gossip. Truro could be suffocating if the wind missed the valley and only blew through the dense woods that dressed the green hills. It made the atmosphere claustrophobic. They looked on a Cuban in their midst with irony, the town had encouraged the diversity of the Empire's trade down its wide river for centuries. But it was the incomers who were expected to change, not the Cornish and acceptance took a long time. He would never have made it. Of course if her husband found out it would be the end of them. So they met once a month. Timed with her menstrual cycle. It was important. She didn't want to fall. Their affair lasted a year and in that time they had a passion that raised her spirits and kept her sane in the dark house where she lived.

He left when the rain started. It rained for days and people watched the sky fearfully. They walked with webbed feet, breathing water through their gills and baring gifts to

Neptune. A sudden cloudburst could cause the two rivers running through the town to grow in fury and if the water pouring down the streets met a spring tide ripping up the estuary, it was disaster. When the floods came, lives were lost and businesses were ruined. Her life was ruined anyway. At least she had Angel.

1

Flo's nightmares were recurring and tonight she was there again, walking across the landing in the house. Or was it towards the river? She heard shouts. A woman's scream for help sent a cold fear through her body. Her stomach knotted as the blood pumped through her heart willing her to go on. A door. But she couldn't push it open. A great energy was leaning on it from the other side. She could see the light seeping onto her feet showing the dust trapped in the floorboards that should have been swept clean by Nan. The light changed. It became a pool of light on the river thrown by a gas lamp on the bank. There was something in the water, a shape moving in the darkness. She knew if she moved towards the light it would reveal itself. Just one step that was all it would take. But she woke, her nightdress sticking to the small of her back. She lay motionless allowing the terror to recede into the darkness. She listened to the house creaking, the rain barely touching the windows and her father shutting his wardrobe in his bedroom. Outside she knew a thick, grey cloud would be so near to earth you could reach up and grab it. The perpetual Cornish mizzle. However much you wrapped up it found a way to penetrate your skin until the dampness became part of you. Flo breathed in the liquid air as her dream became a memory filed away with the others. One day the pieces would fit.

Her nightmare was still clinging to her clothes when she woke Angel. Their father was not up which was surprising. To be free to leave the house without his warnings. What relief. Visitors were already packing the streets and gawping at the sights. And why not? Boscawen Street was a riot of colour. Gill's the draper, a forest of evergreens. And not to be out done Messrs Andrews and Co. had 'God Bless the Prince of Wales' in large letters over their shop awnings. The Royal Hotel had a glittering star high on top of the building and it seemed to Angel as they passed to be sending out silver streamers like the star over Bethlehem.

'Tell me again, Flo? The king will be here?' said Angel, her perfect face turned to her sister.

'It's the Prince of Wales, the Duke of Cornwall.'

'Does he belong to us?'

Flo laughed, 'Not quite. He's coming to lay the foundation stone for our new cathedral. Truro is to be a city.'

Angel was nonplussed. The word city meant nothing to her. She felt slightly put out.

'But will the elephants be here?'

'Don't you worry. This afternoon is the circus procession,' said Flo as they walked over Old Bridge, 'and many other events.'

On the other side of the bridge workmen were erecting a huge archway with pulleys and ropes, shouting to each other as the wooden beam swung over the top of the supporting pillars. They slotted the last piece in place with a slow precision to reveal 'Welcome' written in gold letters across the front. Angel's mouth was a round o of amazement.

'Can we see the rest of it Flo? Are there more arches?'

'Lots of them. We'll see it all later. Come on with you.'

She picked her up and put her on her hip. Angel was safe with Florence, her five years of life protected.

When they reached the fields by the river bank the little girl wriggled down and charged up the grass to find cow parsley watched by wary sheep. She stretched out her arms and yelled feeling the damp breeze on her face.

'Be careful,' her sister called, 'you'll fall.' But Angel was already tugging at a plant.

'This one is still joined to the world, Flo.'

Together they pulled until the roots gave way and they toppled backwards.

'Whoops,' said Flo brushing twigs and earth from her skirt.

'Whoops,' copied Angel.

Flo hugged her. 'Shall we send messages?'

The river was tranquil today. The brown banks etched with a black line dividing the sloping woods from the iridescent water. Herons idly beaked at the edge. Sometimes when the wind blew the smell of salt carried up stream and they could taste the sharpness of the ocean. The sea was never far away. It was born within you if you came from Cornwall. A small cargo boat appeared around the bend from Malpas. They heard the sailors' calls as they picked their way across flat stones and outcrops of kelp to a solid patch of sandy shore.

Flo bent the stalk of a leaf trapping it in the opposite end and handed it to Angel.

'I shall make a wish, Flo.'

She squatted down and shut her eyes.

'I wish I could remember Mama.'

Flo stroked her sister's hair. Angel had been a few months

old when their mother died. She had no memory of her. For Flo it was different. The shock had been immense. The drama of the fatal evening had been erased from her consciousness as if she had woken from a coma. It was the beginning of her nightmares.

'She is in heaven now and she will be watching you.'

Flo had said this so many times it had become meaningless. The small girl looked serious for a moment as if it was expected of her and then her face became triumphant. She pushed the leaf into the water.

'Mine will get there first.' It shot downstream taken by the strong current and Angel clambered from stone to stone following its progress.

The boat was nearer now. Flo could see the coils of rope curled neatly on the deck. It was empty of cargo and sat high in the water. At the bow a bearded man stared ahead, his eyes set as if he had the horizon tattooed on his forehead. She had seen it in fishermen's faces many times. The shifting, rocking sea steadied by a man's gaze so the land could only be encompassed by a pint of ale.

She patted a strand of hair behind her ears as gulls swooped on thermals, shrieking the arrival of another boat laden with fish. Angel was now playing in the mud and was covered in it. They had to go home or their father would be angry with them. And they didn't want him to be angry.

2

Nan reached the downstairs entrance of the tall house on Lemon Street and closed the door. The smell of polish filled her nostrils. Everything shone like amber. The twisted newel posts, the Chippendale music stool, the feet of the Maple Mogadore gent's chair and the mantelpiece over the fireplace in Mr Trevern's study. There was so much she could never dream of owning.

She climbed the stairs to the kitchen, warm from the night time range and went into the parlour to fetch eggs. He would be having his usual. Fried eggs, hog's pudding and a bit of bacon. Mr Trevern liked his eggs, just so. Like his appearance. His shirts had to be starched whiter than a swan's feather. His shoes a perfect mirror. These things mattered for his position in town as owner of the best photographic studio for weddings and portraits. And more importantly as a major shareholder of the China Clay Company. The Treverns weren't gentry, they were trade. But he had the world by the ass, thought Nan. His girls had everything they needed. Although it wasn't right the way he watched over Flo and Angel. He rarely let them out of his sight.

She cracked two eggs in the lard frothing in the pan. There was a lot to do today. They had to make bouquets for the front door. Mr Trevern would want the house to look the best in the street. And Angel's outfit had to be ironed for the photograph.

The bacon was sizzling as Flo and Angel appeared at the kitchen door.

'We've got lots. Look, Nan!' said Angel.

'They are fine my handsome.' She flipped the hog's pudding to seal the blood and stuffing of it. 'Come over here and wash those hands. You're proper dirty.'

Nan put the breakfast in the oven while Angel dumped the bundle of flowers on the table and went over to be scrubbed.

Flo picked up a wild orchid and placed it against a fern. She noticed the contrast of shapes and colours and it pleased her. The way the crisp green leaf unravelled and formed a background to the orchid, the colour of a horse's eye. She longed to be able to photograph the patterns. Photograph them from different angles. View an ordinary object with new eyes. She knew she had a gift for seeing things. The way light filtered through the trees and speckled the ground, how darkness was never black but many hues of grey. With her hands she would frame a picture of the hens in the back yard as they listened to her father calling, their heads cocked on one side. If only she could set up a camera in these every day places the pictures she could make! But her father would dismiss her ideas. He was happy to paint a background of hills and fences onto a canvas and place the clients against it. She knew there was another way to do a portrait.

'How big is an elephant, Flo?' said Angel as she joined Flo at the table.

'A full grown one is as high as this room.'

Angel's jaw dropped.

'And,' said Nan, 'it could trample you down with one foot.'

Angel made a sound of fear and joy.

'And what's more,' added Nan 'they make a noise like...'

She stopped mid sentence as Mr Trevern came into the kitchen still in his dressing gown.

'You're back, thank the Lord.'

He smiled indulgently at Angel and touched her head.

'Will the Princess like these?' Angel asked holding up a crumpled flower.

'She will, my cherub, she will.'

He kissed his youngest and touched a spray of honeysuckle, his blemished hands showing the years of mixing chemicals.

'Your mother loved this.'

Flo watched him closely, gauging his mood. She wanted to ask a question but she had to choose her moment. For some reason today he seemed more approachable.

'Papa, for the reception, I was wondering if I could wear Mother's pink dress? I know she would have wanted me to look my best and I have nothing that is suitable.'

'Are you mocking me, maid?'

She had made a mistake. There was an embarrassed silence broken only by Angel's boots scuffing her chair.

'I'm sorry, Father.'

Mr Trevern barely moved. He tried to prevent the anger mounting inside him. His favourite child was here. Control, control.

'No one must touch your mother's things. Do you understand? No one!' He tried not to shout and the emotion gagged on his teeth flaming his cheeks.

Nan lowered her eyes, her wreath of flowers on her lap. He stared at her. Wretched girl, why was she always there to witness his outbursts? How often did she gossip and tell the private story of the Trevern household. Damn her.

He stormed out of the kitchen and up to his bedroom, locking the door behind him. He had a pounding headache as usual and he poured some quinine tonic into a glass before knocking it back. He returned the glass beside a bowl of water on a small table and caught sight of himself in his shaving mirror. His ginger-flecked hair stuck up in different directions like cactus spikes. Usually by now he had combed it over to hide the bald patch, trimmed his beard to square the jaw line of his round face, eaten breakfast and arrived immaculate at the studio.

The pink dress Flo had asked for lay on the bed. He had chosen it earlier, before dawn highlighted the gap in his thick curtains. Sometimes it helped. If nothing else, he imagined his wife's scent was still there, trapped in the folds. He had placed it carefully on the bed, the gathered lace top on the pillow, the skirt flowing over the eiderdown and lowered himself onto it, pushing and grinding his crotch, the silk slipping through his fingers as he strained with effort. After a few minutes he had banged the pillow with frustration. There was nothing. As if he had been severed at the waist. All hope of satisfaction gone. Like she was. He knew what he was doing was wrong. He was sure it was a sin. But he couldn't stop. As long as her dresses sprang from the wardrobe needing his comforting touch, as long as she tormented his nights, he kept trying. God help me, he thought. He picked up a framed photo of Isabella. Angel was the image of her mother. He sank to his knees.

'Dear God, I pray for the soul of my dead wife and for my daughters, for their safety in a world full of demons and I pray especially for my Angel, she is my only love in these long and lonely days. Look down on my family with kindness, so that they may be spared the everlasting pain of hell. And Lord, I must show more kindness to Florence. Amen.'

Mrs Curnow chatted nervously as Mr Trevern surveyed the dress shop, Angel by his side. Behind the curtains Flo was shown a blue and white evening gown. She could not believe she was there. Her father had suddenly said, 'Come on then, down with 'ee to Mrs Curnow's.'

Finally she realised he meant it and she wanted to get it done quickly in case he changed his mind. If only the woman would lace her up faster. She felt herself going red as the corset was pulled tighter to make an hourglass of her figure. Mrs Curnow slipped the dress over her head and adjusted the skirts before she made an entrance.

''Tis handsome, sir, she was born to wear it,' she announced in her best sales manner. And then she added, 'It was for another maid but unfortunately they moved away.'

'It looks fair to middling to me Mrs Curnow.' Mr Trevern picked a thread of cotton from his check suit.

'No, Father,' said Flo, her distrust making her blush even more, 'it is handsome and I like it very much'

Angel rushed over to Flo and grabbed at the dress, 'I want it. Can I have it Papa?'

'You've got yours,' said her sister gently pushing her away.

'Now there's a child who knows her mind. Come here, come to me.'

Mr Trevern held out his arms and Angel dragged her feet towards him. He lifted her on to his lap.

'You haven't got this dress, but you know what you do have?'

'No, Papa.'

'You've got me.' He tickled her as she squirmed and giggled.

Flo watched their closeness. Aware of her father's hands touching Angel's waist, the pleasure in his face as he buried his head to blow in her neck. He looked up at his eldest daughter and for a moment seemed found out like a child caught in the corner of a garden with a mouthful of dirt. He quickly let her go.

'Pack it up for us, Mrs Curnow, before I change my mind.'

'Thank you, Father.'

'What am I?'

'You're a good father.'

'I'm a good father and don't you forget it.'

Mr Trevern reached inside his coat for his wallet.

'And I hope the evening is a proper job Mr Trevern,' said Mrs Curnow pushing Flo back behind the curtains, 'it's not all of us that's been invited.'

'You're right there, Mrs Curnow. We have to keep the riff raff away don't we. Come on Florence, don't be long.'

Flo stroked the surface of the satin dress. The low neckline was daring. The way the waistline was pulled in with a small white bow, the gathered material over the bustle at the back. She marvelled at the details like an amateur scientist discovering a new fossil on the beach. And the corset. The 'specialite' corset as Mrs Curnow had called it. A necessity if you were going to wear this particular style of dress. The corset was stiffened with whalebone and steel but was comfortable enough to sleep in. Or so Mrs Curnow had said. She would endure the agony of her squashed ribs to wear this dress. She would endure her overwhelming shyness to wear this dress. Her nightmares would dissolve into water. She smelt a sea change.

3

The cathedral was a building site with one structure, the south aisle of the old St. Mary's church, still standing and in use. The decision to develop St Mary's church with its ornately carved roof, rather than build the cathedral on a new site had brought out strong feelings. The ancient church was to be knocked down and many believed the prayers from the thousands of services that had been held since the sixteenth century were embedded in the stones. Souls would be lost. Spirits would be wandering. Mr Bubb, the clerk of the works heard much abuse as he set up his theodolite in Old Bridge Street to survey the sight.

'Bugger off,' an old woman yelled, 'leave our St Mary's alone.' But order had prevailed and most of the church had already been demolished.

Mr Trevern was anxious. His skin glistened and his hands were in constant motion. Out of all the photographers in Cornwall he had been chosen to photograph the blessing of the foundation stone. He had one moment. Only a few minutes had been allocated. If he missed it he would never live it down. He had called a rehearsal and asked his friends to help him.

He set up his mahogany, plate camera behind the

decorated enclosure and Mr Pasco, the owner of the Royal Hotel, pretended to be the Prince of Wales walking in a stiff, military manner.

'He looks as though he's crapped himself,' Mr Ellery whispered to Silvanius Parr, the banker with the odd moustache. The two men sniggered like boys and shared a swig of brandy from a hip flask. Mr Ellery was the clay pit manager and not of the same class as the other shareholders although Mr Trevern had to admit he'd been clever with his money.

Only Mr Fairfax, the solicitor had not arrived. He had sent his apologies for his absence, he was busy. Mr Parr knew where he was but he was keeping quiet.

Mr Pasco poured water on the stone and gave an impromptu speech.

'Get on with it, Alfred,' said Mr Trevern frustrated, 'I don't need to hear what they say. The ceremony will begin directly.'

Angel curtsied, wobbling as she came up to present her imaginary bouquet. Mr Trevern called to them from beneath the camera cloak to hold their positions. He clicked the shutter.

A few hours later the Duke and Duchess stood on the platform surrounded by a cordon of police drafted in from London to control the crowd. Flo was there to assist her father. She was trained by the best. He repeatedly told her so. She knew how to expose and develop the plates while the collodium was still moist. She knew the chemicals needed for coating and fixing the negatives. The scales, weights, glass measures, funnels and the pail to fetch rinsing water if none was available. All these things she remembered to pack on the cart. It was a taxing job to make a picture outdoors. No wonder her father preferred to be in his studio.

The Duchess was gracious. She had been informed about the photograph and waited the time needed for the exposure as Mr Pasco had done. Flo rushed the plates to their tent and fixed them with potassium cyanide. She wished her father would invest in one of the new cameras with dry plates and roll film. She had read about them. The magazine camera where the plates were mechanically changed after each exposure. But her father had no inclination to learn a new method. Why should he? His customers didn't complain. How else could he have bought so many shares in China Clay and furnished the house at the top of Lemon Street.

Flo saw the images were clear and distinct. He had done a good job. In certain ways he had talent. After his many painting expeditions she often found a canvas that would look good over a mantelpiece. A worthy painting, precisely executed as if he had been in his studio, views of Falmouth from the castle or portraits of Angel at Malpas, a snaking river behind her. Customers sometimes persuaded him to sell them. They felt they were bettering themselves, culturally uplifting their status. It wasn't Royal Academy but it was within their price range and from one of their own.

Angel leant out of Flo's bedroom window as the elephants walked past the house. One of them smelt the river and lifted his trunk anticipating a wallow in the water.

'Ooh,' said Angel, covering her ears with her hands, 'they make some awful noise Nan.'

A bear on a chain walked past and a tumbling clown, smoking fire eaters and a juggler on black and white stilts strode like the giant from St Michael's Mount. The circus was followed by two members of the Truro Operatic Society holding a banner that spanned the road, it read, 'The Stupendous New Opera, *The Pirates of Penzance* by Her Majesty's Royal Command, 8 o'clock Tonight.'

Flo suddenly noticed the young man holding the other end of the banner. He was dark in the Cornish way. Like a Spaniard with blue eyes. Strangely he seemed familiar. He looked up at the window and spotted her. An image flashed in her mind. The man was running. Racing through fields. Brambles and bushes catching on his clothes. It was a desperate bid for escape and somehow she was involved. Inside, a coiled spring snapped open and flooded her body with heat. Premonitions were part of her. She was used to them. She knew the boy next door would be run over by a bolting horse, its eyes bulging white as it dragged a broken gig, ricocheting and crashing across the cobbles. She saw the house in Lemon Street long before Mr Trevern moved his young family from their rural cottage in Kenwyn and once she saw Jesus holding out his arms to her. Her mother had discovered her in the garden, her hands together in prayer and rushed her inside and put her to bed, not understanding her daughter's gift. Flo kept quiet about Jesus and now that she was older the memory had become confused. Maybe it had been her mother he was beckoning and her childish mind had not wanted to accept it. Suddenly she was thirsty and she ran down the stairs and through the kitchen.

In the back garden Flo pumped the pure tasting water from the tin-rich ground into a jug. Tonight she would see the *Pirates of Penzance*. Her father was taking her. Not because he'd chosen to take her, but because she'd been invited by the Mayor. The invitation sat on his desk, 'To Mr Quentin Trevern Esq and daughter, two seats for a performance of Gilbert and Sullivan's Opera to be followed by Supper and Dancing at the Town Hall.' Against his better judgement Mr Trevern had relented. How could he refuse the Mayor?

4

Mr Trevern was agitated. He stood in front of the gilt mirror in the hallway fussing with his white bow tie and winged collar shirt while Nan, on her knees, polished his shoes.

'That's no good girl, put some rub into it.'

He had bought his boots from Barret's in Church Lane especially for the evening. They were elastic-sided, kid boots galoshed with fine French porpoise made by a London cutter. They felt good on his feet and he stood taller. It's the shoes that sort the poor from the rich he thought. The shoes gave him confidence, made him the man that he had worked hard to be.

'If we're late they'll hang me from the nearest yard arm.'

Flo handed him his seal black hat.

'I think we'll be in good time, Father.'

Mr Trevern scrutinized the back of his tail coat.

'You are to be on your finest behaviour tonight, 'tis a grand do, full of the bettermost class of people and they know all the airs and graces there is to know.'

'I shall try, Father.'

Mr Trevern paused for a second, 'But is that good enough? Eh?'

He laughed that laugh, the sound that always suggested

she was inadequate. How she wished her father would give her confidence. Over the years he had worn away at her and now she had no shield to protect herself. She could feel wetness in her nose. Tears could fill her eyes at any moment. What was she thinking of asking for the new dress and attending an evening of such importance?

He brought out a tiny jewellery box.

'Nearly forgot, I bought you this to wear.'

She opened the present and inside was a brooch of curled, gold leaf set with drops of amethyst like essence of violet.

'Thank you, Father.' She kissed him lightly on the cheek, the feeling of helplessness giving way to familiar despair.

'With one hand he takes away and with the other he gives,' thought Nan as she got up from her knees. The black boot polish had stained her fingers, but she pinned the brooch to the top of Flo's dress careful not to dirty it.

'Well let's be off. I will be waiting outside for 'ee.'

And he walked to the front door and disappeared into the sunset evening.

'I'm nervous, Nan.'

Nan took hold of Flo's hand and squeezed it.

'You look grand Miss. And that's a fine dress. It fits like a glove.'

The two young women were locked together for a second in a friendship that gave strength to both of them. And then Flo was gone. Off to the bettermost place where Nan could never hope to be.

The theatre heaved. A bowl of top hats and gowns. All checking to see who was there and who wasn't. All of them breathing a sigh of relief. Outside there was a crowd waiting and their inclusion would be noticed. The event was a divider, elevating one group above another so that those who hung from windows and jostled for another sighting of the royal couple became the hoards to be pitied and to know their place.

Mr Trevern moved along the row to their seats in the circle and settled down with his programme. Flo felt light headed. Perhaps Nan had pulled the corset too tight. Mr Trevern gave her a pair of opera glasses.

The royal party arrived in their box and waved before the orchestra played *God Save the Queen*. The curtain went up and the gas lights trapped in their copper shells at the front of the stage spilled an orange glow over the audience in the front rows. Everyone 'ooh'd' and 'aah'd' at a large schooner. Built by the stage carpenters it looked as if it could be launched tomorrow. Behind the boat was a large backdrop of sea with painted jagged rocks jutting into waves and dotted around the stage were various members of the Amateur, Operatic Society dressed as pirates. The audience settled down and the orchestra, small, but accomplished, began the overture.

'Pour oh pour the pirate sherry,' the chorus sang.

Flo scanned the actors with her glasses and saw the young man from the procession, his face covered with make-up, animated with song. She could see more clearly how handsome he was, the fine line of his nose and his generous mouth, how his black hair flopped over his eyes so that now and again he had to move it away with his hand. He had a spark, something that singled him out from the others as if he should be centre stage. It wasn't only his good looks, it was an energy, a likeability. He was the kind of performer who was attractive to every woman in the audience and although you knew he knew it, you forgave him. He was a star. And with every entrance and exit he became Flo's star. He looked over the lights at the audience and it seemed he was singing just for her. She was transfixed.

Mr Pasco made his entrance as the Major General and with the technique of a professional he banged the boards with his foot. The gas hissed through the pipes running under the stage as the dust trapped inside fell away. The sudden rush flared the lights which illuminated his face for a few brief seconds bringing him into focus. The audience clapped. Mr Pasco was well known in the town and was much admired as a singer with the society.

'I am the very model of a modern Major General…' Mr Pasco sang with rapid troppo forte, his eyes overhung by heavy brows concentrated towards the royal box.

Mr Trevern glanced at his daughter beside him. The light on her face seemed to magnify her features. For certain she looked more like him. Her pale skin and auburn hair. Her figure was not rounded enough to be thought beautiful but somewhere in her features, maybe across her eyes, there was something compelling. She had become distant and withdrawn in the past year as if trapped in a cocoon. He cared about her, no he loved her, but there was a wall between them and he had no energy or inclination to knock it down. Many times he had tried. Approaching her room to bring her water or a book, wanting to talk but unable to. He feared she had premonitions. She sniffed the air and knew what was coming. Once when he was a boy he had visited Land's End with his mother. She told him to be careful, it was witch country. The raw wildness of the cliffs and moors alarmed him but it was the sea he remembered most. The sea that changed its moods without warning. It could be crystal blue and green; a thousand diamonds in the sun and in the passing of a cloud, a storm could wrench the guts from you.

The sea was mighty, a giant whale thrashing its tail against the fortress rocks where yellow lichen clung. It was too emotional for Quentin. And the people were different. They were miners full of death and superstition. Pallid, hunched men digging for tin under the roaring ocean, listening out for the knockers, the ghosts of dead men. He wanted to run back to Truro and the folding hills. His father had said the river was like a woman. Land,s End was a roaring man dragon with seas that tossed ships into the barnacled rocks like chicken wood flotsam. He remembered the roar of the waves sucking in and out of the barnacled coves, spitting phlegm as if the dragon were breathing. And in the bleak granite town of St Just every woman he passed had the evil eye. He feared his daughter had it too. But in truth he feared she remembered what happened the year Angel was born. The night his wife had died.

Flo nodded to him to show him she was enjoying the show, her eyes lit up in a way he hadn't seen before. No, he needn't worry, she didn't remember and tonight she looked different. The make-up of her face made sense. You could almost say she was beautiful. Mr Trevern felt pride. He was a lucky man to have such daughters. It was important to keep them close within his sight and not let them feel their wings spread.

After the performance he led Flo to a large reception room in the Town Hall and they paused in the doorway to take in the scene. She let out a cry of amazement. Mr Trevern looked pleased. The council knew he had a good eye and had consulted him over the decorations. The long room was covered in swathes of crimson satin caught by perfect green bows at intervals along the walls under which gilded chairs and tables were positioned for the ladies to sit on. In the centre of the moulded, ceiling rose a hundred painted candles in a gigantic candelabrum dripped wax into solid gold cups. At one end beneath Truro's coat of arms, a table covered in linen was loaded with a blackened, roasted pig, its mouth gaping from the spittle, chickens piled high on silver platters, small pieces of Turkish Delight like chunks of pink glass and fruits, apples, pears, quinces, dates and figs. At the other end, beneath two tall palms in pots a string quartet was playing and couples were already dancing.

'It's perfect,' said Mr Trevern proudly.

In a corner, Flo could see her father's friends swigging port.

'Let us go and say hello to the appropriate persons. Are you prepared, Florence?'

'Yes, Papa.' Her voice sounded as if it was echoing under a bridge.

'Alright are 'ee Quentin?' welcomed Mr Ellery, 'and good evening Florence, you are looking special this evening.' His nose shone with drink.

'Good evening, Mr Ellery,' said Flo shyly.

'That singing was grand,' said Mr Trevern surveying the room as it filled up. Servants dressed in eighteenth century costume began to circulate offering guests champagne.

'The opera's just opened in London so I'm told,' said Mr Fairfax. 'My brother went to the opening night. He said it was a fairly inauspicious occasion.'

Mr Fairfax was originally from the Home Counties. It had been an important decision to move to the West Country. His family were appalled. To visit Cornwall for a holiday was acceptable, but to live amongst the ignorant people was not. But he had been adamant, he loved the mild climate, it was good for his heart and he had made a reputation as a clever solicitor by representing a couple of shipping companies with insurance claims. He had won good compensation so he was considered an asset to the town. And he had learnt that Cornishmen were far from ignorant. This was the country of Humphrey Davy who invented the miner's safety lamp and of Andrew Pears from Mevagissey, founder of the Pears' Soap Company. These men came from a tradition of explorers and inventors, Captain Bligh and Richard Trevithick. They illuminated lighthouses and discovered manaccanite and fifty years ago Goldsworthy Gurney had made the longest journey by steam in the world, from Bath to London. They were not to be trifled with. A brave canny people with a sense of humour that could bring down any pretension in a man in seconds.

Ellery gulped his glass of port. Mr Fairfax's superior tone annoyed him.

'Inauspicious! You up-country folk don't know what you've got, take it all for granted. And what's more, you're all down here. You buy up our land, our hotels, and our businesses and not content with that, you marry our women. Won't be the Cornwall we know afore long, you mark my words.'

'I'll have you know, James,' said Mr Fairfax defensively, 'I have been welcomed into the bosom of this city with open arms.'

Mr Ellery's eyes glinted. 'Only because you brought a bit of gold with 'ee. Take you twenty years before your neighbours will let you call this city home.' He took a step backwards, the drink bringing on an aggressive tone.

'What you need James is a plate of our delicious food over there. Take the edge off your lip. You're squared up like a bottle of piss,' said Mr Parr.

Mr Ellery searched for the door. 'Talking of piss, Silvanius, I shall just be a moment.' And he lurched across the room. He would go down the grand staircase and out into the night to find an alley between the houses. He might even light his cigar. This was a special evening and the thought of the first inhalation of smoke, acrid at the back of his throat as the tobacco high kicked in, would make it perfection.

The Barker came into the room and banged the floor with a stick.

'My lords, ladies and gentlemen, a warm welcome, if you please to the most illustrious, most talented hosts for this evening's reception, the Amateur Operatic Society of Truro.

Flo searched for the young man among the performers still in their costumes but she couldn't see him.

'And an especially heartfelt welcome to the lead soprano, the delightful, the splendid, the breathtakingly beautiful, Helena Day.'

Helena Day stepped forward and curtsied as everyone applauded.

'She's wearing too much make-up and is plain as teddywater,' Mr Parr remarked. Mr Fairfax agreed.

'And to the three singers, the like of which, I beg your indulgence here, we have never before experienced in Truro, the handsome and the talented, Alfred Pasco, Russell Bell and Terence Prado.'

The three men bowed to more cheering, each taking their turn. Flo now knew his name. Bell. It sounded like a note he had sung in the opera. She hadn't met any family by that name, although it was not surprising, her life was so governed by her father and the society he kept.

The quartet began to play again and Alfred Pasco joined his friends. He was a kind man with a hearty laugh and a loud tenor speaking voice that could be heard in the farthest corners of the Royal Hotel. One of his teeth flashed as he greeted his friends with a broad smile.

'Splendid performance, Alfred,' congratulated Mr Trevern shaking his hand vigorously.

'Thank you, Quentin, I had some sweaty moments, but I don't think it showed.'

James Ellery, having negotiated the room by carefully avoiding the feet of the ladies sitting on chairs, rejoined the group.

'Well done, Alfred. It was a proper job in my book.'

Flo caught a glimpse of Russell a few feet away chatting to the other singers. He seemed smaller than he looked on stage and she could see immediately he was a working man. His hands were broad and beaten and his face browned by the weather. It was his eyes that were extraordinary, as if the sky and sea had mixed together in a freakish blue, an accident of nature.

'The prince was whisked away pretty quick. Is he back to London?' asked Mr Pasco.

'He sent his apologies to the Lodge. I believe he's staying with Lord Trevelyan.' Mr Fairfax viewed the room. A small victory gained with this information.

A shot of anger punctured Mr Ellery. 'See I told you. Why doesn't he join the reception? Because they think we're too countrified down here. We don't have a brain in our heads as far as those up country lot are concerned. We're slow and dull, too damn dull for a prince.'

He swayed backwards. Mr Trevern caught him and put him upright.

'What do you say, James, to having a sit down?'

'Just leave me be, Quentin, stop fussing.' And he moved away to lean against the wall.

Russell took a glass of champagne from a passing tray and looked across at Flo. He smiled, his eyes creasing up with recognition. She turned away to check if her father had spotted the moment. She could feel Russell's gaze on her back, hot like a beach in summer. The room did a turn on a painted horse. It stopped for a second and she was in Russell's arms.

'I'll say this,' said Mr Trevern, 'it's been good business for Truro.'

They raised their glasses and toasted 'Truro.'

'And to china clay.'

'The dividends will be going up,' Mr Parr said smugly. They all felt quietly elated. Another year of profit. Another year of luxuries.

'Only the elephant dung to pick up,' Mr Fairfax managed a smile. 'Someone will make a few shillings. Who's got the contract I wonder? No doubt as a banker, Silvanius, you'll be offering a bloody good rate of interest?'

Mrs Parr swept by in the arms of the town clerk. She leant back and peered at her husband. One of her ample breasts peeped out of her taffeta evening gown, a white mound of flesh with the darker circle of areola just visible at the edge. Undeterred she pushed it back.

'Good evening, Mrs Parr,' Leonard Fairfax raised his voice above the music.

Mrs Parr smiled at him graciously and continued dancing, a stately galleon sailing down the room, her slight, confused partner whisked around as if she was making a syllabub.

'That's a mighty fine woman you've got there, Silvanius,' said Mr Fairfax appreciatively.

'You're not married to her, Leonard.'

Mr Pasco held out his hand to Flo.

'Perhaps Miss Trevern would like to dance?'

Flo hesitated but her father said, 'Go on. I don't know how she'll do, Alfred. This is her first outing in public.'

Her stomach dived with nerves. All memory of the steps taught to her by her dance teacher evaporated. Mr Pasco sensed her apprehension.

'We'll do just fine, won't we, Florence?'

On the dance floor Flo tried to follow him but she was wading through treacle. She did catch up steps to keep up with him, her eyes on her feet.

'Look at me my dear,' said Mr Pasco kindly, 'it will be easier.'

She felt a fool. Why couldn't she bend with the music as she had been taught? She knew the dress had been designed to flare briefly to show her slim ankles and if only she could move with the rhythm, her waist would look so small a man could put his hands around it. She was too nervous. Too slow to carry cold dinner as her father frequently said. She wanted to shrink into the satin walls away from her father's critical eye and from Russell Bell who might hate her for her clumsiness.

'That's right, my girl, you're getting it,' said Mr Pasco encouragingly.

Russell and Helena danced confidently past and he caught Flo's eye. A flash of something. There it was again. A spark of knowledge, faint and baffling. Nothing you could pinpoint, just familiarity.

The music came to an end and there was a patter of applause for the orchestra before they started up again. They would be playing all night for an agreed price with two breaks for food and drinks so they decided to get the waltzes out of the way first.

Russell excused himself from Helena and had almost reached Flo's side when Mr Trevern appeared.

'Excuse me, Alfred, I've had enough, there comes a time when you stop listening to people jawing and start hearing your own body complaining.'

He grabbed Flo's hand firmly, pulling her with a sharp tug. She felt the strength of him through her wrist, running up her arm, sending a pain to her shoulder. She looked down. Her feet had been chopped from of her body. There was a sudden tear in the dress as she tripped forward. The sound was like a dagger in her side slicing through layers of skin. It was a clean cut as if a piece of meat were carved in one downward movement. She could hear the blood rushing through her ears, seeping out of the flesh and sinews as she fell. Her head hit the floor, her arms splayed out and her legs grossly tangled in the folds of the skirt. Her father's voice was in her ear.

'Get up, maid,' he said quietly.

Some of the dancers clustered nearby to see what had happened. People peered from the chairs and heads came to together for remarks and gossip.

Flo couldn't move. She had a pain in her foot but the real pain was inside, somewhere between her stomach and her throat, dulling her senses.

Russell looked down at her and she gazed at his concerned face, only half aware it was him.

'Are you alright, Miss Trevern?'

Her father dragged her to her feet and with a smile pasted on his face he called to his friends.

'She's some awkward girl. No harm done gentlemen. We'll be away then.'

Flo wanted the ground to subsume them, but even more than that, she wanted God to strike her father with a bolt of lightning so he might fall into a smoking, charcoal pit. She barely noticed Russell had walked with them to the door. Clamped to her father's arm they made their way down the staircase and out into a night chilled by a north wind.

5

Nan wiped the table and went to the sink to wash the cloth. The marvel of running water from a tap. It's convenience. No fetching and carrying. Pumping it out from the communal well and hauling it back. The weight of it. It took two of them in relays to get enough. And then it was gone before you knew it, used before the last child had eaten and her father had washed the white clay from his arms. She sighed. It had been a long day. She had played hide and seek with Angel before persuading her to get ready for bed and sat telling her stories about piskeys and spriggans.

'But what do they do, Nan?'

'I've told you a hundred times, Miss Angel.'

'But I want to hear it, please, Nan.'

'The piskeys are good people. They take a baby when the mother hadn't cared for it and return it washed and dressed up in pretty clothes like an 'oss marine.'

'And what do they look like?' Angel's face was wide open with listening.

'They are as small as a mouse and as old as the oldest man down to the alms houses. They have wigs like grey lichen and on top is a red cap. But do you know what else?'

'Yes, yes,' squealed Angel.

'Go on then.'

'They have white weskits and green stockings and shoes with big buckles made from dew drops,' said Angel seriously.

'That's right, dew drops like diamonds. And they plait a horse's mane for stirrups and ride all night.'

'All night,' repeated Angel, her mind racing with pictures as she saw the exhausted pony in the morning with ribbons tied to its tail. Secretly she was already checking her father's horse every time the gig arrived at the front door. Once she was sure she saw an intricate plait in its mane but she wasn't tall enough to see clearly.

'And now you close those eyes Miss Angel and dream of the piskeys and the good folk who will take care of you while you sleep.'

Nan had closed the door and gone back to the kitchen where she sat with an oil lamp sewing and darning listening to the loud tick of the grandfather clock in the dinning room and wondering if some day she would marry and have her own baby to care for.

Mr Trevern and Flo returned earlier than she expected and Flo had rushed upstairs. Her father went into the drawing room and slammed the door. She heard the brandy decanter being poured. She worried about Flo and wanted to knock on her door. The master had been staring cold so something must have happened.

She tiptoed to the bottom of the stairs and listened as she had done many times during the evening to make sure Angel was asleep. This time she listened for Flo. But she heard nothing.

She picked up her shawl and wrapped it around herself. The night air would be fresh and she had a half hour's walk to her parent's home. Mr Trevern appeared in the doorway. His eyes seemed darker than usual.

'You'll be off now,' he said brusquely.

'Yes, sir.' Nan headed to the servants entrance.

'Be sure to pull the door shut,' he shouted after her, 'the other night it wasn't closed and all and sundry could have claimed us.'

'Goodnight, sir,' called Nan and she hurried out, wanting to get away from the atmosphere that was always present when Mr Trevern was in the house.

She stood for a moment breathing in the sharp tang of Carvedras smelting works before making her way across Boscawen Street. Not long ago they had markets running through the middle of the road. Sheep and cows were driven through the town and put in pens. But slowly as the houses became shops and tourists brought in by the new railway swelled the population, the farmers' market was moved to Castle Hill and the calling of cows was no longer heard in the centre of the town. She hurried into River Street past Mr Trevern's studio shop with its display of picture post cards and photos of weddings and christenings in the window and started to climb the steep hill to a row of cottages at the top of the city. Ahead of her in the gloom, a man on crutches wearing a worn, soldier's uniform slowly made his way towards her. She stopped barely recognising his face.

'Adam Pollard is that you?'

The man ignored her, all his energy and concentration needed to swing his legs forward.

'Adam? It's me, Nan Peters. I heard you were back. You know me don't you?'

Adam barely lifted his head, defeated by the hill and his useless limbs.

'Let me be, Nan.'

She stood aside as he shuffled past. She watched him for

36

a moment, saddened by the change in him, before walking purposefully on.

Flo lay on her back in bed. The covers were drawn up to her chin, her body rigid under the sheets as she replayed the scene at the reception over and over until the feelings of despair became a form of self-mutilation. Her body seemed to be oozing fluid onto the rug by her bed, her cells decomposing, eaten from within by bacteria that had become the enemy. Nor could she stop the process. She had been turned to marble. To move would crack the edifice open and leave her in pieces. She concentrated her thoughts, trying to stop the repeating images of the fall. She noticed a pitcher of water and bowl on top of the chest of drawers. One side almost black in contrast to the china whiteness lit by the moon. It was a painting made up of squares and rectangles of light, one section superimposed onto the other so you could see through to the shape beneath. She moved her hand and touched her hip where she had landed. There would be a bruise tomorrow. Tomorrow. Nothing but emptiness. The getting up and washing. The dressing and eating breakfast. The learning and her father's studio. Her father's abiding presence. The worms within began eating again. Their munching sounded like corn popping in an oven. She lay still trying to evaporate into the room to escape the invading army.

The door opened quietly and then shut. Mr Trevern brought the glow of an oil lamp beside her. He didn't talk for a moment but looked at her thoughtfully before sitting down on the bed.

'Oh Florence, why are you such a disappointment to me?' He spoke gently as if his words were words of love, 'To make such a spectacle in front of the people who are most important.'

'I'm sorry, Father.'

He circled his hand in the air.

'Your mother was so beautiful, so gifted, a rare jewel. When she danced she floated like Chinese silk. So many wanted her but she chose me.'

'Yes, Father.'

'Everything I do is for you, Florence, you know that doan' 'ee.'

'Yes, Father.'

'I want only the best for you.'

'I know, Father,' said Flo, wishing he would move off the bed. His closeness felt uncomfortable.

'I don't know what I've done to make you so...so...'

He trailed off, frightened of opening a gap through which she might crawl to reveal her knowledge of the past.

'I will try harder, Father,' she whispered, 'to be what you would like me to be.'

'Ah, Florence.' Mr Trevern patted her hand and moved away from the bed.

One of her eyelids had been flickering uncontrollably; she worried that he could see it.

'Mouth closed like a jail house door, Florence. We don't want people knowing our business.' He waited for a reply.

'Of course, Father.'

'Sleep sound then.'

She rolled over onto her side in a foetal position and wrapped the bedclothes tightly around her in swaddling comfort. Somewhere in the fog of her memory she could hear her parents in their bedroom, their voices raised. She couldn't make out the words, only a distorted sound of anger. Her mother shouted. Flo tried to run to her but the noise faded and the voices became the sound of waves crashing onto a beach. She let herself be drawn in and out, floating with the tide. The moon had been blocked by cloud and the mysterious darkness of the shifting sea numbed her as she slowly dipped into sleep.

6

I t was Egypt rising out of western fields as if the pyramid builders had touched the Cornish landscape with their ancient vision. The clay pits dotted the skyline with their creamy points of chalky clay and to those who did not realise the sweat and low wages that went into creating them, it was a magical sight.

Flo and Mr Trevern climbed a hill beside one of the pits. With one hand Flo hung onto her hat while the other held a hankie across her mouth to stop the dust going up her nose. Her father struggled in the wind carrying his camera and tripod.

'Here, Florence, take this will you.' He handed the tripod over as he searched for a good position, 'What about this spot?'

Below them the pit opened out, a white gash in the earth crossed with a double incline railway running in straight black lines to the top of its own pyramid. A clay bearing stream of water from a hose flowed down the rocky slope to a channel at the bottom where a group of men were separating the clay from the sand. From high up they seemed to Flo like ants, carrying and pushing, breaking and loading, silhouetted against the mountainous back drop. While above, the pump of the beam engine moved gently up and down extracting the valuable profit.

Mr Trevern was distracted as if the climb had disorientated him. His face had turned a pale white from the dust and he looked ill.

'Well? What do you think, Florence?'

'I think it will be good, Father. I shall go and get the tent.'

He sat down on a flat rock. Why had he agreed to this? His shoes were filthy and no end of brushing would get his suit clean. The other share holders had asked for photos to show how efficient and modern their pit was becoming. They wanted people to see the clay drying out in the new 'air dry' sheds, the women cutting the best of it into squares like pats of butter and the wooden, hooped casks being loaded onto railway trucks heading for the port at Par. And pictures of the workers too. It would appear in the newspaper. Good publicity for the company. The bosses and their happy workforce leaning on their dubbers and shyvers.

But today he had no energy. The climb had worn him out and he had an angry headache again. He lit a cigar and watched Flo making her way down the hill, her hat blowing back from her face. She was almost running, stumbling in the pot holes. Why didn't she slow down? She could hurt herself. The wind suddenly sent up a fog of clay temporarily blinding him and when he looked again she had gone.

Way below, Russell worked hard in the sunshine as he shovelled the stent into the next skip waiting in line. He had taken off his shirt but sweat still poured down him. His friend, John, worked beside him. It was not a time for talking. Not when every muscle in your body ached as you broke and dug the clay from the mica and quartz. Nearby

41

was Jack Peters. At forty he looked fifteen years older. His hair was almost grey and his eyebrows sprouted like sea grass. The joints in his knees creaked as he directed the water on the decomposed granite. Sometimes the captain took pity on him and let him prop the hose on wooden supports so he could roll his baccy and let the blood seep back into his hands. And if he's lucky thought Russell, when he's past it they'll keep him on as the 'mica man', gently hoeing the fine sand out of the channels in the drag pit. Russell took out a scarf and wiped his face. That was not going to be his future, working in the whiteness with his throat scarred by clay dust. His music had spoken. In his pocket was a letter.

He glanced up at the beam engine high above him. A figure was running across the overburden of the top slope. She reminded him of the solemn girl he saw at the Gala. He had spotted her at a window in Lemon Street where the wealthy families lived and it was strange, but he felt as if they had met before.

She reached the bottom of the hill and suddenly her hat blew off and he could see clearly it was the same girl. Her hat did a jig in the wind and before he could lift his arm to wave, she was out of sight.

'Get away!' shouted John as he picked up a stone and threw it. A thin dog with ribs showing through a dull coat had trotted over with a wagging tail, its face a wide smile of panting tongue. The dog yelped and limped away.

'No need for that,' said Russell under his breath as he sorted the mixture of quartz and tourmaline too hard to be washed down by the jet of water, 'it's one of God's creatures.'

'What? You want to be lying on your back with foam spitting from your mouth?' argued John.

'He was alright, that one. Just a stray.'

John shrugged and pushed the loaded truck along the

tracks to the incline railway.

He was a hard man, thought Russell. For three years they had worked along side one another and they had bonded. John was the senior man. He had started as a kiddle-boy, warming the pasties and lighting the kettle for the men's tea. When Russell arrived John had shown him the ropes; how to cut corners and avoid the flack, the times to keep quiet and when to complain and how to save your skin if the rock face moved sending devastating boulders to the workers below. And in return, Russell gave John his songs in the wet, winter evenings as they cadged lifts home, clay solidifying on their boots.

A hooter sounded and the men downed their tools for lunch, many sitting where they were working, unwrapping their pasties and sinking into the rock face as if they were part of it. Sam, a scruffy boy in his early teens scampered among the men.

'Wrestling match, south field, Thomas brothers.'

'Fancy a flutter, John?' Russell looked across at his friend.

'It's only a device to get you to part with your money. Don't go in for gambling,' said John.

The letter in Russell's jacket burned against his chest. The words were seared on his brain.

'I could do with a win, I have to go up-country to London.'

He gave the envelope to John who fingered it gingerly as if it would attack him.

'Well what do 'ee think 'en?'

John examined his boots wanting to hide his embarrassment. Finally he said, 'I don't tell many Russell but I can't read.'

Russell wondered why he hadn't known before. John had been taken out of school and put to work when his father died but surely he had learnt to read by then. School was compulsory however hard parents tried to stop it.

'Don't have the seeing of the words. It's all of a jumble on the page, see.' He pointed to the letter. 'Still, it's not everything. I've got by. And I've more sense than most of these half wits.'

'Do you want to know what it says?'

John chuckled. 'You go ahead my cock. You tell it to me. Because if it's to do with your singing I want to know.'

'They write,' said Russell still not believing it, '"The D'Oyly Carte Opera Company invite you to audition at your earliest convenience."'

John whistled and stared at his friend. 'They must have heard of you.'

'"We await your reply with anticipation."'

'Fancy wording.'

'They talk like that in the opera world, John. It's different from down here and I want a part of it.'

Someone shouted from the top of the pit to join them. Russell knew his savings were in a purse on his belt. A big win would mean he could leave tomorrow and he was strong enough to wrestle with the best of them.

Outside the beam engine Mr Trevern was deep in conversation with Mr Ellery as Flo arrived with two heavy baskets.

'Good Morning, Miss Trevern,' said Mr Ellery touching his hat.

Her father looked at her grumpily, 'We'll do the picture from here, Florence. I've changed my mind. No need to haul it up the hill.' His headache had worsened and he wanted to be at home with Angel. If they hurried he could spend the afternoon with her. Maybe take her to the beach and tonight he might venture out to the Royal Hotel for a bit of beef and a drink.

Flo could hear shouts nearby as caps were thrown in the air.

'I don't approve of it, Quentin,' Mr Ellery nodded in the direction of the field, 'losing all their wages but there's no stopping it.'

Mr Trevern shook his head. 'They'll be on their knees praying for forgiveness come Sunday.'

Flo put the baskets down with relief.

'They must have been a weight for 'ee,' said Mr Ellery, 'there's nothing of you.'

'She might look a weakling, James, but she's tough as old ling.'

Flo rubbed her strained arms. Her father had no idea the effort it took to carry the equipment. Sometimes he treated her as if she was a boy.

'You stay here, Florence, and wait for me. I'm going to have a geek at this magnificent new engine we've just bought. Don't you move mind.'

Flo relaxed on to a bench and felt the gritty wind on her cheeks. The sun was so hot it could almost be mid summer and what a summer they would be having. All the signs were there. More shouts from the field attracted her attention. Through the open window of the engine house she could see her father lighting another cigar.

The flat space had been cleared of stones years ago and was worn by countless fights where the bare feet of the Cornish wrestlers had made patches of white gaps in the grass. In the middle of a wide circle of workers, both men and women, two brothers were locked together in the ancient art of combat recorded since the first Celtic tribes arrived on the finger of land jutting into the Atlantic Ocean.

The brothers' hands were firmly gripped on each other's wrestling jackets. Thomas was bigger and stronger of the two, a black haired giant with a long moustache and a pig tail down his back. Joshua was dark as well but smaller. He stared at Thomas with a seething hatred.

'There'll be blood there,' muttered John as they made their way around the circle, 'there's a women between them.'

The two wrestlers shook hands, the signal to say they were ready to fight. John watched them prowling, their arms held away from their bodies, judging each other's energy.

'Well are you going to tell me?' asked Russell.

'It was last year, Joshua took up with a girl and mighty keen he was too. But she hankered after Thomas and he be only human. He finally gave in and had her. Joshua will never forgive him.'

There was a loud cheer as Thomas threw Joshua flat on the ground.

'A back, a back,' shouted the referee holding up his stick.

Joshua struggled to his feet. 'You're a cheating bastard, Thomas.'

'I don't want to hurt 'ee,' said the big man. He hooked his leg around Joshua's right leg and lifted it high behind him and gently shifted his weight. It was easy to knock him over. He'd been doing it since they were children. Joshua tried to maintain his balance but Thomas was too strong and he toppled over again.

'A back, a back and a win.'

Joshua angrily took off his wrestling jacket and pointed his finger at his brother's face.

'I ought to push your nose through your ass.'

'You listen here, we're blood and no woman should come between us.'

'She was mine,' yelled Joshua and he strode out of the ring shoving people out of his way, 'I wish you were dead.'

Nearby Russell could see the man keeping a book as he started to pay out to a group of winners. He counted out his savings and walked across to him.

'Anyone else want a beating?' shouted Thomas holding up the jacket. Russell began to take off his boots as John joined him.

'You must be full weight without a wrapper to think you can beat that girt sod, he can turn proper ugly.'

'I've put some pennies on my chances.' Russell held up his hand to attract the big man's attention. 'Here, over here.'

Thomas peered down at Russell, a Goliath to David. He chuckled.

'You haven't the strength to beat a grasshopper, my handsome, but I'll give you a go.'

'You might have a surprise then for I'm keen as a scythe,' boasted Russell.

'Come on 'en, let's be having you.'

The two men squared up before getting into the first hitch and the Stickler held up a scarf and dropped it to the ground. As they dodged and came together grabbing each other's jackets and kicking up dirt with their feet, Russell seized his moment. He neatly turned Thomas' moves against him, tripping the heavy man into a fall. Thomas hit the ground with a surprised look on his face. There was puzzlement amongst the workers. Thomas had never lost a hitch before.

'Foul, foul,' yelled one of the workers, worried he was going to lose his wages.

The referee barged over to the man, waving his stick threateningly, 'A back, I say, anyone say different?' The man held up his hands in a conciliatory gesture.

Just one more thought Russell, one more and I'll be turning my best side to London.

'Three pins,' said the Stickler firmly.

Thomas walked carefully around Russell preparing himself for the next move. His pride had been dented. His brother's words had hurt him and he had to take it out on someone.

At the edge of the circle Russell could see Flo half hidden behind an old man with a torn waistcoat and battered hat. A part of him wanted to stop the fight and talk to her, find out why she was there. He was sure she had never seen wrestling before.

Sam was suddenly there, skipping with feet on hot coals. He could smell the boy's unwashed hair and stagnant boots.

'Come on, Cap'n, you can beat him, but he'm well poor tempered, watch it. Here he be!'

The champion wrestler darted towards Russell. For such a big man he moved lightly like a dancer. Russell could hear him grunting in his ear as they shunted back and forward, eyes popping, feet scrabbling for legs. The crowd were concentrated, waiting for Russell to fall. And it came. With a roar of anger Thomas picked Russell up and tossed him over his shoulder in a Flying Mare. The workers were ecstatic. A Flying Mare was rarely seen and it was a win. They waved their caps above their heads and cheered.

'He looks like a dying duck in a thunderstorm,' commented a woman standing beside Flo, her hands sticky with clay. They watched Russell spin over the big man's shoulders, his arms spread like bats wings in a graceful flight. Flo was afraid he was hurt. Thomas had hung on to Russell's jacket as the rules stated and landed squarely on his chest. She glanced over her shoulder to the engine house. In the distance her father was pacing outside, a stopwatch in his hand.

At the edge of the field Russell lay face down on his stomach, his head twisted to one side. He could feel pebbles and stones under his chest, pressing into the holes in his trousers. Every part of his body clamoured. He coughed as the air filled his lungs again. John bent down masking his concern with a grin.

'Stupid bugger, I could have told you.' He rolled his friend over and began to inspect his ribs. Russell groaned.

'That's my savings gone. All of it.'

'Your singing up to London will have to wait, boy.'

Russell was mortified. Now he would have to wait another year to save enough funds. How could he have wasted it on a moment of ego? The money was to go to London, not to give the other workers the thumbs up as they returned to the pit. Daft as a wagon horse, he thought. He had been practising his audition for months until the notes were part of him like a new skin, he had been determined not to lose the opportunity. His mother would be angry with him. From a distance he imagined he could hear the opening notes of *Cavalleria Rusticana*. His brain must have been affected by the fall. The music became louder each note beckoning the next until evolving out of the music he saw Flo's face.

'You'll live till you die,' said John as he finished feeling for broken bones.

'That girl was here, the one I told you about, Florence Trevern.'

John didn't answer for a second as he helped Russell slowly to his feet.

'Jack's Nan works for them. Stuck up lot if you ask me.'

'She has – something.'

'I've heard that before,' John laughed and patted Russell on the back.

'Ah, ha, don't do that.'

'You'll survive.'

Russell limped down the field as Mr Trevern and Flo left in their dog cart, the horse straining and pulling along the deep, rutted lane. She hugged the camera oblivious of Russell who watched her go by. He let out a low whistle.

'No chance there, my handsome,' said John, 'she's a maid that is caged.'

'I don't know where you got to, Florence. I told you to wait for me,' said Mr Trevern accusingly, 'I hope you weren't watching the wrestling.'

'My hat, Father, it blew again.' She turned her head away so he couldn't see her lie.

'Hum.' The cart fell into another hole.

''Tis awful that the council have not fixed this road, I shall have a word with Councillor Roberts. A disgrace.'

Flo could see the spring growth running riot along the high, granite hedgerows. She loved the way the course grass covered the stones, a creeping, living carpet that sought out the fissures and cracks, providing a nourishing bed for moss and Cornish pinks. In the old days tin miners would walk the walls to work when the roads were impassable. The surfaces were worn flat into paths by their footprints. But now the stones were built high by farmers protecting their crops from the sea gales, structures that defined their territory and ownership and no one was ever seen again walking the ancient walls.

Ahead of them in the narrow road was a passing space with a seat where travellers could wait for lifts or rest on their way from Truro to St Austell. Flo could see a couple sitting close together, the boy lifting the girl's face towards his lips.

'Eyes on the road ahead, Florence. Gid up there,' Mr Trevern barked and the horse picked up pace, hooves thudding on the highway.

She caught a last glimpse as they kissed and she envied them. A memory of her mother filtered through the mist in her brain. Her skin was like a faded poster, filigree paper peeling off in layers, a hole where her mouth should be. The memory became clearer. Isabella had been distracted the year before her death, she seemed to be play acting. The role of mother that came so easily to her was forgotten. She was impatient and short tempered. Flo had tried everything to get her attention and felt confused and rejected. Maybe it was because Flo was no longer a child, she was thirteen and into double figures? Perhaps this was what happened when childhood slipped away. Was her mother jealous? There was discord in the air. The memory was of a particular day. Her mother had asked her to check her hair at the back before going out. Be a good girl she had said. Take care of Angel. Take care of Angel. As she had opened the front door Flo had run to her and hugged her around the waist. Her mother lightly pushed her away and then kissed her.

'Did you hear what I said?'

'Yes, Mama, I will look after Angel.' Flo had felt she would never come back.

The carriage jolted into another ditch and the camera shifted from her hands. She snatched it back and looked to see if her father had noticed the near accident. But Mr Trevern was blind to everything; to the shooting spring around him, to his horse trotting loyally its ears pricked forward and to the turmoil of his daughter, as she prodded the shell that enclosed her in an aching bid for freedom.

7

A faded sepia print. The woman held a white parasol and glared into the lens giving nothing away. She could be any woman in any town with the same backdrop behind her, with the same motivation, a portrait for the family so she might be remembered when she was gone. Her grandchildren could show it to their children.

'Look there is your great-granny.' Small faces would marvel at the details, the old clothes, the staged position, the unexpected emptiness of expression. They could search the face for likenesses and perhaps find themselves, feel comforted, a connection with the past that placed them where they stood in time.

The shop bell rang and she quickly put her mother's photo back in its box where her father had hidden it.

'Florence, they're here,' her father boomed and she had hurried into the studio.

The members of the Amateur Operatic Society dressed in their *Pirates of Penzance* costumes were ushered in by Mr Trevern.

Long into the previous night Flo had tried to prepare. The thought of seeing Russell Bell again made her stomach churn with anticipation but she felt embarrassed he had witnessed her fall. She was certain he would not have any interest in her. So as the performers lined up she melted into the background.

Her father began to organise the company, arranging them in front of a backdrop he had painted the day before. It mimicked the stage production, although Flo thought her father's effort was much better. There was flair in the way the cutter's sails blew gently in the wind and the colours of the waves as they swept backwards and upwards to a crest of frothing foam. The patterns and planes of the rocks were in different tones of grey and smokey green like celadon porcelain. He interpreted the myriad shapes on the beach in the same the way that Flo understood them and when she first saw it, she allowed herself a moment to appreciate her father's gift. A pure flash of belonging. The prince should have seen this set, painted by Quentin Trevern.

Mr Trevern handed Flo a piece of paper, 'I've drawn where they should be standing, make sure they are in position.' And he disappeared behind the drop and started to bang a nail into the wooden supports.

Flo made her way down the line of singers adjusting a hat here, an arm there, barely lifting her eyes from the sketch in front of her. Somewhere in her periphery she could see Russell apart from the others, his foot resting on a fence that was part of the set.

The sketch in her hand was shaking and a fear spread over her: the old fear that she was not good enough, not attractive enough. She had let herself be vulnerable to her feelings and only disappointment was ahead. She earnestly studied the diagram as she bent down and moved Russell's foot to another angle. A tickle in her throat made her cough.

'Shall I fetch you some water?' Russell said.

She stood up and the closeness of his body unsteadied

her. He reached out to catch her and she sighed. Not loud enough for anyone to hear, but she could hear it. It sounded like the sea on the shoreline, gently lipping the sand.

'I have no need of water, thank you.'

'You recovered well after your fall, Miss Trevern? I hoped you were not hurt.'

'And you have recovered from yours?'

She was surprised at how confident she sounded. Or maybe it was defensive.

'Ah, so it was you.'

Suddenly she was frightened.

'Please, if my father found out I saw the wrestling it...'

He interrupted her, 'At the Gala I wished to dance with you.'

His eyes were a trap and she had fallen into them. He pressed his false moustache firmly down on his upper lip. Flo couldn't help smiling.

'What is it?'

'Your moustache, when you were singing it moved. But you carried on so valiantly.'

'Yes, I kept singing.'

'Yes.'

'You must have been watching only me then.' He smiled and it felt to Flo as if he could see right into her.

'I enjoyed your performance very much,' she said, feeling her cheeks go red.

'I'm afraid I sang a few bad notes, although I practise every day. There are songs that go better than others. It happens.' He pulled a face as if to say, that is life.

There was something indefinable about him. The way he deferred without losing dignity. A confidence that came from knowing he was good looking and yet a humility from doubting his singing technique.

Mr Trevern was banging more nails behind the set and Helena Day, who had been placed in a curtsy with her finger pointing upwards under her chin, began to stagger. Mr Pasco paced restlessly.

'I hope you're not going to take much longer, Quentin, this costume smells some musty and Helena looks like she'll pass out if she stays in that position much longer.'

'My apologies, ladies and gentlemen,' Mr Trevern raised his voice so he could be heard, 'I shall be with you soon.'

One of the chorus groaned.

'Are you getting on with it, Florence?'

She jumped as her father's voice broke into the golden oasis that was Russell. He leant towards her and she could feel his breath shaving her ear.

'I must see you again,' he whispered. 'Please.'

The urgency in his voice surprised her.

'I don't know, I – '

'Just half an hour. Tell me where.'

One of the other singers was staring at them knowingly.

'My father would never let me,' she said quietly.

'For pity's sake, Quentin.' Mr Pasco threw his hat on the floor. Flo quickly moved away from Russell as Mr Trevern reappeared from behind the back drop.

'We are now ready ladies and gentlemen to take the photograph.'

'Thank the Lord,' said Mr Pasco relaxing into his position as the Major General.

8

I sandlewana. The name sashayed across the light thrown onto the tavern floor by an oil lamp and shimmered before him. Perspiration trickled into his eyes as if the grinding heat of Africa had somehow infused the cramped, beamed room where he was on his fourth tankard of beer. Above the low babble of drinking men he heard a young man cry out for water in a dust driven, semi-darkness. He bolted his drink willing it to dull his senses but today the memories could not be blotted out.

An old fisherman, his face carved by the ocean, crossed from the bar to sit beside him

'Alright are 'ee 'en Adam?'

The shouts in his head were louder.

'Izimpondo zankhomo'

The old man nodded. He had heard Adam ranting many times before. Ever since he returned from the African wars. It made no sense but he had a soft spot for the boy. His father had worked alongside him in the Penzance herring fleet. How he would have been shamed to see his son turn mazed, God Bless his Soul.

'It means the horns of the beast. Like that.' He extended his second and last finger at the fisherman. 'They came at us like a beast.'

The dust cleared and Adam could see the ochre grass of an African plain strewn with boulders and gullies. Dominating the skyline, cutting a jagged piece of jigsaw from the cobalt sky was the wedge of rocky mountain called Isandlewana. Chelmsford was wrong. The Zulus were on the move. Twenty-four-thousand of them. Why had he made them camp there?

Adam was with the transport wagons. Urging on the mules pulling the guns through the quagmire tracks. It had rained almost every night since December when he had first been drafted to the Cape. They had left a small attachment at Rorke's Drift and crossed the Mzinyathi in high spirits. Gossip had filtered down that the enemy was nowhere to be seen and after they hauled the guns onto a flat, bottomed punt and waded chest-high dragging it through the swollen river to the other side, the only Zulu in sight was a lone herdsman with his cattle. Some of the boys had charged after him. They would have the smell of roast beef curling through the air that night.

The camp was only meant to be temporary while Chelmsford took one thousand men further on to scour the mountain range beyond. The tents were placed on the slopes of the mountain, the 1/24 Warwickshire battalion facing them, while Adam's battalion looked down across twelve miles of uninterrupted view to the enemy. The wagons were parked in a neat line ready to return to the Drift for supplies if needed.

The order to entrench had not been given and Adam was relieved. It would have been demoralising after the long day's march to spend hours digging the rocky ground and struggling to unload the wagons. And anyway, it was not where the fight was going to take place. It was just a resting position beside the cool water of the Manzimnyama. They were to wait until ordered to join the main battalion. There was enough wood for fires and the gullies would slow down an unlikely Zulu advance. Her Majesty's troops would not be defeated. Africa was to be British.

'King Ketshwayo.' Adam spoke the name slowly, pronouncing every syllable as if each letter were a weapon. The fisherman stood up to buy another drink.

'Do you want another boy?'

Adam blinked. Reflected in the old man's eyes were a long bladed stabbing spear and a cow hide shield. The spear was held high above his head. Adam raised his arm to protect himself.

'It's alright my cock, you be back home now.'

Adam handed his glass to his father's friend without a word. He was still amid the stench of guns patching his uniform, carefully pulling the course thread through his five buttoned frock with its regimental facings on the cuffs and collar, the scarlet cloth against the yellow grass with the relentless blue above him. The uniforms were not made for Africa. He sweated until he thought he would pass out. One of the boys who had fought through the Cape wars told him to dye his white helmet with tea to make it less of a target and as he polished the brass badge he thought of Nan. How her body called to him. The way she looked at him directly in the eyes, unafraid and strong, not like other girls with their coy smiles and signals he couldn't fathom. She would be his one day when he returned. They had not spoken of it but he meant to marry her.

His job was to remain with the wagon supplies and only at the last call was he to fire his Martini-Henry rifle with the piece of hide sewn around the stock to protect his left hand from the burning. Sometimes he wished he had a lunger with a socket bayonet. Protection from the African spear.

Rumour had it they were tipped with poison. You stood no chance. Just a graze and you'd be a gonner. The spear and the lunger. Iswandlwana 1879.

At eleven-thirty the next morning he was checking the mules, filling their water buckets, giving a pat here and there, for simple as they were, he had a feeling for the animals, when one of Chelmsford's men rode into camp. The rider stopped at Colonel Pulleine's tent. The orders to move out, no doubt. But despite the talk among the men the order was never given. Instead Adam found himself unloading the guns from the carts to support a group of soldiers sent to protect the north side of the camp. The talk was still of a small skirmish. It was only a local response to the British troops and soon they would be on their way to join Chemlsford on the main battlefield.

Half an hour later and Adam was squatting behind the empty gun carriage shivering, the sound of gun shots reverberating around the landscape. His mouth was caked and dry, he felt sick and he prayed feverishly under his breath. Terror was not what he expected. Back home he had seen himself bravely facing the enemy, his boots polished, his uniform sparkling. No one forced him to join up, he had wanted to fight. Be a hero. Bring back a medal. He had not imagined this misery, the smell of fear dampening his armpits, goggle eyed and frozen to the spot.

They came at them in Zulu formation, the horns of the bull. The main thrust of the army was the body of the animal with two separate groups making the horns that would eventually meet up and surround the camp. There were thousands of warriors with guns and deadly spears. Strong, muscular men, bare-footed, feathers streaming behind them in the wind, loping like leopards, capable of running a man down and slicing him apart in seconds. Pulleine's troops let loose an attack of gunfire and the Zulus collapsed into the grass and dongas, some dead or wounded but most of them sliding down to find protection.

Above their war wail, Adam could hear, 'Qoka amatshe'. One of the gunners beside him whispered, 'Catch stones.' How could they catch stones thought Adam? Catch stones?

The old fisherman watched Adam's smile of wonderment.

'They meant they would catch our bullets, see? Stop them with their hands. Can you believe it? My God they were some brave men.' His expression changed and he gazed into his glass. And then he shouted, 'It was like Hell.'

The barman looked over angrily.

'If he goes on making that noise he can't stay. I've had enough of him.'

The old man waved his hand at the publican in a soothing gesture.

'Adam, my boy, you've got to be quiet.'

Adam looked at him for the first time as if he could really see him.

'No one knows, Grandpa.'

The screams returned. He was hiding under the cart as the Zulus rushed the camp. Soldiers passed him fighting hand to hand, steel and limbs clashing, blood spurting on the dust, glistening entrails like pieces of meat discarded from a lions kill. The cries of the retreating regiment panicked the animals. They reared up on their tethers until they too were stabbed in a frenzy of flesh and splitting bones.

The Zulus had been waiting. For days they collected together, not lighting their fires for fear of giving their position away, waiting for their war ceremonies to begin. They listened to their leader King Ketshawayo breathing courage into them, building up their stamina to face the

61

British defences. Many of them knew the guns they carried were useless. Obsolete Old Brown Bess's dumped on their unsophisticated world. Home-made bullets and no training made accuracy difficult. They had to rely on their wits, the forces of nature to run sure footed amongst the rocky stones. A quick wound from the spear. Watch them fall. Cut them open to free their spirits giving safe passage to the after life. Prevent them from harming the living. The way of the Zulus.

Adam peered through the dust. A mule had escaped the killing and was trotting behind a formation of soldiers making a last stand by another munitions cart. He crept towards it, gagging at the brains spilling from the head of a dead soldier, his face blackened with gunpowder.

He called softly, 'Here boy, come here.' The animal came towards him recognising his voice.

And then vaguely he saw a movement from the corner of his eye. A flash of colour. But he couldn't remember seeing the rifle. The scream was deafening and he managed to turn. The warrior held his hands across his face, blood streaming from his eyes, blinded by the back fire from the bullet that had lodged in Adam's spine. With a knee-jerk reaction Adam pulled himself onto the mules back. The flow of retreating army was heading down the track to Rorke's Drift but Adam could see the other horn swarming over the slopes to cut them off. The mule was cantering now, bolting from fear, heading down towards the Manzimnyama, weaving a path through the mayhem, like Moses through a sea of red coats. And then suddenly, the day turned to night. Adam reasoned the dust of the fighting had been whipped up by the plain's winds and been taken like a cyclone into the sky. But it was an eclipse. The moon had eclipsed the sun. Amongst the hacked and open bodies, a soldier thinking he was at Satan's door rose up to cross himself before the cry of one of Ketshawayo's men levelled him to the ground.

Ahead of him, Adam could just make out two soldiers of the Mounted Infantry racing towards the banks pursued by Zulus. In the murky light the horses plunged into the river before they were swept downstream. With a herd instinct the mule followed. The water looked dangerous as they slid down the muddy banks.

'Swim boy,' he shouted, 'go on with 'ee SWIM.'

Adam's lifeless body was weighing the animal down. He couldn't save it although he clung to its neck desperate to keep above water. They were flotsam, out of control, sealed together in a mutual grave and his life unfolded before him. For a moment he wasn't sure if he was real. If he had existed or not. His life seemed so mundane, so ineffectual. As he sank below the surface he randomly picked a memory. It was Nan. They were walking the castle path in Falmouth, her hand curled around his arm, the fresh seagulled wind in their faces, the clear blue sea surrounding them. And now it seemed as if he was floating above her. She was a small dot standing in the ruins of the fortress shielding her eyes as he became particles of air and clouds. He felt happy to know she was watching him. Suddenly he jolted against a branch protruding from the bank and he sucked in the baking oxygen as he hacked up water from his chest. His mule friend was lost beneath the muddy waves.

He struggled to the bank and lay exhausted on his stomach. He had no feeling in his legs. No pain. That would come later in the tented hospital of flies. A man appeared beside him. He could just make out the yellow corduroy of the mounted soldiers.

'Wrong side mate.'

The man put Adam over his shoulder like a sack of corn

and carried him to a horse tethered by the bank. The three of them sank into the river again. The horse swam steadily as the soldier urged it on through the eddies to the opposite bank. Another soldier waited on horseback as they arrived.

'You after a medal or what?' the man snorted

Private Wassal spat out some river dirt.

'Damn Chemlsford, God damn him, he should be shot.'

'He'll be back soon,' said the other soldier dismounting from his horse. 'He'll see the shit with his own eyes.'

The three of them slumped under cover of an African fire bush, the battlefield dripping from their minds like the water from their clothes. On the other side of the river the blood from one thousand-three hundred corpses stained the grass a dirty red. The buzzards were already circling.

Adam looked up at the fisherman.

'The greatest victory in Zulu memory,' he said and then he raised his glass and shouted, 'To our bloody Queen, to her biggest bloody defeat. She hadn't said a word about that had she. Defeat.'

'Right,' yelled the publican, 'that's it. I've had enough. You don't speak of our royalty like that, not in here. You are half witted Adam Pollard and out you go.'

'Let him stay, said the fisherman, 'those poor souls will never leave him.'

But they ignored the old man and two men picked Adam up as if he was a puppet. They dragged him to the door and threw him out. He hit the pavement hard. One of the men snapped his crutches in half and threw them after him.

Adam rolled over, blood trickling from his forehead and began to laugh.

'Sod you,' he shouted to no one. 'What do I care?'

A shadow appeared across his face.

'Oh, Adam,' said a voice he recognised, 'what have they

done to you?'

Why had she appeared now? He didn't want her. It was too late. Isandlewana had dimmed their star. He rolled back on the pavement, cursing.

'Here, take my arm.'

'Leave me be, Nan Peters, you don't want me.'

'You'll wish your cake dough if you don't let me help you, Adam,' said Nan.

Her voice was hard. She showed no kindness that could be mistaken for pity. He hung on to her arm and struggled to his feet.

'Lean on me,' said Nan and she supported his broken body.

9

'Florence, I want you to take the picture to the theatre manager.' Flo wiped her hands and looked at Angel who stood in the doorway of the developing room, a skipping rope in one hand.

'One moment, Father.'

'Here. The photograph of the Pirates Company so take good care of it.' Her father handed her a parcel wrapped in brown paper.

Angel skipped and counted and tried to cross the rope in front of her but she fell on her knees letting out a wail. Mr Trevern picked her up.

'What are you doing, maid?'

'Fell over.'

'Aah, my cherub, don't you take on so.' He planted a loud kiss on Angel's cheek.

'And you be careful, Florence, on the streets. There's a lot of loitering going on. Walk straight by and take no notice of them. Those corner boys have nothing better to do than taunt and be rude to people like us, they've got no fathers see. Young men need the discipline of a good father, and some loving, to keep them steady. 'Tis a poor thing that so many men run from their families and don't face their responsibilities. Those boys don't know how to be men, got no example. So you watch out.'

Flo put on her hat and cloak. 'I do understand, Father, I'm not a child anymore.'

Mr Trevern stared at her unsure of her response. A subtle shift of emphasis. Like the second hand of a clock moving to the next minute he felt a change in her and for a moment he was confused.

'I want to go, I want to go.' Angel danced around Flo pulling at her and pleading.

'No, you're staying with Papa today.'

'I don't mind, Father, I'll take her with me.'

'No. She stays with me. And don't go talking to any chapelgoers.'

'Yes, Father.'

He turned to Angel.

'And you know what I've got for you.'

Mr Trevern sunk his hand into his pocket as Angel looked up expectantly.

'Sherbet dip, sherbet dip,' laughed Angel and she opened the bag and dipped the lolly into the white powder.

Flo looked back and saw Angel, her mouth rimmed with sherbet, happily sitting on a stool as Mr Trevern went behind the camera to take another photograph of her.

The theatre was deceptive. From the outside it looked small, wedged between buildings, its plain façade broken by two moulded masks set back on their stone plinths, one of comedy, the other of tragedy. But once inside it opened up and spread on both sides back to the stage area.

As Flo arrived she paused for a moment and gazed up at the mask of comedy. She could never understand it. It seemed as tragic as its opposite. The gaping mouth was not laughing at all but mocked anyone who cared to challenge it like a devilish gargoyle wishing ill will. She went into the foyer and through a door at the side that took her into a small cobbled alleyway. At the back of the building was the stage doorman's cubicle. He lay with his head resting on a shelf, an empty pint glass pushed to one side.

'Good day to you, sir,' she said hesitatingly.

The man's grey moustache trembled with each snore.

Flo spoke louder. 'Good day, sir, I've brought…'

The doorman let out a loud snort and changed position. Flo thought maybe the theatre manager was in his office beneath the stage and moved past the sleeping man and into the wings. The theatre was in semi-darkness, the curtains pulled back and caught at the side of the proscenium arch revealing flats hanging like pages of a book from the flies. On a rail against the back wall were rows of costumes altered to fit the periods of the changing shows; skirts, dresses and cloaks covered in sequins and fur. Beneath the costumes in neat pairs were slippers with clasps of paste diamonds, varnished hessian shoes coated with yellow paint and leather swashbuckling boots. At the end, hanging on their own, a pair of white, Berlin pantaloons stood out in the dusty chiaroscuro.

A door slammed. Startled, Flo hid behind the curtains as she heard men's voices, one coming from the auditorium the other from the opposite side of the stage. Russell walked into the centre and spoke to Mr Pasco who was settling himself at a piano in the pit.

'It is very kind of you, sir, to help me. You've found the music?'

'Yes. *Tosca* right?'

'You found it, that's handsome.'

'Now, imagine this is your audition. Sing out, my boy.

Are you ready?' Alfred Pasco placed the sheet music on the stand.

'As ready as I'll ever be. If they don't like it I shall be stricken.'

Russell faced the empty theatre, his eyes upwards to the gallery as if it was packed to the rafters. He put his hands together under his chest as Mr Pasco played the introduction to the aria.

Flo couldn't believe she was so close to him again. She could step into the shady light and be in his arms or if she was sensible, tell them she was there, but she stayed quietly in the shadows, wrapped in the curtains watching. There was something about him not knowing she was there that excited her. Like seeing his performance through the opera glasses or taking a photograph, she was safe, protected behind the lens, a voyeur. She could just glimpse him from her hiding place, his ribs expanded to take in the air before the high notes, his hands gesturing with the emotion of the song. She had heard him sing before. In the *Pirates of Penzance* his voice was loud and clear with the rest of them, but today it was different. He seemed inhabited. A spirit had drawn him up and flown him above the music with a frightening passion. His voice woke her, nuzzled her, stroked her in places she never knew existed. What she felt was not from the pages of a romantic poem. No canoodling or small kisses pressed on pages of a valentine card. No rosy arbours. It was not what she imagined love to be. It was like animals. There was a fire between her legs she could not control. She prayed for the music to stop so she could slip away to the busy street, back to the tomb of her father's house. Unconsciously her hand moved down to the burning spot to touch herself, her fingers gently rustling against her dress. And as Russell sang she had her first orgasm.

Mr Pasco played the last note and there was a silence where the applause should have been. Eventually Alfred said, 'Boy you've got some notes there.'

'Thank you, sir. And thank you for playing so expertly.'

''Tis nothing. My hands are like plain meat compared to the fricassee of your talent. Don't you waste it.'

Russell suddenly spun around as if he might have heard Flo panting, wrapped in her hiding place, but then he jumped off the stage and picked up the sheet of music from the piano. The two men shared a joke as they walked up the aisle through the empty seats. Flo remained, her pale face a shimmering oval against the red plush curtains.

That evening in St Mary's church Flo's eyes were tightly shut as she prayed for forgiveness for her sin. Mr Trevern noticed the intense face of his eldest daughter with pride. Her devotion to God was pleasing.

'Good Lord, deliver us.'

'From all blindness of heart, from pride, envy, hatred and all uncharitableness,' intoned the priest

'Good Lord, deliver us.'

Flo knew the words that were coming.

'Almighty God, forgive me,' she whispered.

The priest surveyed his audience in the pews. He paused and with a look of accusation he spoke to each individual as if they were members of the Devil's pack.

'From fornication and all other deadly sin and from all the deceits of the flesh and the devil.'

Mr Trevern's walking stick fell to the ground knocked by Angel's swinging legs. It rolled echoing into the aisle and stopped with a clatter against the opposite pew. The priest tried to see who had disturbed his mantra and waited as Flo crept to retrieve the offending object. The accusing eyes of the church were on her. She felt it was a punishment. She had been found out. And it was more in the finding out that her suffering lay, for as long as her furtive moment was a secret she could carry on enjoying the memory of it. Deep in her heart she knew what she had done was not wrong. Such pleasure had to be God's creation. But she was sure the congregation could see her guilt radiating out of her, like the light coming through the stained glass window of Jesus in the arms of Mary.

Mr Trevern managed a smile to thank her and Angel continued to swing her legs. Annoyed, Flo held them tightly to stop her kicking. The litany was still in progress as Angel watched her elder sister's face sensing there was a change in her.

That night Flo returned to her dream. The river, the gas light hissing on the water, the thrashing shape like a dark monster sending ripples returning to the shore in quick, small crests. And this time she heard the anguished cry. It shivered through her body. If only she could see who it was? The neurons in her brain flashed from point to point trying to make connections but there was a failure somewhere. She needed all parts to be working to make the memory clear. And then in the slide changes of a dream she was in a boat rocking up and down between the sound of Russell's voice and her hot body. She was still dreaming when the boy selling fruit and vegetables from his cart woke her with his calling.

10

Nan rolled out the pastry for the pasties, sprinkling flour as the wooden pin turned and banged against the kitchen table. She felt out of sorts which was unusual for her. The meeting with Adam yesterday had left her marooned. She had always believed that if he returned from Africa they would be together. But no one had prepared her for his state of mind in the aftermath of war.

She had helped him back to his filthy cottage and managed his drunken weight as she steered him towards his bed. The condition of his room shocked her. The floor was a sheet of mud covered by footprints and at the windows tattered pieces of curtains barely covered the light. His bed clothes were damp from a hole in the roof where rain dripped steadily through and a pail of stagnant water sat beneath a table scattered with stale bread. Nan wondered how Adam had avoided the cholera that had swept through the town a few months earlier. She began to clean, shaking out his dirty blankets and she got down on her knees and washed the floor as best she could. Adam watched her, his eyes dull to the world and her caring. There was a moment when she hauled a fresh bucket into the room and dipped a cracked cup for him to drink from, he looked almost apologetic.

'What are you doing here, Nan?'

'You need some help, Adam Pollard.'

She guided his head towards the clean water. He collapsed back onto the mattress and she put his legs straight.

'Where did you come from my lady of the lake?' He looked at her with a lopsided grin and then passed out.

Nan sat on a stool watching him for a long time before she realised her father would be back from the clay pits and want his supper and her mother would need help with her brothers and sisters and there were more chores to be done and more water to be fetched from the well.

Flo came into the kitchen and stood beside Nan as she cut a shape like a boat from the pastry. Flo then took a portion each of beef, onions, potatoes and swede from four neat piles on the table and put them in the middle as Nan folded the pastry over and expertly crimped the top with her thumb. Angel would be wanting a licky one and the leeks were already cut into slim slices.

'Nan,' said Flo breaking into the silence that Nan was always careful to preserve, waiting for her mistress to speak first, 'I wanted to ask you, have you…?'

Nan looked up into Flo's worried face.

'Have I what, miss?'

'I am embarrassed to ask you.'

'What kind of subject would you be wanting to approach?' said Nan intuitively.

Flo could feel her experience of the day before racing through her veins with an incomprehensible victory. And yet here in the family kitchen it seemed like a dream, as if another person had peaked and sighed and touched herself.

Nan carefully phrased her sentence.

'Would this be to do with a man that you have a fancy for?'

'Oh Nan, I have to tell you for I don't know how to behave and he is never out of my thoughts. I cannot believe he noticed me, it's beyond my understanding that he has such eyes for me, and I want to ask you, forgive me. I'm ignorant…of what…happens… and I have feelings I should not have.'

'And who's to say what feeling you should have or not have?'

Nan was touched by her employer's innocence. Flo's question should have been answered by a mother when the time was right. But Flo had no mother and her father would run like a long dog if asked to discuss such a matter. She cleaned her hands on her apron and put her arm around Flo's shoulder.

She lowered her voice, 'I don't know for sure mind, but my mother says if you lie down in the hay grass on a summer's day with the boy you love, 'tis all starry.

'Starry?'

'Mmm like fireworks, no, much more than fireworks, like the feeling you get when you have a chocolate nicey.'

Flo considered this for a moment while Nan took the pasties to the oven.

'I've read Elizabeth Barrett Browning and she says, 'Love me sweet, with all thou art feeling, thinking, seeing, love me in the lightest part, love me in full being.'

'Sounds a bit up herself to me,' said Nan.

Flo looked at her hopelessly, her eyes full of melancholy.

'But even if someday I find – a person – who would marry me, I am not able to love him with all my being. My father would never allow me…'

Nan cut her off, unable to contain her opinions any longer.

'I don't belong to say it, but 'tis awful the way your father…'

Quentin Trevern came into the kitchen, the smell of chemicals like a halo around his clothes. He handed his hat and coat to Nan and looked at them suspiciously.

'And what are you girls whispering in corners for? Upstairs, Nan. Go and see to Angel. Flo has her reading to do.'

Nan hung her apron on the back of the door and went into the hall. Mr Trevern smelt the pasties cooking in the oven. It was a homey smell. It reminded him of his parents' house protected from the outside world and the overflowing workhouses. The wealthy Tweedy family had started soup kitchens during the last depression. He remembered the queues of shuffling men and women and their hungry faces. It was seeing those queues that made him vow it would never happen to him. Not to his family.

'No one can say I haven't educated you to the highest order, Florence. You know maths and poetry and you take a fair photograph. And you have all the comforts for a happy living.'

'Thank you, Father, you do much for me,' she paused searching for a way to tell him she had no friends, 'but sometimes I need…'

'And what is there for you to need?' He looked at her hard.

'You're getting too close to that girl for your position, she is only a servant. There's those who serve and those who pay them to serve. And it's best to keep a deal of air between them.' He opened the oven door and broke off a piece of pastry. 'Mind you she makes a pasty fit for a king.' He went to the back door and looked down the narrow garden full of fruit trees.

'Go and fetch my little Angel? I must feed the hens.'

Flo stood at the kitchen window watching Angel throwing food. Mr Trevern called to the birds and they came running to his feet and pecked at the grain.

'Chick, chick, chick, now don't 'ee be snotty now.'

He bent down to examine one of the hen's feet talking to it tenderly. 'You've got a bit of trouble there haven't you, my lover. Come here, my cherub.' He put his arm around Angel. She stood patiently beside her father as they watched the hen limping away.

Flo noticed her father's hand stroking Angel's back. For some reason it made her feel uncomfortable. If she could find an excuse to bring her sister indoors she would. But she couldn't think of one.

11

The steam from the London train enveloped the passengers waiting on the platform. Two men in black suits stepped into the wet clouds. Each carried a small suitcase. Prendergast was much taller than his companion, Jackson, who grimly surveyed the scrambled station packed with travellers. The season had started and the locals had steeled themselves for the onslaught of visitors. The emmits were not to be dismissed. The economy was beginning to depend on the new tourism. Thomas Cook had long been running train holidays to the West Country and now the beaches of Cornwall were attracting city dwellers choked by the furnaces of the manufacturing North. The building of the cathedral was definitely a draw.

Prendergast and Jackson were not holidaymakers. They had purpose in the tilt of their hats. Finally Jackson nodded towards the exit and they made their way out to the street.

Amelia shifted her weight so she could lean against Russell's bare arm. She could see the dark hair on his chest peaking from his shirt and it excited her. He put his glass of beer to his mouth and took a swig.

'Are you listening, maid?' he asked. She looked

disgruntled and picked at the wooden table.

John was sitting opposite them, his arm cosily around a blonde girl with wide, brown eyes.

'You see, Tosca trusted the wrong person. She should have trusted her lover, but she believed that evil sod, Scarpia. All because of jealousy,' said Russell, 'mind you, if you want a good sing, Scarpia is the part to play.'

'What you chittering on about?' Amelia was out of her depth.

'You see…' He stopped and searched her vacant face framed with a frizz of curly hair.

'Doesn't matter.'

Amelia felt his disinterest. A new development. A month ago he couldn't wait to get his hand up her skirt.

'You've been going on about that bloody opera all night, Russell Bell and to tell you the truth I'm sick as a shag with it.'

'Leave him be, Amelia, it's his hobby,' said John, 'every man's got to have his hobby. I've got mine,' and he pulled the blonde girl closer. 'Shall we have a walk 'en?'

The four of them left the public house and John ducked into an alleyway between two shops. He started kissing his girl.

Amelia unbuttoned her blouse. She reached out for Russell's hand and placed it on her breast.

'You do want a bit of that doan' 'ee?'

He felt the roundness of her flesh and moved his hand to her nipple as Amelia pressed her body against him. This was about as far as she would go. Leave them wanting more was her motto. She didn't want a come-by-chance child inside her before they were married, although Russell was a perfect choice. He was hard working and their families knew each other. He'd soon get the singing out of his system once they were nested. He just needed a little persuasion and she was sure they would be walking down the aisle by summertime.

The sound of men's voices in the street made Russell look up. Mr Trevern and Mr Ellery walked along the cobbles, their canes marking their footsteps as they passed. Mr Trevern glanced down the narrow drang and saw shapes moving. He knew they must be courting couples; the alleyways of the city were favourite places. But he wished they would be more discreet. Bizarrely the kissing and fondling affronted him, made him feel empty. It would linger in his mind ruining the evening, bringing memories he wanted to bury and sharpening pain he struggled to dull. Close it, he thought. Bring the sluice gates down. Only the trickle of water running through the wooden slats was containable.

Russell quickly removed his hand from Amelia's blouse as if Mr Trevern had caught him with his daughter.

'What's up with you?' she said, surprised.

'Tell you the truth; I'm not in the mood.'

'Well la-di-da, he's not in the mood.'

Russell rearranged his shirt and Amelia called after him not expecting to be abandoned. 'Where are you going?'

'Nowhere you can come.'

John and his girl were smooching closely, unaware that Amelia had run off in tears and Russell was walking towards Lemon Street. He stopped outside the Trevern house searching for a face at the window but the heavy curtains were drawn. A thin sliver of light broke the darkness of an upstairs bedroom as he stood under a gas lamp willing Flo to be there. For an hour he waited until the light went out.

The next day, after the long hours of work and the ride back to Truro, Russell opened a battered trunk looking for something suitable to wear. John had suggested his grandfather's best suit. It was left to him years ago and had lain mothballed and forgotten at the bottom of the case. He had never found the occasion to wear it but he was loath to pawn it. Secretly he was keeping it for his wedding day but he wasn't going to tell Russell and risk being ribbed.

Russell found the suit and shook it out. He held it up.

'I can't wear this. Looks like I've been stuffed and stuck down the museum. Smart, John, I've got to act up on this one.'

John had never seen Russell in such a fever. His face was contorted with minute muscles moving around his mouth and although his voice was not raised John could sense that the slightest word out of place would have launched an onslaught of recriminations.

It didn't stop him saying, 'Forgive me, Russell, but is a maid worth all this effort?'

'This one is'.

'Giss 'on.'

'It's true, John.'

'Bugger me,' said John seriously.

'I need a gentleman's outfit. Black with tails. And a tall hat.'

John walked over to the window. The forever sound of mournful gulls circling the rubbish tips at the bottom of the road mingled with the call of the town crier advertising a new cargo from a ship, 'If anyone have a mind to buy good earth coals...'

'I know who has that stuff.' John had an inspired thought. 'Those fiddle players in the orchestra. They've got fancy suits.'

After Russell had stood watching Flo's window praying

80

she might appear like Juliet talking to the stars, he had gone back to the room he shared with his brother in his parents' cottage and couldn't sleep for thinking about her. He knew she was socially above him and it was hopeless to pursue her, and given that her father was her jailer it was even more hopeless. But he had a strong belief that his world could change, one day he would have more to offer. From boyhood he had known he had talent, music was in his bones. The Cornish loved to sing but the difference between him and the other boys in the school choir was ambition. At seven years old his teacher, Mr Hocking, recognising the small boy's ability, brought him to the front of the class to sing a verse from a hymn and on Sundays his mother proudly watched him in chapel as the congregation searched along the pews to locate the strong voice belting out John Wesley's words. On the day the bargue *Emma* was wrecked near Land's End he sang, 'For Those in Peril on the Sea' unaccompanied from the pulpit, moving the congregation to tears, as the body-count mounted on southern beaches.

At home his mother told him how special he was, what a voice God had given him. Perhaps if he practised he could sing in the theatre? But his father dismissed his wife's encouragement. There was to be no future as a theatrical. After his schooling Russell was to learn a trade and contribute to the family. Be a tanner like himself or work at the clay pit, earn proper money. Without her husband knowing his mother saved pennies from the washing she took in and bought her son sheet music and story books of the operas and once he could read, he devoured them, often late at night burning candles they could ill afford. He practised singing every moment he could. His father would banish him to the streets and then Russell would creep around to the stage door of the theatre and beg to be allowed to watch the amateurs in rehearsal. Sometimes they let him sing with them and once they gave him a song to sing on his own. When he finished he felt the surge of satisfaction and completeness as the group applauded enthusiastically. He was hooked. After his voice broke they called at his home and his father was persuaded. He became a member of the Opera Society. So the D'Oyly Carte was not a dream. Their letter had been read and re-read until the folds were deep furrows across the paper. He had replied to the board saying that within the year he would be in a position to audition for them. There was real chance for him to escape the poverty of physical labour.

He had pushed his sleepy brother's arm away as it flopped over him in the bed. Grumbling, the boy took the blanket with him, leaving Russell stranded in his underclothes. He heard his young sister crying for his mother and then the sound of footsteps crossing his parents' room as she went to the crib. After all he thought, weren't opera singers famous the world over? What was wrong with asking to spend time with Florence Trevern. There were many photographers who would be puffed up like a bladder of lard to take a picture of a successful singer. Why should he worry about Mr Trevern? If he was arrogant it came from a single-mindedness not to waste his talent.

It was these thoughts that eventually led him to John's door in search of a suit to wear when he went to the house on Lemon Street to ask Flo's father if he could walk out with her.

The wet granite streets were shining grey and tawny as Russell arrived at a public house by the quayside. It was busy. Four ketches were moored against the jetty and dockers were unloading into the night. At the end of the room tapping his feet to a piano was Bert Trevorrow, his long, greasy hair hanging down his jacket and his fingers stained with tobacco. He had been there a long time. He'd forgotten how long. All day perhaps. He was playing the old songs, 'Going up Camber' Hill Going Down,' and 'The White Rose.' Some of the tunes brought tears to his eyes but as long as the ale was flowing he would fiddle all night, his bow flying backwards and forwards across the strings. It was very different from the music he played in the theatre for the amateur opera.

Russell called to him, 'Bert, my man, lend us your dressing up suit for the evening.'

'Where you be off to 'en?'

'None of your business, my lover.'

Russell massaged Bert's shoulders. 'What you drinking? More of the same?'

'Stand us another two and you can have the suit, though the hat's gone, I don't call home 'zactly what happened to 'n' but I do think one of my Jerseys ate it.'

Bert chortled showing his gums where his teeth had dropped out years ago.

On his way back along Boscawen Street with Bert's suit carefully draped over his arm Russell passed Treleaven's the men's outfitters. He inspected the collection of hats in the window. Top hats, straw boaters, day hats and cloth caps, a hat for every position in life. It was essential if he was to have any confidence visiting the Trevern household he wore the right hat.

His eye was caught by an item placed in a central position in the window, displayed with pride. 'The Acaric' a notice said, 'This sock suspender prevents that Fatal Slipping Down of Sock!' For a second Russell knew his place. To spend his back breaking money on a contraption that would varicose your veins in seconds was a mystery. He read on, 'After a month's use, they'll never consent to be without them, and so kill another of life's little worries.'

Russell fished his money out of his pocket. He could do without the Acaric but did he have enough for a top hat? That was the worry.

Mr Trevern insisted on having a lion's head door knocker. He had seen one in Falmouth when he was a boy and had promised himself, when he had his own property, it would be one of the first things he would buy. It was bright, polished and glowing with importance, when Russell arrived at the house.

He adjusted his new hat. It felt odd perched on his head, uncomfortable. It made him hold his head upright in one position and strangely affected the movement of his face. The concentration frowned his eyebrows and gave him an odd, distracted look. He pulled himself up to his full height and breathed in. The waistcoat of the suit was too tight but he dared not undo any buttons. It would not be acceptable for a gentleman to have an open waistcoat.

When Nan saw Russell she giggled. He looked hurt for a second and immediately she wished she hadn't laughed.

'Why, Russell Bell, and what have you got to do here?'

'I have come to speak to Mr Trevern regarding a matter,' said Russell, his face frozen in rigor mortis

'A matter. Hm!'

Russell removed his hat so he could speak normally.

'Give us a chance, Nan.'

'You stay put here and I'll get him,' said Nan stifling another giggle.

Russell stepped into the hallway busy with landscape paintings and anaglypta wallpaper. He stood on a rug and glanced down at his feet. He hadn't been able to afford new shoes and his work boots looked odd beneath the black trousers of the evening suit. He moved off the rug onto the polished, oak floor hoping for camouflage. Perhaps Mr Trevern would ignore his footwear.

On the wall was a painting of a woman. She sat with her back to the viewer her head half turned in profile, her blonde hair caught up casually with a silver clasp. Draped around her shoulders was a Spanish shawl, red roses against a black background. Her beauty was undeniable but Russell could see how sensitively she had been painted. The strokes of the brush softened and disappeared into her skin. Her aquamarine eyes were delicately flecked with white and she looked into the distance as if someone was calling to her. She seemed so alive. He felt that if he reached out and touched her she would speak. And yet there was something mournful about her, something impermanent, as if she might suddenly drift away like a ghost.

He didn't hear the door to Mr Trevern's study open and close.

'You approve of my work.'

Russell jumped. 'Oh yes, sir. Very fine.'

He replaced his hat and then removed it in a wide, sweeping gesture.

'Good evening, sir,' he said with a bow. He was unused to bowing in a social situation and half way down he wondered if he had gone too low.

'The young opera singer. Good evening.'

Mr Trevern was abrupt wondering what the man was doing in his house in a borrowed suit.

'Have you come to talk about the photograph? It was to

your liking I hope?

'Oh yes, sir, it was magnificent. Yes.'

There was a pause as Mr Trevern waited for Russell to explain himself. Russell took off his hat again. He had rehearsed this bit and felt on safe ground. He bowed again, not so deeply.

'Good evening.'

'Good evening.'

Mr Trevern was annoyed. They had been through the meet and greet formality. What was wrong with the boy?

'Good evening.'

Russell couldn't remember what was to come next. Eventually he said, 'I'll get straight to the point.'

'I wish you would,' replied Mr Trevern eyeing the study. He was half way through the financial report on tin mining shares in the local paper and wanted to look up the percentages.

Flo appeared on the landing above them and peeped down into the well of the hall. She could see the top of a head but it was only when Russell spoke she was sure it was him.

'Well?' said Mr Trevern more aggressively.

Russell drew a deep breath. He clutched the hat in front of him for protection and stared ahead beyond the gaze of the older man.

'I am here to invite your daughter, Florence, to join me for tea at the Assembly Rooms.'

Flo made a small sound and immediately her hand went to her mouth.

Mr Trevern's face never moved. It was as if the question had been spoken in another language and needed to be translated. Russell held his position. A clock ticked loudly somewhere behind him and an itch had developed in his cheek demanding to be scratched.

'Out of the question. Now, will you please leave.' Mr Trevern walked towards a bell on the wall but Russell continued.

'I'll take good care of her, sir, the Assembly Rooms is a respectable establishment, she is proper safe with me.'

Mr Trevern turned like a bull about to charge, although somehow he managed to hang on to civility.

'I doubt that, sir.'

'Be reasonable, sir. My intentions are honourable. I think she would like to have time with a person of her own age who wants nothing but to make her happy.'

'The answer, sir, is no. Her place is with me do you understand? She doesn't belong to go courting and even if she could, do you imagine I would let her gallivant about town with a pauper like you. I know what you are, despite your fancy clothes. My daughter is used to high living, what would she be doing with you but cleaning the clay from your shoes.'

Mr Trevern pointed at Russell's boots. He hadn't got away with it.

'Now get out before I turn you to the doors.'

He strode into the study and slammed door. Russell heard him banging objects around the room and then the sound of a smashed glass. Nan appeared cautiously from the kitchen her eyes as wide as saucers.

'Be gone, Russell, before I get afraid.'

Russell thought he heard a noise from upstairs but when he looked, the landing was empty. Had Flo seen him? How stupid he must be in his new hat and a suit that was too tight. His resolve vanished. He was back in the pit hacking at the clay with his shyver. Heaving the trucks up the incline. Employed by the masters at the engine house. And

Mr Trevern was one of them.

He stepped out into a misty damp night watched by Flo framed in her bedroom window. He paused for second under the lamplight and Flo could see his face. She guessed how he was feeling. Her father was a master at making people feel inadequate.

As he arrived at Lemon Bridge he punched his fist through the hat. He leant over the skummy water clogged here and there with waste and household rubbish and hurled it into the swirling mess. It caught in an eddy and then sedately floated out to the wide expanse of the Truro River.

A knock. Flo did not move from the window as her father tentatively opened the door. He was carrying an oil lamp. There was a slight wind chilling the back of her neck from the half-open window but still she did not move.

'I've filled it up for you. It was close to empty,' he said, knowing she understood it was an excuse for him to come to her room.

He had waited downstairs for what seemed a suitable time after Russell had left before climbing the stairs. He needed to talk to her. He was sure she must have heard him shout and he knew it must have upset her. For despite the unfathomable jealousy he felt, the complex turns and spirals that took him to a place where he wandered without hope reaching out to grab any stray particle of reason floating through the entanglement he had created, he realised she was of age to go courting.

Flo didn't speak. It was the only choice and familiar. To say what she felt was unthinkable.

Mr Trevern coughed and wiped his moustache. It was turning yellow from too much cigar smoking.

'You know that I care for you, Florence?' he said.

'I do, Father.'

'And you know there is nothing I would do to purposely hurt you, but...' He trailed off and looked glassy-eyed at the floor as if he had forgotten what he had come to say, '...but you can't have everything. Life's not like that and if you try to have it all, do you know what happens?'

Flo looked at her father's guilty face. There was something about the way he was behaving that unsettled her. The drop of his mouth after each word. The self-pitying tone that lacked a sense to it. In the deadness of his eyes she saw her own and it frightened her. What was the border between sanity and madness? A blink maybe? A small unnoticed movement? Many times after waking from her turbulent dreams she feared she could become like the rabid dogs that roamed the town with death in their bite. But now she saw it was her father who was in danger.

'I'll tell you what happens,' her father finally said, 'you get destroyed. Ruined. And if you ever think to leave Angel and me you'll never be happy, I can promise you that. So it is best to be grateful for what you have. For terrible unhappiness can turn a person mazed.'

'Thank you, Father.'

The light from the oil lamp threw ghost shadows on the wall as Mr Trevern moved towards the door.

'And another thing. You must remember all we have is each other. No one is to be trusted. We must protect ourselves from others who want to break us apart. It happens when you least expect it.'

And he went out as if a memory had returned and was sticking to his shoes like a piece of blown paper.

Flo crossed to the window and closed it shut with a bang. She drew the curtains, locking out the night air. She took off her dress and stood in her cotton petticoat in front of a mirror in the wardrobe door. She stared at herself looking for any trace of madness. The person in the mirror was someone else. Her eyes seemed to be black stones on the beach after the sea had soaked them to a shine. But there was a missing connection between what she felt inside and the image looking back at her. The other Florence was freer, wilder. Ignoring the rules, she went swimming in the summer when the sun was burning hot. She had heard of a pool in the woods where boys went to bathe and swing on ropes across the brackish water. No one knew how deep the pool was. Some said it was as deep as Dozmary Pool, where King Arthur threw his sword Excalibur and the disembodied hand rose from the surface to pull the blade to the bottomless depths. This other Flo hid in the jungle undergrowth, took off her clothes and slipped into the coolness alone. She felt the drag of the soft water covering her like a kid glove, watched the sun flashing on and off through the trees and saw king fishers swoop on dragon flies as the sound of her naked body passed creamily through the lake.

She stepped out of her petticoat and liked what she saw. The shape of her breasts above her flat stomach surprised her. They were beautiful. With a professional eye she could see how her body was in proportion. Perhaps she was too slim but the picture worked. She began to imagine the impossible. That she could photograph the image smudged in the lamplight. She noticed the curves, the shadows, the soft focus of her skin, the rising shapes. She turned sideways and passed her hands over her breasts and stomach. She trembled as she reached her pubic hair. In the mirror, the other Florence smiled back as the two became one.

12

J ackson and Prendergast hitched a ride to a clay worker's cottage near St Austell. They ate a meal of potato stew and drank cider before planning their strategy.

After dinner Ned showed them to a stone shed in his back yard where they slept on bales of straw with a blanket between them. The discomfort didn't bother them. They had other things on their minds. They could sleep in a pig sty with the pigs if they needed too. If the cause demanded.

The next day they gathered at the bottom of Castle Hill with their small band of supporters for a protest walk through Truro to shout for justice.

As Nan walked back from market carrying a brass pot she had to step aside to let the banner waving procession pass. One of the men banged a drum and they all stamped their boots marching to the rhythm. A young wife put a leaflet in Nan's basket and she glanced down at it.

'Clay Pit Workers Unite,' it read, 'Join the Union Today.'

Nan screwed up the paper and threw it to the ground. Ahead of her an old woman came out of her front door to find out what the commotion was about. She was carrying a bucket of slops and as she looked at the words rippling across the road, challenging everything that made her life safe, she instinctively hurled her bucket over the nearest convert turning him into a stinking mess. That'll learn them thought Nan. This is Cornwall where no Union men are. What would they need with that nonsense? Let the Northerners wallow in it and the bloody Welsh. It wasn't for her.

Nan reached Adam's cottage and opened the door. She placed the pot on the stove but its golden brassiness looked out of place in the dirty room. He lay on the bed with soulful eyes watching her as she started to clean and scrub.

'What you doing here, Nan?' he said abruptly, his voice breaking into her soapy concentration. She could work away as much as she liked he thought but she won't change a buggering thing. I will stay here until I quail away to nothing. Until I'm a pile of withered, useless bones. And she will never understand.

Nan stopped scrubbing. She was half way across the floor and it was coming up well. It just needed a bit of care and Adam's room would be a home. She had already wiped the grime off the windows and stuffed old newspapers around the cracks in the frames. Flo had given her some pieces of material and there were new curtains nearly finished. She would light the stove before she left and he could sit griddly by the fire and warm his damaged legs. She would take care of him. Bring him back to life.

'You need some help, Adam, and I'm the one to do it.'

She poured more water onto the boards and pressed the yellow soap into the brush.

'I'm alright on my own. You don't have to be doing for me,' he answered irritably.

He dragged one of his legs from the bed to the floor and winced with the effort. His exasperation grew.

'It's done now. Just go.'

'No, it's not finished yet.'

She watched him lift his other leg across the bed. He

reached for his crutches that he had managed to strap together with rope. He couldn't walk far on them. They would give way under his weight before he reached the town. But they helped him move about the cottage and allowed him to sit on the step so he could give a few coins to neighbours who passed. He always had beer in the mornings. Filled to the brim. He could taste it on his lips now. Feel the liquid anaesthetising the boredom of the day.

'I don't want you here, Nan, go on! Go away!'

His voice was rough and his eyes burned in his sunken face. He never thought of himself as a ladies' man and yet Nan had waited patiently for him to return. What had she seen in him with his big nose and his skin dotted with freckles? His father used to say, 'A brackety cheild is a healthy cheild.' Meaning somehow his freckles would help him survive the hazards of childhood. Healthy! What did he know. At least he hadn't lived to see his only son's shame. To see him weak and malingering. A coward who ran away.

'Did you hear me. I don't want you here.'

Nan hid her hurt by scrubbing harder. If the floor was clean everything would fall into place. Adam's legs would heal. He would forget the trouble in the land of savages. They would be happily married and have many children. He bent over her willing her to empty her bucket.

'Look here, Nan.' His voice was gentler, more cajoling.

'You don't understand what it does to me. Seeing you coming and going and me sitting here like a dead dog. Just think woman.'

'But I like to be near you.'

'No! No! You don't understand.'

Adam stumbled to the door and banged it open with one of the sticks. His voice was louder, more aggressive as he pointed at the sky.

'You can walk where you want. Run where you want and see places I'll never see again. I'm useless. If I didn't have my pension, I'd be begging on the street. What do you want with me?'

'You are my man, Adam.'

She spoke firmly with the no nonsense tone she used for her brothers and sisters and there was a certainty in her words that silenced him.

The sun appeared through the door and a block of light showed up the vanilla colour of the clean boards. He could smell the bleach rising and it reminded him of his childhood. He saw himself jumping off the rocks at Malpas with his friends, kicking his legs and sinking into the verdigris water, the light fading above him, taunting the younger ones to come and join him before clambering out dripping naked to jump again and again. He wanted to forget. Forget the athletic man who thought nothing of walking ten miles to watch the wrestling. Why didn't she go? He could be sitting on his step by now waiting for Tregorro or Tonkin to bring him beer. Not confronted by her obstinate devotion.

'Before I went away we were never promised, Nan,' he said almost inaudibly.

He leant on the door frame not wanting to see what his words had done to her. To look into her crumpled face would be too much.

13

I t was a back street cottage like any other with a peeling front door and black curtains at the windows. He wasn't sure he should be there. Usually he was at home with his daughters by now. At least he had persuaded Nan to stay overnight. Although what use she'd be in the event of an intruder God only knew.

He peered down the street to check no one had noticed them but the rows of cottages were mute and unseeing. Faintly he could hear noises inside, laughter and a piano. The drunken faces of Ellery and Pasco swayed before him their eyes alight, their faces like beacons. Parr was fairly gone too. Only Fairfax appeared sober with a strange aloofness as if he were above it all. Foreigners thought Quentin, they're all the same.

'This is it,' said Silvanius Parr and he fumbled for a bell.

'Now are you sure?' said Mr Trevern, 'I'm not going to knock and have some woman glower at me like a hen 'afore day.'

Mr Fairfax stepped between them and thumped the door with his fist.

'Oh yes, this is most certainly the place.'

The men waited expectantly. Mr Ellery farted loudly.

'That's better out than in,' he said in a high pitched

giggle. He was past tipsy now and there were two Treverns moving in a mirage before him.

'For God's sake, James, can't you keep your emissions to yourself?' Annoyed, Quentin moved away as Mr Ellery began to sing.

'I've seen 'em, I've seen 'em, I've been in between 'em and the hairs on her dickey dye doe hung down to her knees.'

Alfred Pasco joined in with harmonies in his deep baritone voice as they repeated the verse.

Quentin wanted to leave. It was a mistake. The others had persuaded him when he was tipsy with port at the Royal Hotel. He was sober now and a shifting uneasiness had settled in. He pictured Angel lying in her bed, her eyelids closed and fluttering with dreams. She had probably waited for him to say good night and he had disappointed her.

The lamplighter stepped from the pavement into the road to pass the group of top hats blocking his way. He had finished illuminating the town for the evening and was on his way home to his wife. He kept his eyes on the ground. He recognised all of them but he needed them to understand he had not seen them. Quentin quickly put a scarf over his face. The others were still singing embarrassingly loudly and his worry increased. There was sure to be someone who would look through their curtains and spot him. It would not be good for business. Men would not like their wives to be photographed by a beauty lover.

'There's no one answering, James, I'm off home.'

Mr Parr caught his arm. 'Hang on they'll be here directly.'

The door suddenly opened and a woman appeared with a face that looked as if had been scraped from the bottom of the ocean. Her white painted skin was pitted with marks like lichen on rocks and on her head was a matted, orange wig.

Her rouged lips chewed mechanically on a piece of tobacco. Instinctively Quentin recoiled from her. He covered his nose with his handkerchief as if germs had sprung out of her pores instead of perspiration. There was something about the red, gaping hole of her mouth that disgusted him. It was the mouth of an octopus, a rotating orifice that would grind you to minced meat if you were stupid enough to get caught in it. The woman grinned knowingly and held out her palm.

Mr Ellery paid the money and they stumbled over each other into a narrow hallway. She led the way into a shabby room lit by candles packed with men drinking and smoking. A few tables and chairs had been placed at one end looking towards a small raised stage with a piano in the corner. A young woman appeared in a cotton blouse, her breasts hanging loose as if she had fed too many babies. She directed the men to a table and plonked down a jug of beer. Quentin sat uncomfortably on the edge of his chair.

'I'd heard of it, but I'd never seen anything like it before,' he muttered to Silvanius Parr.

'It's been here years. Backalong times there were two of them. If you weren't proper prudish, Quentin, you'd have been with us last time we came. Hang on a second, the show begins!'

The man at the piano began to play 'She was poor but she was honest'. The piano was out of tune and the song, barely recognizable. From a door at the corner of the stage two girls appeared and glided enticingly towards the audience. The men hooted and whistled.

'Get them clothes off,' shouted Mr Parr.

Quentin looked at him in amazement. He'd never seen this side of Silvanius before. He hunted for the exit. Just a few strides and he'd be out but another group of men had squeezed themselves into the room and were raucously cheering, swinging their glasses above their heads, blocking his way.

The girls peeled off the top layer of their clothes as they routinely went through their dance. Quentin could see they were very young. About thirteen or fourteen. Barely out of childhood. Although their movements were sexual their blank faces showed a strange detachment as if their bodies belonged to someone else. A feeling of disgust and anger welled up in him. It shouldn't be allowed. He would report it to the council tomorrow and have the place shut down. These girls' souls would be saved. What father would allow his daughter to be performing in such a disgusting manner. He remembered Florence at this age. Her small limbs and boyish figure and it wouldn't be long before Angel... His vision blurred in the candlelight. The stifling atmosphere was making him feel faint. One of the girls had blonde hair and golden skin. It was Angel smiling at him and rotating her hips, her arms making movements in the air. He shook his head and swilled some beer around his mouth, he felt faintly sick. Drunkenly a man lurched onto the stage and tried to grab the girl but a burly heavyweight pushed him back to his seat. The audience booed and shouted.

The girls were down to their corsets urging the men on. Mr Parr's face glistened.

'That's some beauty. What I'd do to get my hands on that new flesh.'

'If you scrape the paint of her, she's no more handsome than a frying pan full of arseholes,' said Mr Trevern trying to avoid the gyrating show before him.

'What's the matter with you, Quentin? Relax. Enjoy the natural talent of Truro. It's what you need. You've been on your own for too long'

'This is not to my taste, Silvanius.'

The girls were moving around the tables touching the men as they slowly undid their corsets. One of them approached Mr Parr and sexily shoved her boot in his lap as he furtively tried to undo his flies.

'Come here, my beauty, have a look at what I could give 'ee.'

The girl playfully kicked him. The men clapped as she moved on to Mr Fairfax. She ruffled his hair and he tried to touch her legs. Artfully she twisted away and moved on to Mr Trevern.

For a second she wasn't sure if she should find another punter. Occasionally she came across a man to be avoided. A man who had hate in his eyes. He would slash her open before she could get his flesh in her mouth and leave her dead and bloodied. Another statistic for the city's moralists. Another beauty down. There was something about this man that made her uneasy.

But the men were cheering even louder, needing to be satisfied. The girl glanced at the woman in the wig who watched with hawk eyes by the door. She trailed her hand along the back of Quentin's neck and then turned around waggling her bareness at him.

He tried to get up but Mr Parr pulled him back and held him firmly. The girl lowered herself onto Quentin's lap grinding into his legs. He thought. he could smell her genitalia. He was sure it was a dirty smell and it engulfed him until there was no air in the room to breathe. He looked around wildly and jumped up in a fit of nervousness knocking beers from the table and the girl to the floor.

'Get off me, get off,' he yelled.

As the minder began pushing his way towards the table Quentin waved his cane blindly and cleared a path through the sweating bodies. The girl angrily stuck up two fingers at him.

Mr Fairfax's impassive face, a ribbon of smoke trailing from his cheroot was an out of focus photograph. The last thing he saw as he escaped the room.

It was only when he reached his front door and slammed it shut that Quentin realised he had run all the way. He bent down and hacked into his handkerchief. He knew he should go into his study in case Florence woke up and found him but he couldn't move until his ankles had stopped hurting.

As he raised his head he came face to face with Isabella. He hadn't looked at the portrait so closely for years. He didn't know why it wasn't put away with the others. Probably because it was painted with her eyes focused elsewhere so there was no danger of her watching him. But tonight the chance encounter drowned him with memories which he surfed wave after wave until he slumped in a chair. He took off his hat. It had left a red circle around his forehead and the usual headache was developing. He went to a cupboard in the kitchen, knocking bottles of medicine over in his hurry to find his quinine and he swallowed a large mouthful before climbing the stairs and creeping along the landing. He paused outside Flo's door to listen for a second and then opened the door opposite.

Angel was lying on her side with her thumb in her mouth, her bedclothes pushed away revealing her legs beneath her nightdress. A circle of dolls, their vacant eyes wide in their ceramic faces were daring intruders to harm her. He walked over to the bed and had to stop abruptly to avoid stepping on a miniature table and chair that had fallen from a large doll's house. The front was swinging open and he could see by the light on the landing how each replica room had been played with, as if the occupants of this other tiny world had suffered a great storm blowing pictures to the floor and kitchen utensils to the bedroom.

Quentin watched his daughter sleeping and his heart broke. He wanted to eat her she was so perfect. He had an overwhelming urge to reach out and stroke her, hold her tightly until her translucent silkiness moulded to him, until she became part of him so that the love he felt inside would not be coloured by the pain of her separateness.

He leant close to her face, listening to her small intakes of air and kissed her cheek. She stirred and lay on her back, her arms outstretched, her legs apart. Even with her underdeveloped body Quentin could see how like her mother she was, the slim hips and long legs. He remembered Isabella, her body ready for him, her legs parted and her pelvis thrusting upwards. He never realised how much a woman could enjoy being with a man. He had known only one girl before her. True she had let him roughly poke his fingers between her thighs before she flounced away pretending it had all been his fault. But he had been a virgin when he married. It was Isabella who seemed to know what to do. She had taken him easily into her body opening herself up as if she was made for him.

He reached out and touched Angel's legs. A flame licked his groin. He moved back alarmed. Angel's face had changed. She was the girl in the brothel thrusting her nubile body towards him, calling him to caress her, giving him signals to go ahead and enjoy her. The flame vanished and Angel shifted position and curled up on her side, her legs tucked together again, thumb back in her mouth. She mumbled an unrecognisable word in a dream, her childish voice breaking the silence and then fell into a deep sleep.

A pulse was pounding in Quentin's head. Why hadn't he seen his daughter's sexuality before? What further torment had the Devil sent? Hadn't he suffered enough with the emptiness that dogged him day after day?

The dolls stared accusingly, their black eyes his judge and jury. Ashamed, he looked down at his hands. He wanted to touch her again but something had happened that frightened him. It had to be forgotten. He drew the covers over her and tucked the bedclothes under the mattress before leaving the room as hushed as he came in.

14

Nan slipped quietly into the Lemon Street house. She was late and she hoped that Mr Trevern had already left for his studio so she wouldn't have to brave up to his glowering face. There was no one at home but she waited in the hallway, listening to make sure. The air was thick and stuffy as usual. Mr Trevern worried about germs and refused to have any windows open. How the mistress put up with it she didn't know.

The thought of Flo's relationship with her father made Nan tut as she opened the door to the kitchen and plonked down her basket. What a life the girl lived. It wasn't right and now, by all accounts she had an admirer. It wouldn't come to much but surely the poor girl could enjoy it while it lasted. As she stoked the fire and hung a partridge in the larder she continued to shake her head. The drowning of Mrs Trevern had made headlines all over Cornwall. She had been walking by the river and her parasol had blown across the water. In an attempt to reach it she had lost her footing and fallen into one of the many pools concealed in the river bed. Her skirts had dragged her under and the treacherous currents pulled her downstream. But it was all conjecture. A journalist's story. No one actually saw her drown. She had been found white and bloated, clumps of sea lettuce in her hair, face down on the mud flats at Tresillian. Mr Trevern was called to identify her while Florence stayed at home to take care of the newborn baby. Her body was blue and full of gashes, weeds were wrapped around her face and part of her leg was missing. Nan had heard it from the fisherman who found her. When he returned Mr Trevern howled and raged with grief but told Flo that her mother had looked like the painting of Ophelia by Millais. She had been lying on her back, her face lifted upwards to Heaven, the palms of her hands open like Jesus on the cross and red and blue flowers were lodged in her dress. She was still beautiful. This was all before Nan had come to work for the family and in the four years she had been there, the tragedy was never mentioned.

She forced some wet clothes through the mangle in the basement and put them in a laundry basket to take out to the washing line. She found it strange that Florence rarely spoke of her mother. She assumed the shock had been too much for her. It was not an unusual reaction. She had heard of a man who suddenly was struck dumb at the loss of his wife and was dead within the year.

A creak of floorboards made her aware there was someone moving in one of the rooms above her. She carried the washing up the back staircase and reached the hallway. She could see the sitting room door was open. Surely it was too early for Mr Trevern to return to the house? If she didn't get the pasties on soon, they would be eating boughten ones and he would complain for days.

Flo was in the drawing room with a book on her lap. Nan could see her copper, braided hair against the black of her high collar. She was always in dark clothes. Nan never understood why. She was too attractive to look like a widow. She turned, surprised at Nan's sudden intrusion into her private reverie. She looked as if she'd been crying, her cheeks were puffy and her eyes red.

'Oh forgive me, miss, I thought you were down to the bookshop,' said Nan.

Flo looked away. Now there was no hope for a relationship with Russell her feelings had diminished into a small, tight knot in her stomach that sometimes sent feelers like vines creeping upwards to freeze her face. She touched the faint frown line on her forehead.

'I've been reading *The Water Babies*. It's very sad but rather fine too. There is a chapter called 'Tom's journey to the other end of Nowhere'. And I've been thinking,' she paused and closed the book on her lap, 'unfortunately it is how I feel.'

'Sounds like a good book to me, but I don't think you should get in such a stewer as you do.'

Nan went over to the window and boldly threw it open letting the salt-laden air fill the room.

'Smell summer coming,' she said and an idea popped into her head. She picked up a plate left by Mr Trevern the night before and stood in front of Flo demanding her attention. Something had to be done.

'Come to the Flurry dance with me,' said Nan. This was not a request you could easily ask your employer. Although there was a friendship between them Nan was always careful to keep her place.

Flo stared at her for a moment and then said, 'Mr Trevern would never allow me, you know that, Nan'

'You can't live without partying, it's not natural.'

'There is nothing I can do.'

'Don't you give up so easy. If he has objections then let him have them. But you and I are going.'

She held Flo's hands and added, 'He won't know we're gone.'

'How?'

'We'll find a way.'

'Oh, Nan, do you think…?'

'I shall do a spell.'

'I can't, Nan. If he found out my life would be impossible.'

'Have faith my handsome, we will go. And do you know who might be there?'

Flo examined Nan's face wanting to believe what she was saying but wondering if it was too much to hope for.

'That's settled then.'

Nan smiled, a wide slice broadening her round cheeks. She would make sure Russell was told. Put the two together however mismatched they were. Maybe it was meant. The spirits had chosen it. And if that was true she would be rewarded for her match making.

Flo was suddenly worried again.

'What is it?' said Nan.

'But I don't know how to do the Flora dance.'

'Is that all? Then I shall have to show you Miss, won't I?'

Russell searched for John among the sea of heads crammed into the hall. He had been depressed and too heavy with failure to find a way out. With each blow of his shovel he'd tried to shrug it off, but it shadowed him from the clay pits to the bars and back to his room. Not only had he to wait for his audition, now he had been banned from courting Florence Trevern. And worse. Arabella had been chasing him, coquettishly promising more. Casually bumping into him in the street, flashing her turquoise eyes, sticking out her tongue and giggling in corners with friends as if she'd heard how he'd been turned to the doors by Quentin

Trevern. He ignored her but she didn't seem to mind until finally he lost his temper and gave her a shove. She'd fallen over and hurt her knee and he picked her up leaking with remorse. She yelled at him but it didn't stop her finding him again.

His days were filled with Flo. He devoured the thought of her. She drifted in and out of his dreams where he imagined her in his arms and he woke with wetness and frustration. And now he had to meet John and the Union men. He had no interest in it.

Finally he saw him sitting beside Nan Peters's father and made his way down the line of workers on the benches.

'Didn't think you were coming,' grunted John rolling a leaflet into a cone in his hands. Russell squeezed in beside him.

'Where are they from?'

Jack Peters answered the question.

'Somewhere up North I'm told. Bloody foreigners if you ask me.'

Jackson and Prendergast stepped onto the platform and the room quietened. The two men were different from the Cornish workforce, they were like Vikings, red-haired and tall with strong Yorkshire accents. Their audience struggled to understand them and an irritation spread.

'Men of Cornwall,' said Prendergast, 'no doubt you term us agitators. We are pleased to be called it, for there is such a thing brothers, as righteous discontent.'

One of the clay workers called out, 'Why don't 'ee go back to where you belong.'

There were cheers from a group of men at the back who had only come to barrack and jeer. Prendergast ignored the heckler and waited for the interruption to die down.

'Men of Cornwall, you are putting up with the worst

wages in Britain, but you are working in one of the wealthiest industries in Britain.'

'Get your arses back where you belong.'

Prendergast raised his voice, 'You are too content down here for your own well being. Don't you know your fellow workers in the North are protected by unions?'

'We don't want unions down here,' said Jack Peters with dignity.

There was a pause as Prendergast sat down and raised his eyebrows to Jackson who took his place. His friend surveyed the hostile room for a second and then said, 'Men please listen to me. I am bringing you good news.'

The mood subtly changed. A natural public speaker, Jackson had the knack of talking to each worker individually.

'When your children are asking for new boots because the damp coming through the holes is rotting their feet, think of the master's children, think of the clothes that adorn their backs, for while you remain unorganised you'll never need a handcart to carry your wages home.'

'God bless you,' shouted an old man, his voice resonating with the truth of his childhood.

'I know trade unions are not known to you yet,' said Jackson warming to his subject, 'but if only half of you were true men and would come out in protest, it would be enough to force that fancy lot with dividends burning fires in their pockets to pay you fairer wages. Men, you workers, who dig, wash, dry and load the clay with the sweat of your backs, earn a meagre wage because the toffs, that tell you their earnings are swallowed up in working expenses, are pocketing the surplus to pay for their own luxuries. This is unfair to any man's comprehension. The time has come for action.'

He reached his finale and his voice rose to a crescendo,

'The time has come for all men to join forces and with one voice speak out against the masters. Listen to my message and act on it. Be not afraid for your voices to shout, we have had enough of your lying.'

A few men were on their feet with shouts of agreement. Jackson knew he had found takers but not enough. This was a tough meeting. What was the matter with them? He lowered his voice. A technique he had learnt during his years of campaigning to make a crowd listen.

'Join us, my friends, join our union and have a more prosperous and happy life.'

The Yorkshiremen stepped from the platform to polite applause. The clayworkers folded back to make a path, examining them as if they were a strange species from another planet.

John patted Jackson's back as he passed. 'You are welcome here as far as I'm concerned, captain.'

'We need all the support we can get.' Mr Jackson said intensely and he shook John's hand vigorously before moving down the hall.

'Why do you want to get involved?' asked Russell picking up his cap.

'Dignity, Russell. It's all about dignity.'

John's heart felt lighter. For the first time in his adult life he was excited. Jackson and Prendergast had touched a nerve, a core of resentment that had built up over years of working the pit. Horizons appeared in front of him and he wallowed in the expansion of his world. They were giving him a voice and out of that voice came power. A feeling he was not accustomed to. He liked it and wished Russell could feel the same. But he wasn't going to argue tonight

The driving rain hit them as they left. A storm cloud had

burst over the hills and water was pouring down the gullies at the side of the road. Russell turned up his collar and considered the clouds knowingly.

'It will be over soon, God willing.'

'We haven't had a flood for years, boy. My father remembered them. Took away half of old Truro and my uncle with it. They found him nearly down to Falmouth. The river was like a raging beast so they say.'

'I smell trouble in the air, John.'

John laughed. 'The only trouble I've got is that blonde up on the Penzance Road.'

'Not fallen for her have you?'

'Nah. Last time I asked her out, her face screwed up like a duck's fart.'

They reached a cross roads as the rain reduced down to a mizzle and John broke away up River Street. Russell waited until his friend was out of sight and walked quickly back to Boscawen Street unusually deserted at this time of night. The rain had kept people inside. There would be no scroungers on street corners in a downpour. Lemon Street was on the right. He slowed his pace. A meeting with Mr Trevern was the last thing he wanted. But he saw only the lamplighter poised with his long stick, static in the moment of igniting.

The Trevern house was half way up the road and he found a shadowy entrance to hide in. There was a light in Flo's bedroom. The curtains were partially open and he could hear singing. She appeared in the window moving and turning, humming the Flora dance.

15

I picked her up and put her into the trap. Well, she was laughing like a piskie to know we were off to the beach. It was a rare feeling to have her close and all to myself. Some warmth she was doing to me. I got in beside her and patted her sweet, fine head. 'You hang on to Papa.' I said and she held my arm. Her small hand grabbing my coat. So I sent the pony on and we must have looked grand trotting away. My neighbour, old Cocking, waved at us. I know what he was thinking as he has no children of his own. That cheild is growing like a fern she's so handsome. It was a sunny day and the pony went well all the way to Falmouth. She wanted an ice cream so we stopped on the top by Castle Beach. My word she looked happy when she saw it. She took a mighty bite at it and what happened? Well there it was all down her pinafore. So there I was with my neckchief wiping away the muck and there she was crying her eyes out. I held her to me tightly and she stopped her bawling and squirmed away from me. Though I knew she did like my affection. She pronounced she was ready for her bucket and spade. 'Oh are you my lady.' I said and let her go on ahead.

'I'll be there drekkly, you wait for me at the bottom,' I called to her and she ran down the steps that zig zag to the beach. The lizards scurried away proper quick from their sunbathing on the stone walls when they saw her coming. Ha!

I picked up my easel and canvas and our basket of victuals and we found a perfect spot by the rocks so she could play in the pools and I could see her clearly at all times. The tide was out so it was a proper job. I helped her out of her dress so it wouldn't drag in the water and she was before me in her petticoats, the sight of her melted my heart for she had a look so like her mother's it sent me into a shiver and I had to take a swig of the stout Florence packed for me. I lay on our blanket watching her playing with her fishing net.

Pink, I'm sure the ribbon she was wearing was pink? Or was that her mother's? The day we left the house and walked to the river. How harsh I was on her. I was some angry. Like a bear with a sore head. But I must speak no more of this.

Well, she waved to me and held up a shell. ''Tis a good one,' I shouted.

She threw it back into the pool begrudging me as children do when parents try to join their imaginings and she carried on poking and prying for crabs and the like. I placed my easel in front of her and unfolded my travelling stool. The sun was mighty hot. 'Twas busy all to mix my paints before they dried. I was to do a portrait but oh my, the problem to get her to be still. In the end I summoned her to dig me a hole to the other side of the world.

'If you dig deep enough you might touch Australia where the kangaroos live.' She surveyed me as her mother might have done.

And do they have elephants too, Papa?'

'No my handsome, they come from India which is part of our empire. Queen Victoria is the Empress of India.

'I shall be an empress one day.'

'You are already, my handsome.'

I painted as fast as I could. She said, 'You don't belong to be painting me, Papa. This day is a saint's day.'

'And you don't belong to be telling your poor old papa what to do young lady. Stay still for a second, my sweet.'

I traced the line of her soft lips with my brush in the air while she posed for me as I had taught her to do. Before my eyes her darling face took shape. The colour of her eyes had changed with the sea behind her. Might they be turquoise? I couldn't remember. Why can't I remember. Did she remember? Her hair was like corn. But not. Not corn. A field of corn. Many different shades of yellow from lemon to cream. Just fleck in some white here and mix it with brown. That will do it. Isabella. Isabella. I could see her shimmering across the canvas, under her parasol, dipping her hand into the sand letting it run through her fingers while I painted long into the afternoon until it was a blind man's holiday, too dark to work.

'Papa?' I must have slept for a while. 'Papa, look.' She was showing me another shell, it was perfect in its rosiness, 'For Flo.' And she skipped away to the pools.

At that moment I happened to glance at my easel for I could not remember if I had finished my work or not. And, Oh Lord, forgive me, my heart stopped its beating, for on the canvas was a portrait. It was the face I had seen before me on the sands. Of this I was sure, for I have no recollection of anyone else but her.

Flo had noticed her hand was shaking as she packed her father's picnic hamper. The pasties were well wrapped and placed in the bottom along with yellow saffron cake, creamy butter in an earthenware dish, ruby damson jam Nan had made the year before from the tree at the bottom of the garden and a tub of clotted cream you could stand a spoon in. There was just enough room for his bottle of stout. She had reached to pick it up and nervously knocked it to the floor with a crash. Nan came rushing into the kitchen from the larder carrying lemonade.

She put her finger to her lips 'Sssh!'

'He'll see it.' Flo felt the tip of her fear flick its tail and slash across her face.

'Don't you worry. I'll clear it up. Get another one.' And Nan took the broom and quickly swept the glass into a corner. She is cool as a cucumber thought Flo. And whatever spell she had cast, had worked. The day before the Flora dance her father announced he was taking Angel to Falmouth and she should go with them. But in the morning Flo refused her breakfast and sat pasty-faced at the table. Mr Trevern said she should stay at home and anyway he'd prefer to have Angel to himself as he wanted to do another portrait of her.

He could be heard in the hall calling to Angel to put on her coat. There was a loud knock at the front door.

'The carriage is here, Nan,' Mr Trevern bellowed, 'tell him to leave it outside and I'll pay him directly.'

Nan and Flo went into the hall where he was slowly doing up Angel's buttons one by one as the little girl stood passively waiting.

'We'll be back after six.'

Flo kissed Angel and said, 'It'll be grand on the beach. Bring me back a shell.'

'It's a pity you can't come, Flo, it's a fine day for the seaside.' Mr Trevern had spoken casually as if he wasn't bothered by Flo's absence but in her guilty state she missed his tone.

'I'm certainly queasy, Father.' She blushed with the lie.

'You do have some red face on you,' said Mr Trevern straightening Angel's straw hat.

Nan returned from talking to the stable boy and they all went outside to the pony and trap where Mr Trevern heaved the basket and easel into the back. Then he picked up Angel and placed her on the wooden seat beside him. He took up the reins and Flo and Nan stood waving with relief in the doorway.

Suddenly Mr Trevern stopped and patted his waistcoat.

'I've forgotten my cigars.'

'I'll fetch them for you, sir.' And Nan rushed inside.

They had watched the pony pull away and trot up the road as Angel waved and waved, first to them and then to their neighbour Mr Cocking who came out on his doorstep to see what was happening.

'I thought they'd never go,' said Nan with relief.

Then they went up to Flo's bedroom and retrieved a round box from under the bed. Flo took out her hat. It was decorated with cream lace and a pink ribbon that Nan had been sent to buy for her. Around the base were flowers she had collected with Angel on their weekly trip to the riverbank.

'Phew,' sighed Nan,' that is one fine hat.'

'Nan, I'm not sure whether to go or not. I am so afraid. I've never done anything like this before.'

Nan put her arms around her.

'Cornish women be brave and stubborn, come on with you maid, we are high living today.'

They had walked to High Cross to board the coach hoping not to be recognised but they needn't have worried. Most people were rushing for the coach or setting off in gigs, thinking only of themselves.

Flo looked furtively around as she climbed onto the back seat. There was no room in the front, eight people had crammed beside the driver and the cabin was spilling over with faces. The hats alone took up much of the room.

She leant down and helped Nan clamber over the big wheels to the seats in the open air on top. The four horses snorted and shifted as more people found spaces and the weight increased on their wooden harness. A steaming smell of manure filled the air and the women were careful where they trod. The children were not. A mother quickly took a small boy to wash his boots in the horse trough before the driver blew his horn. Flo watched a couple of foolish lads leap on to the side and cling to the windows as the coach groaned forward. Somewhere in the back of her mind she had imagined Russell would be with them.

Nan touched her gloved hand. 'He'll be at the Furry to be sure.'

Flo's face was like an open book to Nan.

16

The roots of the Flora dance were back in the mists of time. For centuries the inhabitants of Helston had danced to welcome in the spring and celebrate the triumph of life over winter when the struggle to survive was at its most acute. It was both Celtic and Christian, a perfect blend of pagan and the Bible. The Romans inherited it and dedicated it to their God Flora and the church, not to be left out, used it to celebrate the feast for the appearance of St Michael, Helston's patron saint. St Michael was supposed to have appeared four times, twice in Rome, once in France and once at the Mount in Penzance. He got about Nan used to think, but then she preferred to believe the legend told to her when she was a child, it had much more of a ring to it. A fiery dragon had appeared over Helston many, many moons ago and dropped a large stone which fell to earth and landed on an empty piece of land without killing anyone. The people split the stone into pieces and used it to build more homes. Ever thankful that their town was not destroyed, they celebrated their deliverance by dancing through each other's houses. This story made much more sense to Nan than the church stuff. Although surprisingly, given its history, the Flora dance was very formal, sedately performed through the crowded streets of the ancient town.

Any drunken behaviour was met with the appearance of the town constable who dragged offenders before the magistrates.

Flo and Nan waited in the packed road for the dance to begin. Disappearing around the corner, a line of women faced a line of men dressed in suits and top hats. This was the first dance of the day. By invitation only. The women were in their best frocks, their hats decorated with bluebells and hazel twigs as tradition required. All eyes were fixed on the town clock where the small hand was ten seconds away from midday. Behind them the band waited too. As the town clock chimed, the big base drummer, who was very experienced with the dance and had never in forty years missed the opening beat, thumped his stick hard onto his drum and the dancers began their steps.

Russell was determined to meet Florence. He had polished his boots, put on his cap and arranged a ride with a farmer who picked him up on the narrow, winding road to Helston. Today he was going to find her.

He pushed his way through the crowds as the dancers in the road solemnly turned and bowed and linked arms. The whole of Truro was here. How he longed to get away from its crushing society. The gossip and the social game playing. The knowledge that everyone knew each other's business. The feuds that could span a century. He longed for anonymity. The casualness of a stranger brushing his arm. Eyes without recognition passing in a street. The world was out there waiting. But he needed Florence by his side. He found Nan leaning against a lamp post.

'Where is she Nan? You told me you'd bring her?' He tried to hide his anxiety, although if he had thought about it why should she be there. Her father would never allow it. Nan gave him a winning smile

'We've come on our own. Her father is away to Falmouth. Be careful, she doesn't want to be seen by too many or they'll be trouble.'

'Where?'

Russell was exasperated as he searched the people weaving along the pavements. She pointed above her and as Russell followed her gaze he saw Flo leaning out of an upstairs window. It reminded him of the first time he had seen her, framed in the window of the house on Lemon Street.

He called, 'Flo I'm down here.'

Either she didn't hear or she was too shy to answer but she moved away, back into the room. The door to the house was open and he took off his cap as he went in. The hallway was gloomy with a red tiled floor and dark wood panelled walls. He could hear chattering in the parlour room and through the kitchen door at the back he saw a square of light from the garden. It was not one of the dance through houses. She was safe here from busybodies. There was a rustle of skirts and she came down the stairs. In the dimness she didn't recognise him at first and she lowered her eyes to pass him politely.

'Miss Trevern?' Russell said. She stopped surprised at the sudden, unexpected closeness.

'Mr Bell.' He was standing across the door.

'Would you consider a walk with me Miss Trevern? Somewhere quiet where there is no one to know you.'

The sound of the Flora music came closer. Some wisps of hair had escaped from under her hat. He wanted to brush them away. She put her hand to her forehead.

'Are you feeling well?'

'Yes thank you.' Her voice was small and without any confidence.

119

'We'll go this way.'

Feeling his hand on her arm she had no resistance and he took her out into the busy street and up a steep road to a gate, leading to a garden of a private house opened to the public for the day. It was quieter here, the trees were the colour of green apples and a path cut across the lawns by immaculate flower beds. At the far end an old man sat on a bench talking to a dog held on a piece of string. The dog's head was on one side listening as if they had been in conversation for years.

Russell walked Flo to another bench placed in the shadows of some sweeping willows. She sat down leaving an appropriate space between them. They were silent for a while neither of them wanting to talk. What peace she thought. The sense of belonging. Not a random collision of fate as two people slam absurdly into each other, but a benevolence, a soothing syrup of certainty that was pre-determined. She thanked God for sending him to make her circle complete.

Russell leant towards her and stopped before he reached her lips. She didn't move. He leant closer until she could smell the craving on his breath and then he stopped again. She took a picture of herself, her eyes closed, her head tilted to one side like the young woman she had passed on the road back from the clay pits with her father. Days came and went before he kissed her. She heard herself moan as his lips touched hers but she couldn't be sure. It might have been the branches moving above them.

As Russell pulled back he was suddenly without confidence. An overwhelming shyness had overtaken both of them. Finally Flo put her hands to her face and said, 'Oh.'

Russell felt helpless. It was not through inexperience for he had had a woman before. Most men found a girl who was willing. It was a tradition in Cornwall for girls to try out their potential husbands before marriage and country girls were known to walk down the aisle proudly with their rounded bellies on show. No, it was not the rawness of a new woman that had made him unsure. It was the depth of feeling he had for her. This was a girl who needed to be wooed and he wasn't sure he had the etiquette.

A bluebell on her hat lay dislodged across the brim. He leant towards her. Thinking he wanted to kiss her again she pulled back. She didn't want to be thought of as easy.

'No, it's this,' he said and picked the flower from the ribbon.

Flo removed her hat to see what he had done and pressed at the pins making sure the other sprays were secure.

'Perhaps, Mr Bell, you could let me have it and I can put it back where it belongs.' She sounded quite formal like a school mistress talking to a naughty child. Russell laughed at her serious face.

'Well what did I say that was so funny?'

'Nothing.'

He realised he might have upset her. She was looking down the path towards the gate. Any moment she would get up and leave.

'Miss Trevern, look!' He crammed the bluebell in his mouth.

'No!'

Russell slowly munched through the bitter taste enjoying the amusement in her eyes.

'Ah. Lovely.' He swallowed with a gulp.

Florence burst out laughing. He liked it. Her pleasure was bewitching. He trapped the sound and parcelled it up for the future.

He looked towards the main entrance as the noise of the

Flora dance drew nearer. He could see the children who hopped and fooled around trying to keep one step ahead of the formation come tumbling through the gate. In a few moments the dancers would be snaking around the garden in an ever diminishing circle until they jostled tightly together waiting for the final thump of the drum to be released from the dance.

'Come with me.'

Russell took her hand and they ran to the other end of the lawn through a narrow shortcut in the hedge used by animals to gain access to the night-time garden.

'I want to show you something.'

They slowed down and made their way through a dribble of Flora crowd coming towards them before Russell stopped in front of a church.

'Mr Bell, I feel I should return and find my maid,' said Flo.

God's stern finger pointing at her accusingly for her indiscretion was not what she wanted. The very thought of going through the heavy doors filled her full of dread but Russell pushed one of them open and took her inside. The potent smell of incense filled the air and drifted upwards in fragrant rings to the vaulted roof. Paintings of apostles surrounded by putti with golden wings hung between gothic pillars. The nave was aglow with candles and it seemed to Flo like a thousand flames were lighting up the darkness. This was no Methodist chapel.

As they sat down on a carved oak pew, a boys' choir began to sing. She had not seen them at first or perhaps they had drifted into the choir stalls without her noticing. They made a pure, high sound that was exquisite. Russell held her hand and linked his fingers through hers.

'Quae pax, quae requies,' he whispered.

Flo was surprised. 'How do you know Latin?'

'These days, my han'some, even the poor get educated.'

'My apologies, Mr Bell, I did not mean to.' She answered him quietly, embarrassed that she had underestimated him

Russell put a finger on her lips.

'But there are many things I have not learned that you have learned.'

'Have you been here before?'

'I used to sing with a boys' choir. We had competitions. But Helston always won.' He smiled wryly, 'Now you know why.'

Russell noticed her pensive face. Perhaps he had been too forward. She seemed frailer than he had imagined. He longed to make her feel safe, to smooth out the sheets and lie her down between them. Then he would lie on top so they were not touching but they could feel each other's bodies through the soft linen.

'Perhaps we should go now?' said Flo anxiously. As they left the church a shout from the road brought Nan towards them.

'Are you coming to have a dance then?'

'We're there already,' Russell called back.

'Thank you,' Flo touched his hand lightly marking their new intimacy.

'We will find time to be together again,' he said.

Flo was waiting at the door as Mr Trevern carried a sleeping Angel into the house.

'She had a fine time,' he said as he laid his daughter on the chaise long in the drawing room.

'Now don't you disturb her mind. She's been running and playing with sandcastles all afternoon. I don't call home the last time we had such a good day.'

He touched Angel's cheek with the back of his hand and his face softened, the hard lines rubbed out until the young Quentin emerged. Had he ever looked at her that way? She couldn't remember. She heard her mother's voice calling her name and she half turned expecting her to come bursting through the door.

'Dinner will be soon,' Flo said as Angel stirred, 'I'll get her washed, Papa.'

Mr Trevern disappeared into his study as Flo led a reluctant Angel out of the room.

'She is proper winnard,' he called, 'she'll turn ugly in a minute.'

In the hallway Flo noticed the canvas propped against a chair. She called back to him as he put on his velvet slippers.

'Is your painting good, Papa?'

'You don't want to look, maid.'

Angel was whining. A noise that jarred the orchestrated silence of the leaden house.

'You go up my child. I'll be there directly.' Angel rubbed her eyes and climbed the stairs.

Intrigued, Flo checked the study door before unwrapping the cloth which covered the painting. It was not often her father refused her a glimpse of his efforts. He liked to hear her praise. She was sure it would be another picture of Angel to go with the many others. He had been offered good money for them. Pictures of golden-haired children blowing bubbles or patting dogs were fashionable. Angel on a Cornish beach eating an ice cream would sell well in the London galleries if he could find a way of letting them go. He always said his painting was only a hobby.

The cloth was tied with coarse string and Flo struggled with the knots. Angel's tone upstairs reached fever pitch.

'In a moment, Angel. Calm yourself.'

She pulled the last fold from the painting and gasped at what she saw. The composition was the usual one. The blue waves in the background, the colour meeting a flawless, blinding sky blended away at the horizon to a salt white line. The sand, a bright yellow, dotted with red brushstroke parasols. Hunched shapes of families sheltering from the sun. There were dogs painted carefully with a fine hair brush sniffing along the shoreline and sitting right of centre in the foreground, a straw hat framing her face, was her mother, her green eyes staring at her as if from a photograph.

Flo caught sight of her father in the mirror coming towards the hall.

'Go and see to your sister, can't you hear her calling?'

Flo stared at him for a second and then hurried upstairs.

At dinner Mr Trevern appeared to be in a trance, his jaws moving in a circular motion as he chewed the part of his moustache his teeth could draw into his mouth.

'I found a shell,' Angel brought out an empty limpet shell from her pocket and put it to her nose, 'smells like dead fish.'

'Get on with your food, child,' said Mr Trevern, his eyes moody with other thoughts.

'But I bought it for Flo. See Flo.'

'Didn't I say put it away, be done with it.'

Angel, quiet now, sat on two cushions, her legs dangling and waving in the air beneath the table. Nan came in with a tureen and began to serve soup. Flo searched her father's face for clues. Did he really believe he had painted Angel or was he being deliberately evasive, knowing she would never challenge it if she questioned him?

Nan dipped a metal ladle into the mutton broth and clumsily knocked the spoon against the bowl.

'Gently, gently, that is fine bone china, Nan.'

'Nothing's broken, Father.'

'If I say she's to be careful, she's to be bloody careful and I don't need you to tell me otherwise!' he exploded.

Nan and Flo exchanged looks and Angel stopped drinking her soup. Which way would his anger take him now? Mr Trevern frowned. The headache was making his brain shrink inside his skull like a rock pool drying up on a hot day. Small fish flapped and gasped for air and seaweed had turned to black, arid straw. He fixed on Nan. How he hated her. The plumpness of her. The listening ears of her.

Nan put a loaf of bread on the table. Something inside her was beginning to rebel against the tyranny of her employer. She hadn't reached breaking-point yet but her fear was being replaced by a dumb defiance. She could now meet his cold stare and not feel attacked.

'I shall be more careful with the china in future, sir,' she said and she picked up the bowl and left the room.

Mr Trevern wiped his mouth with his napkin. It had QT embroidered on a corner and he kept it rolled in a silver ring.

'My apologies, girls, for shouting. Your poor father has a headache. Eat up then. And Angel uncross those knives, it's unlucky.'

'Are you angry with me, Papa?' asked Angel, her lip wobbling.

'No, my child how could I be, you are my life, my reason for living. And Florence.'

He stretched under the table and grabbed both their hands. Angel's expression changed and she slurped her soup happily. Flo quickly took her hand away and unconsciously wiped it on her skirt. Then she shivered with pleasure remembering Russell's mouth on hers.

Before Flo tucked Angel in bed she told her they were going to search for the doorway the pixies used. Every house in Cornwall had one. A hole the builders forgot to fill in to allow the small folk an entrance and exit. A door to bring luck and make dreams come true.

They searched the house carefully, down on their hands and knees feeling along the skirting boards, balancing on chairs, scrutinising the corners of the rooms from ceiling to floor, even moving some of the heavy, walnut furniture just in case a tiny hole might reveal itself. Mr Trevern would have banished them to their bedrooms if he had found them but he was safely in the Royal Hotel with his friends. Only one room remained. The attic at the top of the house where Nan slept when she stayed over. Angel crawled along the walls and dived under the wrought iron bed covered with a red and white patchwork quilt. There was a shriek.

'I found it Flo. Look! Look!'

Flo slid under the bed and joined her sister on the floor. From the skirting board, a long crack in the wall ended at the window frame where the paintwork had chipped away in places leaving the wood bare

'See?' said Angel, her finger pointing to a spot where damp, grey circles corralled the flowers on the faded wallpaper.

And there it was. A simple dot of light between the exposed brickwork and the frame. An escape route. A stream shining into the gloom that was not controlled by their father. It was freedom. Flo rested her chin on her hands and for one transforming moment her life had a future. She knew it was nonsense, a fairy story, superstition borne out of ignorance and yet she believed it. She looked at Angel's bright face beside her.

'There it is my love. Now we must remember to put port

and a pasty out for them. We have to keep them happy.'

Angel was beside herself. She danced around the room clapping her hands.

'Don't make too much noise,' said Flo, 'they might be here already.'

Angel regarded her sister seriously and with the tone of someone in possession of an arcane knowledge she said, 'No Flo, the pixies only visit in the middle of the night.'

17

Adam was in the shadows outside Nan's cottage, a short distance from his own. It had taken him forty-five minutes to pull himself up the road. A passing soldier wanted to carry him on his back. He recognised Adam was a veteran and he had crossed himself, thankful it was not him twisting and staggering on a pair of broken crutches. But Adam waved him away and cursed and the kindness of strangers turned to anger.

'Well bugger you 'en,' said the soldier and he made a sign he had learnt in France meaning, 'you see this finger? You know where you can stick it.

Adam leant against a gate and watched the man saunter down the hill. His fearless youth forging a path through the breeze, a newly-built ship breaking the waves of the Atlantic.

And now he was at Nan's door exhausted. He didn't knock. He hadn't officially asked Jack Peters if he could court his daughter and he feared the response. He was right to. Nan's father would have said no. If Nan were to marry him he would be a millstone round her neck.

He looked up at the inky sky. A half moon hung perfectly and the air was a sweet mix of fruit trees and manure. A pig squealed across the street. He took out a hankie and blew his nose. He suspected Nan had gone to the Flora dance and although he knew he had no right, he had spent the day in turmoil, imagining how she might have behaved. He was confused, afraid to need her but enjoying her devotion and the thought she might have squandered it on another man made him boil.

The front door opened and she came out to throw water from a bucket. She paused, sensing there was someone there. He walked forward into a flicker of candle light spilling out from the hall and she let out a cry.

'Oh Adam, you frightened me something awful.'

'Where have you been, Nan?'

He grabbed her arm and she felt his fingers pressing into her flesh. She struggled to get free but he hung on to her.

'What's the matter with you? Let me go.'

'You were up to the Flora Dance weren't you?'

'Yes, I went.'

He could see the prints of his grip, white on her skin. She would be bruised tomorrow. A memory of him to carry all day.

'You never told me you were going.'

'How could I tell you, Adam?'

'You're just like the rest of them. You don't care. I waited all day for you.'

'How can you say I don't care?'

'You come and do those things for me and it means nothing does it? I was alone. You left me alone all day! How could you leave me to suffer?'

'You told me we weren't promised, Adam.'

'But I never meant it, you know that. You come easy, go easy maid.'

Nan searched his face. A trace of alcohol was on his breath but no more than usual. Aware her father could be beside them at any moment she spoke in a whisper.

'What is wrong with you?' His face contorted with anger.

'Dancing were you? Of course you were. In and out of the houses, a man, stinking like a buck, his arm round your waist. Talking up a load of old ledden for you to lie with him.'

'You be quiet now.'

Nan quickly looked over her shoulder to the cottage.

'You must go now.'

'You're as cunning as a fox and you know it.'

'And you're so full of hate you've forgotten how to be nice. It makes you selfish.'

'Me? And how do you allow that? It's you the selfish one!'

There was a pause. Adam stared at her willing her to answer.

'Alright I'll tell you what you want to hear, we had a good time. It was some fun. I danced all day. Is that what you want to hear? Well, is it?'

The door banged and Jack Peters appeared. Adam flattened against the wall.

'I heard shouting, Nan. Best you come in.'

'I'll be there directly. Just feeling the spring.'

'Not too long now.'

Jack smiled fondly at his eldest and went inside. There was a sound of a child laughing and then it stopped.

A strange sensation poured through Adam. Something he wanted to prevent but had no strength to control. He wanted to cry. He battled to keep the dam from bursting as he turned to go.

'Forgive me, I was mistaken. I thought you were mine, Nan.'

She closed the door on him and he stumbled down the road as quickly as he could, his face determined. He knew a place where he could sit drinking by a fire and he had a few pennies from his pension to see him through the night.

Russell had not wanted to have a meeting with the northerners. In his mind they were interlopers come down to stir things up. There was no need for the hard tactics of experienced trade unionists in Cornwall. Most of the clay workers were content with their pay. There was a relaxed feel to life. 'I'll be there drekkly' meant, 'I might be there next week.' As long as the sun shone and the vegetables grew and a salt breeze comforted your walk to the pub, what need was there for a strike?

In John's cottage he watched the two strangers light their pipes and wipe their smarting eyes from the fire. A beam of light from the window carried smoke upwards to the blackened ceiling where two rabbits hung, their opaque eyes cruelly stopped by an illicit snare,

'Any more tea you party want?' said John, warming the pot on the Cornish range.

Mr Jackson gave him his cup. 'Will you join us, Russell?'

Russell shifted uneasily on his feet. He hadn't sat down because he wanted to spend as little time with them as possible.

'I'm not convinced it's the right way. Most of the men don't want this strike, John.'

'We've got to persuade them. It's not just for us. It's for our children's future. And for the future of society. This is a great cause, Russell, and we've got a chance to better the lives of all the workers in Cornwall.' John glanced over at Mr Prendergast his eyes shinning.

Russell was bewildered. It seemed that overnight John had changed. Newly converted, he had all the fervour of the anarchists. And all of England was afraid of the anarchists. There was no arguing with them. Anyone who stood in their way was hacked down and the gory mess justified in the name of the cause. No one wanted revolution.

'We don't like trouble down here.'

'We have to fight for it, Russell. You be weak as a wranny!'

Prendergast smiled at John indicating he had said enough.

'It's important that we keep our heads in this. There won't be that sort of trouble. There never has been with us. Just a fair hearing for the men's grievances.'

John interrupted him, 'They'll not negotiate. They stink like fitchers with money and they're not going to let us get our hands on it.'

'John,' Prendergast puffed on his pipe and the smoke thickened the room until Russell had to narrow his eyes to see him clearly, 'John, we're hard working decent men. I've nothing personal against the masters so long as they give us a fair deal.'

'Strikes in the social world are like wars in the political world. Both are crimes unless justified by absolute necessity.' Jackson's rhetoric jarred on Russell's ears and his dislike of the union grew.

'Ah well, there is the point,' said Russell, 'I don't believe we've got the necessity see.'

'Not got the necessity?' John raised his voice riled by his friend's reticence. 'What are you chittering on about, Russell? Look what you take home. It's not enough. According to these men here, we could double it. Clay is used for much more than making pots. It's in paper and rubber and paint. Who gets the profit 'en? And it's a hard job for a man.'

Russell retied a bootlace. He wanted to side with John. Normally he would have done it out of loyalty but the pit was not going to be his life. An audition had been offered. He only had to save enough money for his fare to London. He had no right to be involved in local politics. He was getting out.

'It's the only way, Russell, you must see.'

Mr Jackson started reciting.

'We know we've got a cause, that's honest, right and true; we thought t'would win applause, if nowhere else, from you.'

All eyes were on Russell. Irritated, John said, 'We'll ask you again. Are you with us?'

Russell put on his cap.

'Mighty sorry, John.'

Later that evening in the Royal Hotel Quentin had a drink with James Ellery and Silvanius Parr. Their mood was grim. Silvanius Parr studied some figures written in perfect, rounded numbers in a leather bound accounts book.

'We're alright for a couple of months. We can carry it.'

James Ellery's cheeks were a purple, red colour. Quentin thought he might explode at any minute into a pint of bloody, frothing foam.

'You might be able to carry it on your piece of paper,' he said pointing at Mr Parr, 'but 'tis me in the firing line. Where the hell do 'ee think they'll be striking? Up there, I say, up there, at the pit and it'll be my arse that'll get it.'

'We have a fine police force, James. Calm down. It won't get that far. The men don't want it. In fact my spies tell me the Yorkshiremen are ready to board a train back up country any minute now.'

Mr Parr smiled, although beneath his smug exterior he

was worried. He had heard what a prolonged revolt by workers could do to investments. And he was sitting pretty with the China Clay Company. It was growing. They had already bought out three other workings. Only two more companies to go and they would own the whole lot. He often prayed for wealth, down on his knees in church, 'Oh please God, make me rich, make me rich,' and recently he could smell it like a spring tide running up the river.

'We want them here as much as a toad wants side pockets,' he added and he called a pretty waitress over to order more drinks.

Quentin glanced at the window. The earlier soft rain had hardened and wind driven drops splattered against the glass. Vaguely he remembered he hadn't brought his overcoat. Damn! A walk home splashing through puddles. He'd be wet through as he climbed the stairs for his nightly visit to Angel. Just the thought of her brought on a sexual frisson. He couldn't put a name to it or censor it, the feeling existed, and that was as far as he would go.

He picked up his cane and addressed the room with a loud voice.

'Don't know what they're beefing about. They're like pigs in shit. They wouldn't know what to do with more money anyway. What are they going to spend it on. A top hat for the opera!'

The others chortled. He tipped the waitress on the way out, barely noticing her sweetness.

In the morning John, Prendergast and Jackson tried to stop the men before they reached the pit gate but most of the leaflets explaining the objectives of a new trade union of clay workers lay on the ground. Russell passed a large poster pinned to the fence. It read 'STRIKE TODAY.'

John held up his hand as he reached him.

'Here take it,' he said angrily shoving a pamphlet in his chest.

'What are you doing, John?'

'A lot more than you.'

'This is not a good idea. There's no one going to join you. Come into work with us its not too late. Forget about this agitation, my friend.'

'Can't call you a friend, Russell. Not any more.'

Russell walked away before John could see the hurt in his eyes. How the force of politics could condemn the personal so quickly. A chasm had opened up between them. The long friendship born of common background and a shared work place had made them brothers and now, overnight, they'd been torn apart. It was only in that moment he realised how much he loved John.

18

The note from Russell reached Flo through Nan, who furtively took it out of her apron as if she'd been down to the Lizard wrecking for a ship and was telling Flo there was valuable cargo to be found. He had written to ask her if she could take his photograph and he explained the opera company in London needed to see what he looked like.

She quickly sent a message back telling him she would let him know when her father was out of town and he could come to the studio. The session would take an hour and he must arrive at the shop after she had put the closed sign in the window. He must tell no one of his visit.

Nan returned with a question, 'He is between the driftwood and the hardwood at the moment. He can't give you nothing to do it. Lost all his savings at the wrestling. Like they do!'

'Why would I need paying, Nan?'

'I am off like a star-shot to tell him,' Nan said.

Flo called after her. 'Tell him to be sure to wear dark clothes. Tell him it photographs best.'

Two weeks later Flo looked at the clock behind the counter on the shop wall. A bit early for closing but she needed to prepare. She was excited, not only because she longed to see Russell again but today was an opportunity to create a portrait in her own style unfettered by her father's methods. She knew most critics viewed photography as a poor relation to art. Her father pompously relegated it to neither art nor science, 'It's just a mere reproduction of reality,' he often said, 'it doesn't teach or fire the imagination or lift the spirits like the great pictures do in the Royal Academy.' Sometimes if he had time he would try and copy the Old Masters he'd seen in books. He was very impressed with a photograph by O. G. Rejlander, a painter like himself. It was called *The Two Ways of Life*, an allegorical composition with Industry on the right, Dissipation on the left and Penitence in between. The semi-clad figures draped in biblical robes, the light flooding through a rounded arch as if leading to heaven were seeped in moral comment. Although many people were shocked by the degree of nudity. 'Now that,' her father would say while working in the developing room, 'is high art, maid, and Prince Albert saw fit to buy it for our queen. It hangs in her study. Imagine! It's only a photograph. Be thankful, Florence. Without this camera here we'd be as poor as a coot. Whatever they say about photography, a toad is a diamond in a duck's eye.'

But she had also read the arguments against *The Two Ways of Life*. The thirty negatives used. The joins painstakingly retouched and re-photographed and printed on paper seemed to her artificial. The aspiration of many members of the Royal Photographic Society to produce a photograph that could be judged with the same criterion as a painting was a waste of time. It was a scissors and pastepot job. There was nothing original about it. She wanted a photo to stand on its own. Without comparison.

As she went to the shop door to turn the wooden sign to

closed, Mrs Frith the caterer suddenly barged in. She was a large woman wearing a jaunty, spoon bonnet with silver chrysanthemums which was far too young for her. Her day dress was green taffeta trimmed with fur. The combination was a muddle but she had neither the taste nor sensitivity to put it right. She ran a successful tea shop making the best Saffron buns in Truro, often supplying council events and parties with delicious home grown food. She considered herself to be a personal friend of Mr Trevern'

'Oh, Florence my handsome, is your father there?'

'He's away to St Austell with Angel and I was just closing up.'

Mrs Frith was cross. She was very fond of Mr Trevern for reasons that were obvious to every spinster and widow in town. He was not a bad-looking man for his age and on civic occasions smartened up nicely. The family had it easy, they lived like fighting cocks. Who wouldn't want to bag him? Although she had to admit in the five years since his wife drowned he had not made one sniff in her direction. Or in anyone else's for that matter. She thought him too sensible to start looking for a young wife. For as she often said there was nothing as foolish as a middle aged man fawning over a bit of fluff. Some people said his heart had been broken and would never mend. An early grave was predicted. Never mind she thought, bit by bit as the cat said when she swallowed the hatchet, I'll manage it, be it a tight fit or no.

The door opened and Russell sidled in. He pretended to sift through a box of postcards on a stand near the window. Now and again he caught Flo's eye and made a face behind the enormous shape of Mrs Frith.

'Well you tell him, they've settled on the twenty-fifth, a May wedding. He's not booked is he? I'll be proper mad if he can't do it.'

Flo walked over to a large diary on a high desk.

'He's free on that date. I believe my father has put your name there already.'

Mrs Frith ignored Flo, the words coming out of her mouth like the rubbish flowing down the river, some of it caught in eddies, other pieces blown out to sea to be lost forever.

'They say this photography be too dear a thing, but I say you'm be as daft as a carrot half-scraped not to spend the money. 'Tis a picture postcard to keep on your mantelpiece, a likeness to have even when they've fledged and flown.'

She took out a scent bottle and dabbed behind her ears, 'To think my poor dear Samuel didn't live to witness the wonders of the modern world. He was too young to be taken. I raised three cheilds on my own and she'm a brave woman, I've heard said. Your father do know the difficulties of doing 'un. Poor man, him left with two daughters and not a sister in sight to help. And now my eldest is to be wed. Well God be with them. Their children will be born into a new city and a new age. The hope is there won't be the wars to bring 'un down.'

She looked confused for a second as if she wasn't sure where she was going and Russell politely opened the door for her. She thanked him before trailing a waft of rose water behind her.

'You'm be as daft as a carrot half-scraped,' said Russell copying Mrs Frith's walk.

Flo shushed him and led him through to the studio. The scenery from the opera photograph still covered half the room; large and imposing the turbulent sea contained inside four walls. Mr Trevern had found customers preferred it as a background rather than the many country scenes he could provide. It appealed to their sense of identity. The sea

140

defined them, gave a meaning and boundary to their lives. Cornwall had more coastline than any other county in England and better than the church God, the sea was God in nature as the Celts believed. The drama of it infected everyone who lived in the granite, clustered towns where the smell of fish polished each doorway and the bell calling out the lifeboat brought families to their knees.

Russell felt awkward. He needed his photograph to be taken, the D'Oyly Carte had written to him requesting it, but also he wanted to see Florence again. And now he was certain she liked him he curiously felt naked before her and the eyes of her camera. Flo moved purposefully around the studio, her skill and technical knowledge made her even more attractive. She had a level of concentration that he understood. It was the same for him when he sang.

'Where do you want me?' He tried out extravagant poses, his nerves making him play the fool.

'No, not like that.'

'Why not? I think I look gallant, like a soldier in the Boer war.'

'But you want them to take you seriously, don't you? I mean as a serious singer.'

Russell looked chastened. 'What would you like me to do, my girl? Well? Shall I smile?'

Flo's voice was muffled beneath the camera cloth.

'No, but I would like you just to be you,' she poked her head outside, 'somehow.'

'Ah.'

Russell sat on a small bench and looked at the lens. Flo checked the upside down frame telling him not to move because she had his head and shoulders in view. The more she examined it the more the space between them became jagged and fractured. Light flooded in from one side of the camera. She pulled the cloth closer to her. Where was the light coming from? The demons were always there when she least expected them. Branches swayed above her and she was catapulted through a dense tunnel of misshapen trees bent over in the wind like Japanese Bonsais. Russell ran after her calling her name. She shouted loudly to tell him she was waiting for him, but he couldn't hear her. He ran and ran. Why could she see his fear so clearly?

Russell dragged the camera cloak away from her.

'Are you alright, Flo?

'Yes, I – I lost my breath for a second. It can get hot under there.'

He took her to a chair. She sat down trying to catch her breath not wanting Russell to know about her vision. How could she explain her gift? And it was hot in the studio. The morning sun had warmed her face on the way to work. She wished she had worn a cotton blouse and not her thick, navy jacket.

He stroked her back and after a few minutes she jumped up.

'We must begin. My father will be home at eight.'

After she had taken enough plates she quickly went through to the other room to develop them. Russell followed her. He picked through a pile of discarded wedding prints lying on a table beside her.

'They look well content with themselves.'

'They don't look real do they? The expressions on their faces, it's all an act for the family album or the mantelpiece where Mrs Frith will put her wedding picture. We'll never know what they are thinking. If they're happy or just plain bored. Which is more likely.' She laughed and Russell wanted to hold her but she carried on talking.

'Julia Margaret Cameron said, "There is no one wanting

to record the greatness of the inner, as well as the features of the outer man". Isn't that grand?'

'Who is she? I never heard of her.'

'Why should you? You have no reason to know her.'

Russell shrugged his shoulders as if to say, are you going to tell me?

'She was a fine photographer who died last year. I admire her portraits very much and the famous people she captured. You can't imagine how many. Mr Browning and Mr Darwin, Edward Burne-Jones, Mr Millais; and she had a style with her pictures. Her camera was very close on their heads like this,' Flo held up her arms one above the other as if she was making a frame around Russell's head, 'Her lens was like an eye looking into their souls.'

'And is that how you've done me?'

'It's how I would like to do portraits, so I hope so.'

'I'm not sure you should know me that well,' said Russell sending her up.

Flo gazed at him for a second frightened she was going to lose him.

'But I would like to.'

She continued to print his picture onto albumen paper toning it with chloride of gold to improve its permanence and then lifted it up to show him.

Russell studied the closely cropped, soft-focus photograph. His eyes appeared luminous and enquiring.

'Do you like it?' asked Flo nervously.

'It's...it's...'

'I think it's...you.'

'Yes,' said Russell leaning over her shoulder to get closer to her, 'you've found me.'

He brushed her cheek with his lips.

'So soft,' he said.

19

Mrs Parr heaved and groaned with pleasure as Mr Fairfax bounced on top of her. He buried his head in her large breasts and sucked a nipple. Since spotting them rising above her dress at the Opera night dance he had yearned for her.

'Oooh you're a proper man, Leonard!'

'No more than you are a woman, Mrs Parr.'

Silvanius was obviously not supplying the love and care she needed for why else would he be a regular at the whorehouse. And why indeed would he want a prostitute when he had this succulent, soft mountain at home?

'You're my platypus, Mrs Parr, my big duck-bill platypus.'

'Aaah, don't you stop now.'

Mr Fairfax resumed his love-making with frenzy. They had met two or three times since he'd sought her out at the Truro grammar school grand opening. The school had been relocated to Tregolls House, a magnificent ivy-clad building which used to be owned by Robert Tweedy of the Truro banking family. Leonard had contacts with the Tweedys in London and Silvanius knew them too, so he was fairly certain Mrs Parr would be accompanying her husband for tea and a meal in the marquee. In the afternoon there had been a furtive kiss by the ornamental pond in the lush garden and a promise of future meetings. Today was another forage into her undergrowth.

There was a loud knocking at the door. Mr Fairfax was an inch from Mrs Parr's face.

'Perhaps they'll go away.'

The knocking continued urgently and he leapt out of bed scrambling for his clothes. He went over to the window.

'Oh.'

'What is it?' Mrs Parr emerged from the sheets her hair spread over her face.

'With regret I have to tell you, dearest, it is your husband.'

She dived under the covers while he opened the window and looked down at Mr Parr.

'I'm sorry to disturb you, Leonard, but you must come directly; there is a most important meeting.'

'You've caught me at my afternoon nap, Silvanius.'

'Well get dressed, they're expecting us.'

'I'll be with you in a jiffy.'

Mr Fairfax had the window nearly shut when Mr Parr shouted, 'Oh and Leonard, tell my wife you won't be back for some time.'

Mrs Parr made a small noise as if she had caught her fingers in a door. She flopped back onto the pillows, abandoned like the *Marie Celeste* as Leonard rushed from the room.

The major shareholders meeting was at the Royal Hotel in one of the heavy, wood panelled rooms used for various civic functions. Alfred Pasco had made sure there were jugs of mead and pieces of cold mutton available. He knew this would be appreciated for lamb was in short supply. He had

145

heard of the first shipment of frozen mutton from Australia to London on the SS *Strathleven* a few months earlier and marvelled at the possibilities for hoteliers like himself. What menus he could create! He had already bought a copy of Alexandre Dumas's *Grande Dictionnare de la Cuisine* but frequently failed to find the right ingredients for the recipes, so it sat unused on a shelf in the hotel kitchen while the cooks served up local ham from Cornish Blacks, hogs' pudding and all kinds of stews. Today for dessert there was whortleberry pie and Cornish cream.

Mr Fairfax stepped into the rich foyer of the Royal Hotel with its blue and red tiles covered with a Persian rug. Ahead of him was the wide, carved staircase. A small palm stood in a brass plant holder on top of a fine mahogany table with an inlaid wood design. Nothing but the best for Truro's premier hotel.

He took the stairs two at a time and arrived at the open door. Seated around a vast square table, were the major shareholders of the China Clay Company.

'You're late,' said Mr Trevern with a scowl.

'My apologies, gentlemen.'

He was brought up in court, pigs one end and he the other, thought James Ellery as Leonard sat down beside him.

'Are we all settled?' Silvanius Parr assumed natural control of the meeting. Being director of the most successful bank in the city meant Mr Fairfax, a mere solicitor, was out-ranked.

'As most of you are aware a dreadful thing is happening. We've got half the workforce wanting to strike, a small number of them are doing so already, and the other half wanting to work and being punished for their diligence by the anarchist pickets. Something must be done. I can see our profits running down to Falmouth.

'Plymouth more like,' said Alfred Pasco puffing on a large cigar.

Mr Parr was annoyed at the interruption and glared at Mr Pasco. He fingered his drooping moustache which grew like pieces of liquorice from his top lip. He longed to have bushy hair that covered his mouth like the hanging gardens of Babylon but he had never succeeded. In fact he had very little hair anywhere on his body and consequently it made him feel less virile than other men. He had more to prove. He believed his addiction to the girls in the back street went some way to proving his potency and to keeping his marriage together. Leonard Fairfax was helping too.

'I think we should put a stop to it now,' he said forcefully.

'But how do you mean to do it?' Mr Trevern stared morosely at his plate.

Mr Parr cleared his throat and shuffled the papers in front of him looking for a letter he had received.

'I have heard about the mines in America. A place called Wisconsin where Cousin Jacks emigrated to –'

'Was about forty years ago they all went because there wasn't any work up to the tin mines. Australia had more of the stuff than us. The bottom fell out the market. My grandfather went and his cousin as well, went to a place called Pendavis. Full of Cornishmen blowing holes in the ground,' said Mr Ellery.

'Yes, yes, thank you, James,' said Mr Parr through gritted teeth. Were they ever going to let him speak?

'Well it says here that a lot of Cousin Jacks made a rebellion because the American mine owners treated them something awful.'

'Which sure as hell we do not!' said Mr Fairfax.

'No, that is true, we treat our workers well. They are as pluffy as silk. They have nothing to complain of, and if it

147

wasn't for these agitators they'd be happy on their own dung heap,' said Mr Trevern.

Mr Parr waited to deliver his coup de grace.

'But gentleman over there the Yankee owners of the mines brought the Pinkertons to the strike. Set them on the hoards with guns and truncheons and that stopped their rioting.'

There was a silence in the room. Mr Trevern cut a piece of mutton and daubed mustard over the grey flesh.

Alfred Pasco was thoughtful, 'Sounds like what they do in Wales. Mayhem. Not my way, gentlemen.'

'What's the matter with you, Alfred, you've got more gab than guts,' said Mr. Trevern,

'What else is to be done to stop them?'

A maid came in bringing a plate of thick sliced bread. She bobbed a curtsey to the men before going out.

'Actually, there is another way,' said Mr Faifax as he poured a glass of mead. The sweet liquid was making him sleepy after his afternoon in bed with Silvanius Parr's wife.

'A clever way.'

'Oh and we be not clever enough to think of something then?' Mr Ellery shouted.

The others told him to shut up. The last thing they needed was another Fairfax-Ellery fight detracting from the serious business of an all out strike.

'As you know money will buy you anything you need. Just imagine, gentlemen, a group of men, workers from another mine maybe, or from another town, who perform aggressive actions around the city. They persuade, cajole, threaten, rough up the strikers. In other words put the fear of God into the bastards. I believe this would frighten most of them into working and bring this unfortunate event to a conclusion.'

Mr Fairfax sank back in his chair studying the effect of his words on the faces of his compatriots.

Mr Trevern smiled and toasted his glass, 'You belong to be a politician, Leonard, not a solicitor. A handsome thought and I, for one, am for it.'

Silvanius Parr nodded his head in agreement. Mr Pasco cleared his throat.

'Yes perhaps, to a small degree it might work. But nothing too violent. Not for me. But a bit of pressure to scare them. Yes, yes, that gets my vote.'

Mr Ellery's instincts told him it was a very bad idea. He knew the men better than any of them. He knew there would be retaliations and separate camps. Gangs would form. Whichever way, the police force or the gangs, bloodshed could not be avoided.

'You'll wish your cake dough, Leonard. There will be nothing but trouble.'

'So it doesn't get your vote?'

'You don't know what you're getting into. They may be workers but they are proud,' he turned to Mr Fairfax, 'and there is nothing like a proud Cornishman. They'll find you out, and Lord help you if they do.'

'So do you have any other suggestions?' Leonard had had enough of the overweight clay pit manager and couldn't avoid his icy tone.

'Well,' Mr Ellery hesitated, 'at this moment? No. I can't say I can produce any solutions. I am just giving a warning to you. To all of you. I can't help but feel Mrs Ellery would never forgive me if I didn't.'

'You're fussing, James,' bellowed Mr Trevern, 'will you have it or no?'

Mr Ellery swigged his mead. He wanted a barrel of it. No, not even a barrel would be enough to feed his need for alcohol.

'Yes,' he said, 'I'm for you.'

The others relaxed. Mr Fairfax lit his second cigar.

'Right then, I will see to it that something is done.'

20

Flo made her way through the town to Mrs Bidden's bookshop. She left her father reading to Angel saying she needed to find a new book for her studies on Greek mythology. Mr Trevern had nodded approval. He felt proud that his daughter was well educated in the classics. As long as she wasn't buying French literature. Flaubert was too risky. But it had been worth paying for the tutors that had come and gone when she was younger. He would not be doing the same for Angel. His youngest was solely for him to teach. He cherished the intimacy as she wriggled onto his lap and looked anxiously up at his face asking for his approval for solving arithmetic or reading a difficult sentence in the Bible. In the last few weeks his need for her had turned into a disturbing kind of desire. He would catch Flo watching him as he lifted Angel up and down to bring on her giggles. He dismissed her interest as jealously. He never loved Flo as he loved Angel.

'Don't be too long,' he said. Flo picked up her coat and closed the door on him.

She was not only going to buy a book in Mrs Bidden's, she was also going to meet Russell. On the corner of Fore Street she braced herself to pass a group of boys. Scuffing the road with their boots, cigarettes hanging from their mouths they were like a pack of snarling dogs. There were more of them than usual. Their aggression was obvious. It's the strike thought Florence, they are joining in.

One of the youths produced a flag and waved it in her face, 'Support the strike,' he declared, 'fair wages for the workers.'

Flo crossed the road trying to hide under her bonnet.

'Outward flink, inward stink,' a boy yelled at her. The others laughed raucously and made rude gestures.

Flo hurried down the road. She was used to the catcalls but something about them made her feel uneasy. She suddenly had a vision of the river rising in a storm, taking over Lemon Quay scattering carriages and dead dogs up the hill to the Trevern front door. She let it go. She was too excited.

Mrs Bidden's was in Boscawen street tucked between a jewellers and Johns and Hawken's the outfitters. Displayed in the window was a notice embellished with gold scrolls which said, 'Juvenile suits, knitted knickers, cap and shirt suitable for seaside wear.' For the visitors thought Flo, Falmouth beach would be crawling with strange accents in the summer.

The shop bell rang as she entered the bookshop. A peculiar smell of dried paper, once damp, filled the air despite Mrs Bidden advertising she received parcels of new books daily from London. An assistant was stacking pamphlets on a shelf behind the counter. He wore a worn suit and a starched detachable collar frayed and grubby from over washing. His thin face seemed appropriate for the dark interior of the shop as if he'd just stepped out of a coffin.

'Alright are 'ee? Can I help?'

'Greek books?' said Flo almost inaudibly. The assistant directed her to the back of the shop. She had managed to get a message to Russell asking him to meet her after his day's work. She had his photograph to give him. Russell faked a twist of his foot and managed to persuade Mr Ellery to let him go for the afternoon. His pay would show for it but he didn't care, although he wanted the job in London more than his life he wasn't prepared to give up seeing Flo again.

He thought she wasn't there as he came into the shop and a look of disappointment crossed his face, but she dropped her book to attract his attention and he found her at the back. He went to the other side of the bookcase in case another customer arrived. He stretched his arm through a space on the shelf and held her hand.

'I came, as you said,' he whispered, his voice filled with urgency.

'Yes, I.. I...'

'Do you love me ?'

She could see in his eyes a small movement, his pupils dilating with desire. Unconsciously she acknowledged it. The closer she was to him the more she ached for him to kiss her again and the restraint of their situation heightened and sharpened the feeling. For days, since their last meeting, she had been in a fever, thinking of him. His eyes had come and gone, his hands, his body. The fever hurt. It consumed her. Interrupted her sleep so she would wake hungry for another sight of him. She dug her nails into the palms of her hands wanting the exquisite pain to stop, until the red marks became marks of the crucifixion. And she prayed intensely until she was sure God was exhausted and refused to answer. She was left writhing in her bed. Her hand sliding up and down between her legs begging for satisfaction. But it was pointless. She wanted his skin, his smell, the in and out of him. Only he could relieve her turmoil and lie her gently down, her back arched, her mouth open. She dreamt of a chance meeting in the street where he would press her against a wall and take her suddenly. She would feel the granite stones on her back as he became part of her, dissolved into her. Her longing turned into a fantasy that made it possible for them to be together. She saw her father fading before her, rising to the sky as if a giant fish hook had lifted him up cursing and jigging on the end of it. His eyebrows glowered as she undid Russell's buttons and moved her hand inside his trousers to hear his easy sighs. And when they became like animals she knew she would be cured of her love sickness.

The shop bell rang again and two schoolgirls came into the shop shrieking loudly.

Flo took out a notebook and searched for a pencil in her cloth bag. She scribbled down some words and handed the paper through the book shelf to Russell.

'When we are in love, we often doubt what we most believe,' he read out loud.

'No Flo don't doubt me, don't doubt.'

Outside the evening was closing in. Purple-capped white clouds hung over the hills as Russell and Flo went down to the quays and in a deserted corner between two wooden warehouses, empty of workers for the tide was low and no cargoes were to be brought ashore, he kissed her.

Nan had not spoken to Adam for weeks. They avoided each other and although she spotted him making his way out of Juliffe's, the grocer's shop in King Street, a large crusty loaf wedged under his arm, she had crossed the road so he wouldn't see her.

She had gone home and felt very tearful and when one of her siblings had demanded a piece of hevva cake she shouted and pushed him into the back yard where he sat grubby and sulking till tea time. She went to fetch him with a piece of toast and jam which he greedily shovelled into his mouth. He broke off a small piece and gave it to her and she stuck it on a fork. Together they carefully placed it under the biggest apple tree in the garden to ensure a good crop in the autumn.

Nan's problem was how long it was going to take her to forgive Adam for his aggression. At the back of her mind a thought had occurred to her that the rift might have been her fault. She went to the Flora dance without telling him. She had rationalized he didn't want her anyway so why shouldn't she have gone. But somehow the argument niggled away at her. So she went to chapel on Sundays and prayed she might be shown a sign. Of course her faith was tainted with superstition. If only she'd stolen his jacket she could have turned the sleeves inside out and buried it in the churchyard at night and then as the jacket decomposed Adam's heart would turn and he'd ask her to marry him.

In the end she was practical. He was her man and it was not in her character to give up. So she forgave him and thought of a solution to make his life easier.

She knew one of Lord Trevelyan's footmen. He was a neighbour, one of four sons he'd been a lucky boy with charm and good looks and the Lord had taken a shine to him, plucked him from poverty and trained him up.

'He was proper pleased,' his mother had told Nan, 'full as an egg, dressed up in his uniform and that master was some pleased. Spent days showing him how to lay the knives and forks, teaching him how to pour the wine. Even took him to London last year, introduced him to society and the head butler was well put out.'

Nan had thought this unusual but didn't want to

question any further. It was none of her business.

At the back of the Trevelyan house the languid boy had taken Nan down a path surrounded by beech trees and magnificent magnolias to an old stable. He told her to have a rummage. When she was finished one of the stable lads would take her back to Truro.

'And send my greatest respects to your father,' he'd said with an airy wave.

The stable was a dumping ground full of discarded mare carts, horse rakes and broken furniture. Regency chairs, stuffing trailing from the red cushions like sausage meat were stacked in a corner against a Japanese screen and a cracked vase full of fraying ostrich feathers. Nan poked around moving dusty tables and old cart wheels but she couldn't find what she wanted. Frustrated and covered in cobwebs she heaved a large, ebonised cabinet to one side and there it was. Exactly what she was looking for. Broken and rotting but salvageable.

'What do 'ee want that old thing for?' the stable boy shouted as she bumped and rolled in the back of the wagonette, one hand clinging to the side, the other gripping her find.

'Oh, I have a need for it.'

She smiled and pulled the rattan wheelchair close to her. She couldn't wait to see Adam's face.

Flo sneaked out to meet Russell whenever she could. She told her father she needed time to read and search for books and to her surprise he allowed her an afternoon free every week. She met Russell in the Mechanics' Library, in the bookshop and the opes and alleys of the city. They barely noticed the striking workers huddled in protective groups like sailors against a storm. They met on the narrow New Bridge and hid their faces beneath their hats. The danger of their clandestine meetings became addictive. Once, as she knelt in prayer with her father and sister, Russell sidled into a pew at the back of the church. He held his hymn book in front of his face and only when he sang did she turn, along with others, to see who was making the beautiful sound. Russell had winked at her. When they were together they talked. But mostly he talked and she listened. She heard about his early life and his love of opera and how he wanted to go to Italy and America. She ignored the hit in her stomach each time he mentioned the future. She had no reason to think she would be included. She could only live each day marvelling that they had found each other. She felt lucky. Her love for him was beyond anything she expected. It was enough. She was trained not to ask for more.

She shared her secret with Nan who counselled her to be careful, 'I'd hate to think what'll happen if your father finds out,' and she stoked the stove fire to prevent a hole appearing in the middle. It would mean certain death.

'He is strong, Nan, not only...' she stopped searching for the right word, 'physically, but also in character. He is truthful and knows what is right and wrong. He wants to learn too. I borrow books for him and he reads all night or so he tells me! I don't think he minds that I have more education. He likes to hear me talk about Shakespeare and poetry. He has a feeling for the words. I wish we could go to the opera. He has watched most of the companies that have performed at the theatre, but they don't do the whole story, just selections and it makes him frustrated.'

Nan looked contented to see her so happy but she kept a watchful eye on Mr Trevern.

As May became June, Russell and Flo walked together towards Poltisco, away from the charged atmosphere on the streets, to find a corner of a field where they could be alone. Below them Lemon Quay and Back Quay were crammed with three-masted ships and long barges carrying Peruvian guano. Herons dived into the gooseberry river before landing on trees that swayed gently with their weight.

Russell put a piece of grass in his mouth as Flo leant against his shoulder.

'*Nabucco*. Now there's music. Mr Verdi knew what he was doing'

'Tell me about it.'

'I've never seen it Flo but I want to perform it, I want to sing in all of his operas like I have to eat, it's a longing inside me,' he moved closer to Flo's face, 'like I long for you.'

Flo let him kiss her. He undid the buttons of her dress and touched her breast.

'As smooth as cream,' he whispered.

In the back of her mind she knew it was wrong. She was allowing him to go further than before. But apart from wanting him, she felt curious. In some way the over protective environment in which she lived had made her both naïve and fearless. She was driven to experience what she knew was going to happen in order to be a complete women. It was also an act of rebellion, a payback. The part of her that was completely hers and not her father's she was choosing to give to Russell and at this moment, lying on their coats with the smell of the damp grass beneath them, nothing seemed more natural.

He rolled over on top of her and slowly put himself inside her. Pushing gently he said, 'There,' and then he pushed again and said again, 'there.'

She thought it might hurt. The roughness of seeing dogs and bulls and cows and hearing the cats screaming in the night had made her think it would be a painful thing. But what he was doing brought an arousal she had never dreamed of. He turned her over and lifted her hips so her back was curved towards him. He separated her legs so he could touch her where she had touched herself so many times before. She began to pant. Her legs shook and ached and a heat enveloped her spreading inwards to one blinding point of concentration. And then the aching ceased with a tight cry as he made her orgasm. He laid her on her back and pushed into her, harder this time and she could feel the ground pressing beneath her as he moved faster. She thought she might break for wanting him. She heard him groan. She had not expected that his pleasure should make her feel such love for him.

'Am I hurting you, Flo,' he whispered.

She hugged him closer clinging to him, her legs wrapped around his waist. She felt him deep against her womb, deep inside her for a second before he quickly withdrew, the white fluid spilling over her dress and legs. He breathed heavily for a while and then was still, his head on her shoulder. She stroked his hair and held him in her arms while the afternoon turned soft and weightless. They lay sleeping until the sun dipped behind a cloud and the breeze turned into an offshore wind that woke them. He smiled at her, touching her face and kissing her cheeks, and then he tenderly helped her up. She looked down at the damp patch on her brown, linen skirt as he did up the buttons on his trousers. It was a map of their love. She wanted to keep the stain there like the veins of tin stained the rocks down at Malpas, etched for eternity.

He held out his hand and guided her through the field to

the path.

'Best make our way back separately then.'

Shyness took her, she could barely look at him. Surely now he had known her he would think less of her. He pulled her to him and she could feel the tears stream down her face. 'Oh Flo, don't cry,' he said, his voice thick with feelings, 'I love you something terrible don't you know that?'

Flo tried to wipe her nose. 'I love you too, Russell.'

21

S am, the look-out boy who slept under the trucks in the clay pit, shifted on his rocky bed. The nights were getting milder and he slept well under the stars. His early memories of the crowded workhouse, where he had been left after his mother died often haunted him. Even now he could smell the unwashed sheets and feel the shame of poverty clamped to his back like a limpet. He had often starved. His escape had been a miracle. Mr Ellery had come looking for a boy to be a night watchman and Sam had been chosen. He would kiss Mr Ellery's boots for rescuing him if he would allow him, his loyalty was heroic.

He moaned in a dream and then his eyes were suddenly wide open. The light from several torches woke him and within seconds like a threatened animal he smelt danger.

Six men came down the steep path holding axes and heavy blocks of wood. He heard them talking as they reached the bottom and tipped over a couple of incline skips on their way.

'Just rough 'em up a little.'

One of the men raised the axe above his head and brought it down on the wheel of a truck. The metal sang as the wheel spun away stopping in front of Sam.

He felt his anger rising. If only he could creep out the

back he could raise the alarm but he was rigid with fear. He tried to shrink in the shadows pulling his blanket over his head as the men smashed boxes and tools. One of them piled an armful of shovels beside a large wooden structure used for filtering sand.

'This'll fire up nicely.'

He's got a face like a dead stoat, thought Sam, I shall remember him.

'Aw no, nuff's nuff,' one of the others said, but it was too late and a burning torch was thrown against the wood which flared up, lighting Sam's hiding place like a fairground.

His foot had gone to sleep and he leaned down to rub it back to life. A large piece of granite moved beneath him and rolled towards the group. The dead stoat turned sharply hearing the noise and saw Sam's wide-eyed face clearly beneath the truck. Sam's feet didn't touch the ground as he was thrown onto the rocky surface in front of the men who covered their faces with scarves.

'He was near as the grave, saw 'en all.'

'He's nothing but a boy,' said a younger man with a scar running from his ear to his jaw.

'Children's tongues will cut your throat with a bar of soap, or hang you with a yard of cotton,' said a big man who looked like a sailor. He was cutting an apple into thin slices with a long bladed knife and eating them although he had no teeth.

'He'll not talk will 'ee?' The scar-faced man punched Sam in the mouth. He fell backwards a sickening feeling in his head as blood spilled on the ground. Another man kicked him in the ribs with a heavy boot. Sam screamed and tumbled over clutching his side, the pain shooting around his body.

'What you been doing is wrong,' Sam spluttered.

'And you haven't seen it,' said the man and he booted Sam again.

'Mr Ellery will be on to you.' He staggered to his feet. He knew of an obsolete path at the back of the pit which led to a hole in the rock face. If he could run away he would crawl into it and be like a young cockle in a shell. They would never prise him out.

The men laughed and Sam was surprised.

'Mr Ellery, ha. Mr Ellery is as warped as a planchen.'

One of the other men shoved Sam over again and his head cracked against the side of the truck. The last thing he remembered before a numbing blackness was the face of the stoat man bending over him.

'You talk and...' He drew his knife lightly across Sam's throat.

Later Sam managed to crawl bleeding and hurt to his cave where he curled into a ball and let the pain come in waves. In the morning he knew Mr Ellery would pay for the doctor and be angry with him for hanging out with the dregs of Truro.

A few days later the *West Briton* newspaper carried an item with the headline, 'STRIKE ADJUTANTS DESTROY SKIPS'. Letters were written about the groups of men and their marches through the city. Members of the public who might have been sympathetic to the cause turned their backs and for the working men who still walked the walk past the pickets, there was much sympathy. The war had begun. Mr Fairfax had got what he wanted.

Mr Trevern enjoyed his afternoons alone with Angel, knowing that Flo would not interrupt them. He gave Nan an afternoon free and he closed the shop. The pressure of waiting for the shareholders plan to take effect and the growing resentment from striking men as he walked to the studio was pushing him towards crisis. A lout had thrown a piece of slag from the smelting house narrowly missing his hat. The six-man police force was pushed to its limits and the superintendent demanded the council employ more men. Angel was a world where Mr Trevern could have a breathing space.

He began to remove part of his clothing when he was with her. The house was hot in early summer and he felt relief wearing only his vest and trousers. Angel thought nothing of it. He usually sat on the beach bare-chested with his trousers rolled up to the knees, a paintbrush in his hand. She was more interested in the tickling games he played with her. He would chase her from room to room hearing her shouts of delight before she hid in a cupboard. She screamed as he prowled around looking for her.

'I know where you are hiding,' he called, 'I'm coming to find you.' And she screamed again when he opened the door and groped for her body in the darkness.

'She is as pleased as a cat with two tails,' he thought and he pretended not to find her by making heavy foot falls on the stairs or going out of the back door into the garden.

Sometimes he would pounce and put her on his knee and tickle her legs. His fingers would reach under her dress and he felt the skin at the top of her crisp, white underclothes. She seemed to enjoy it and he asked her to tickle him back. He would lie on the floor and she trampled over him sticking her small fingers in his ribs and tummy. His pleasure was indescribable. Only once did Florence return from her library early and stand pensively in the doorway watching their game. He had quickly put on his shirt while Angel scuttled out of the room to show Flo a new doll he had bought her.

In the evenings he would read her a story and lie on the bed beside her until she slept. Gently he would pull up the covers but once he had delayed so he could stroke her until he reached her tummy. She stirred and said, 'I like that, Papa.' So he continued to massage around the tops of her legs until by accident he touched the small mound between them where he rested his hand, flat and warm. He sat there in wonderment for a long time knowing he had an erection.

22

Nan pushed the old wheelchair to Adam's cottage. Over the past few weeks she had kept it in the yard and carefully restored the cane to its original pristine condition. She had cut and hammered replacing wood and material she begged from timber yards and shops. At the docks she scrounged a small wheel from a boat builder for the back left hand side and knocked it into place. She polished the pitch pine sections on the arms until you could see your face in them and at lunchtime, after packing Angel off with Mr Trevern on a painting trip, she popped into Webb's to buy a piece of wide ribbon. She tied it with a flourish around the seat. She could allow herself a small luxury. Her father was not on strike and still getting his wages. Although even if he had come out, she knew they wouldn't starve. Like every worker in the city they had their cabbages and potatoes growing. Meat might not be on the menu but there was always a fish head to be found on the quay side. Cornwall was not like the industrial North. Many of the striking men were enjoying the break. Basking in the sun on the grassy slopes by the clay pits drinking home-made cider. But the majority of them were now going through the gates every morning. Nan's father had made his position clear and John had turned his back on him. Russell too was out in the cold.

'Politics,' her father said, "Ted'n all the world nor half a parish, and there's families turned against families. Not our way down here, never has been and never will be. Them thicky men are some stupid.' But Mr Prendergast and Mr Jackson were long gone.

Adam opened the door bleary-eyed.

'Oh. It's you,' he grunted.

She had not been far from his thoughts since their argument on the Flora day, but as she had not visited him he had stopped expecting her. He blamed himself for pushing her away with his irrational jealousy. But he was not going to admit it. And certainly not to her. He felt excessively hard done by and wallowed in more self-pity than was humanly possible. Recently he had transferred his loneliness into a drunken sardonic bitterness that few could handle.

'Well are you coming in or what?'

Nan beamed at him. 'I've got something for you, Adam. Now go and sit over there and wait.'

'And why should I?' His tone was defiant and he was annoyed that it had no effect.

'Because you wait, just you wait.' She clapped her hands like a little girl and disappeared

He manoeuvred himself back to a stool by the table and ran his fingers through his hair. He had a headache from an all night drinking session, and this morning he had woken in a pool of his own urine. Why had she come today? He shoved a dirty plate away in despair.

'Well, here it is!'

Nan wheeled the chair into the room and presented it like a fairground hawker chatting up trade for the next show. Adam stared at the object in front of him and made an involuntary movement with his hands. For a second he was speechless.

'Well what do you think?' Nan's smile would heat his room for a winter.

'And what is that, maid?'

'For you, Adam. For me to take you to all the places you want to go. Up to the meadows and down to the bakers. I even think I could push you to Summercourt Fair.'

Adam's face was set like a storm cloud waiting to flood.

'I...I see it has come as a surprise, I...I thought you would be pleased. I dressed it up for you. I think it looks very fine?'

He pointed at the gleaming chair, his hand shaking.

'And you think I want to be like a feeble cheild. Carting me round like a baby. You haven't got your eye in, girl. Are 'ee mazed? Which part of that head of yours thinks I want to sit in that.'

'Why don't you try it, Adam it's proper cosy.'

'I'd rather burn in Hell,' he shouted, 'you've got no thought for anyone but yourself. This was for you wasn't it? You tarted up this chair for you. So you can feel good about yourself. No thought for me! Doing a charity for the cripple up at Hightown. He can't use his legs and I'm the one who looks after him. Aren't I good!'

He pretended to be an old woman gossiping over a wall to an imaginary neighbour. 'Well didn't you hear my 'andsome, he was a coward, yes 'm. Fought in the wars but ran away. The shame of it.'

Nan could see his out of focus eyes and realised he was drunk. A distorted version of the man she loved was in the room and she knew the alcohol would win the argument.

'I hate them,' he ranted, 'all of them, the toffs in the government that wants the hellish wars and the generals safe in their tents making bloody awful decisions. They hadn't learnt a thing. What about the Crimea! Sod them.

And the civil servants who decide the money you can have, which is rightfully yours to own anyway – and I hate you with your bloody charity and this...this...coffin!' He looked at the chair as if he wanted to kill it.

'I'm sorry, Adam, I only meant to please you.'

'Leave me alone, you can take your pity and stuff it where you know best. You're a burden to me. Who said you could torture me? A stone's got more sense.'

'I spent time making it work. I thought you'd be proper pleased,' said Nan in a small voice.

His mouth set in a tight, single line, 'That's what I think of that bloody chair. Whore.'

And he hurled his plate at her. It missed and hit the wheelchair sending it lurching backwards to the doorway.

Nan felt the tears coming and couldn't stop them. They wetted her cheeks and tasted in her mouth. There were very few times in her life when she didn't know what to say. She realised she lived in a world of comfort. Her family supported her with a blind belief in her goodness and honesty. She walked in a protected world of elastic love. If disaster happened there were always hands to help. Truro was a full-blooded city buoyed up by humour. You could live to an old age here. She knew if she didn't leave him now he would drag her down to a place she did not want to go.

'What now? What are you crying for?' He demanded.

'Adam Pollard,' said Nan, feeling her strength return, 'I'm finished with you. You've not an ounce of decency. When I look in your eyes I see two black holes as deep as Dolcoath. You're lost in the ground and I don't know of any rope strong enough to pull you out. I have tried because whatever you want to believe I know we were promised. But I don't want you like this and I can't see you ever stopping your drinking. I don't belong to be with you anymore.'

She dragged the wheelchair behind her and slammed the door.

He reached down to the floor for a discarded bottle of gin. If he could just stretch out his arm he wouldn't have the pain of shifting from the chair. His fingers touched the cold, slippery glass and the bottle moved. He could see a few drops in the thick green bottom and as he fell over and hit the floor the bottle rolled out of his reach, the alcohol trickling through the gaps in the floor boards.

Flo was so absorbed with Russell that she ignored her concerns about Angel and Mr Trevern. She knew her father's obsession with her sister was wrong but she wasn't sure why. She had no knowledge to guide her. His behaviour had become more erratic. His tempers were replaced by a brooding, impenetrable silence. Often when a client asked him a question in the studio she would have to alert him to the answer. She wondered if he was going deaf and summoned up the courage to suggest a visit by the doctor. Instead of the usual defensive tirade she got a sly smile and a pat on the head.

'I'm as tough as old ling,' he said and went back to positioning a sign in the window that said, 'The public and gentry are respectfully invited to inspect our photography. Our splendid Club Portraits exquisitely finished in oils.'

But Flo was happy and Angel and Nan enjoyed the sound of her singing around the house. Her nightmares had stopped and she was eating more, her figure was rounder and more womanly. She kept the thought of her love-making with Russell in the long grass like a perfectly carved scene protected under glass.

Flo had often talked to Russell about Angel and he

suggested that he meet her. It was dangerous but with her new-found confidence and her father's change of behaviour she felt she could control the situation. So they arranged for Flo to take Angel for a walk and for Russell to be passing by at the same time.

The air had been close and buzzing as Flo led Angel out of the city to a village on the outskirts. It was a steep climb for Angel and she complained all the way that her knees hurt.

'They're growing pains,' said Flo, 'we'll be there directly.' But their progress was slow and Flo worried that Russell would be tired of waiting.

She adjusted her straw hat which sat high on her head. Her dress was pink cotton embroidered with flowers and around her shoulders was a silky, blue shawl. Nan had noticed the new clothes and commented on them.

'It offsets the colour in your cheeks. And you deserve to be wearing it.'

Flo had not wanted to ask why she deserved it. She didn't want the past to intrude on her perfect bubble. The blindness of her love was making her brave.

Russell was waiting outside the Wheel Inn as Flo and Angel came into the village.

I was tired when I reached the top of the road. It took a long time to get there and it was tea time when we reached the place. Oh my, I wanted a nice cup of tea and I was proper whiney. Flo promised me an ice cream but I couldn't see a stall. I knew it wasn't the beach. Papa had gone down to Redruth to make a picture of a tin mine, the tin they put on the long boats. Flo said today was a secret day. Just between her and me and the pixies. They might bring me a present through the hole in our house. I think they will. I know they will. But I liked being with Flo more than anyone, more than Nan and much more than Papa. He makes me read and sometimes I don't want to. I just want to play with my dolls. Yes, I've got a new one Papa bought me. Well, she's called Tamasin and she is the colour of coal. She has black, curly hair and red, red lips and around her neck she has a beautiful necklace like pearls. I think they are real, but I haven't told Papa. When we got to the place Flo was talking to a man with black hair and brown clothes. He bent down to speak to me and was very pleasant. His name was Russell. Flo and him took me to a nicey shop and bought me some chocolate and we sat outside on a bench and Russell drank beer and Flo and I drank lemonade. It was some boring because they talked and talked and I just sat. But then the barman from the inn said he had puppies and would I like to see them. 'Oooh,' I said, 'yes please, my man.' So I went around the back where they keep the chickens and dirty things. Those puppies were all acting up to me, licking me and those tails were wagging like rigs. I asked if I could have one and he said 'Yes,' so I took a long time choosing. It was difficult because they were all wanting me. But I was taken with the little fellow. He had one white ear and one orange and he had big eyes. Oh, I liked him best. But when I went back to Flo and Russell, Papa was there and they were shouting at each other. Papa's carriage was in the road and the horse was stomping his feet and eating his bit. Papa looked like a bear with a sore head and he hurt me dragging me and putting me in the cart. Flo was very white and Russell had a stick in his hand and was waving it. Papa shouted more and there were people coming to their windows. I hid for shame. The dog man came out and told Papa to be gone. What? No, my sister didn't run away. Papa told her to get in beside me and in a little while she did. Oh my he was fuming then we went back to our house. He followed Flo to her room and I heard them being proper angry. I sat on the bottom of the stairs with Tamasin and took her clothes off and tickled her

and then put them back on again and then I remembered the
puppy and started to cry because I forgot to ask if I could have
him.

Flo winced as she touched her legs where her father's stick
had lashed her skin. She didn't cry out in case Angel heard
and also her pride wouldn't let her.

He had come quietly into her bedroom as usual and
locked the door. She was hiding under the bedclothes like a
child.

'What is he to you?' her father had asked in a passionate
whisper.

She said 'Just a friend' so softly he made her repeat it.

'And you think to meet up with him without telling me?'

'Yes, Father.'

'You've been gallivanting with that boy haven't you?'

She had no answer.

'You'll tell me, by God you will!'

He hit the frame of her bed with his stick. It made a
zinging sound that seemed to Flo to reverberate as if it was
part of her like her leg breaking or a tendon snapping.

'Don't hit me, Father.' She pleaded. But he grabbed the
covers and pulled them back revealing her bare legs. As he
spoke he punctuated his words with the beat of the cane.

'You're the lowest of the low, a useless, pathetic nobody,
you are nothing and what is more, you are nothing without
me. Do 'ee understand?'

She whimpered and begged him to stop. He caught his
breath and let the cane drop to the floor.

'You are to stay here near by me at all times. If you need
shopping you send that useless girl. I want you in my sight
and if I catch 'ee around and about on your own, I'll skin you

like a pig. And as to that singer, he'll wish he was dead by the time I've finished with him.'

He stormed out of the room and then checked on Angel to make sure she hadn't over heard. She was fast asleep. At least Florence had understood not to cry out. He sat in his study trying to control his breathing. He didn't feel well. In fact he had waves of sickness as he imagined what his daughter might have been up to with Russell. The bottle of brandy he was drinking blurred his mind but finally his heart rate slowed and he was able to think clearly. One thing he knew. Sacking Russell was too easy. He wanted to be rid of him forever. And he'd find a way. He always got what he wanted.

That night Flo's nightmare returned but this time it changed. She saw Russell running. But was it him? No, it was her. She was the one running to the river. She heard the voice calling and saw the body in the water thrashing and beating beneath the murky surface. The lamplight circles expanded and she could see a face. It was a man's face and yes! Why hadn't she recognised him before? She had always known it was him. Her father's anguish dark as a dog's gut. His eyes boring into her, his clothes sodden with mud. He held up his arms to her. No! No! No.

Flo accepted her punishment, she knew it was coming. She had transgressed and broken the rules. The sermon her father had given her was fierce and touched all the triggers. Her old self crept into its familiar place and banished the new princess to the forest. She removed her pink dress and put on her black clothes. The weals on her legs were not deep and they would heal without anyone seeing them.

She thought her father was going to have a heart attack

when he spotted them outside the Wheel Inn and throughout his tirade she was surprised that a part of her felt worried for him. His eyes had blazed and his colour was disturbing. He had all the signs. Only after he calmed down the next day did she think he was going to survive and when he apologised for hitting her she felt sorry for him. He hugged her as if he was in a melodrama. He said if he lost her it would kill him. He spelt out in the clearest words how unsuitable Russell would be as a husband. If she was thinking of running away with him she would live in poverty. And what of Angel? How could Angel grow without her, a young child who had already lost her mother.

'We can't survive without you,' he pleaded, 'we are family, there is nothing more important. Wherever you travelled you would always be thinking that you left us with no one to care for us. There's no contentment in such a life.'

He made her promise never to see Russell again and in the future, when he felt she was ready, he would see to it that she met acceptable suitors. He had not understood she had come of age and he blamed himself for his lack of foresight, he would put it right. But as he left the room she heard her father locking the door from the outside saying it was for her own good. Soon he would let her free. Soon. And she saw her future prison subsume her.

Sometimes at night she remembered her mother. Images that flashed on the wall like a shadow play. Her mother soothing a headache with her hand, gently stroking her forehead, pushing her hair back from her face to kiss the pain away. A day when they walked by the river, her mother dressed in purple silk that rustled and smelt of apples, her pale hand twisting her parasol above their heads. She had lowered her eyes and smiled at a tall foreigner walking past them from the docks, a visitor just off the boats, he had looked out of place striding down the fish strewn quay. And one night she remembered the birth of Angel, the memory swooping down on her like a gull diving at a child's ice cream. Her mother had given birth with no fuss. She remembered the woman who came to help rushing in and out of her parent's bedroom, a smile of glee on her face.

"Tis remarkable Mr Trevern, she's just dropped it. Not often do 'ee witness it. No yelling or shouting.'

She had noticed Flo hiding in a corner, her eyes on the floor and the old woman lifted up her concerned face.

'Like a pea from a pod that cheild fell out my handsome, there's nothing to worry about. She be fine.'

And Flo had relaxed, she'd heard many times of mothers and babies who died in childbirth. But deep down she knew her sibling would survive. She had already seen her golden haired sister, watched them sauntering through the tall grass hand in hand. She went in to find her mother sitting up in bed serenely, the baby wrapped in a white towel marked with patches of blood. Mr Trevern leant over and kissed his wife's cheek.

'You did well, maid, just dropped it I've been told.'

'It was meant,' Isabella said drowsily.

'Yes, my darling.'

But her mother turned away from him, her face to the wall.

'We'll be gone, you must be tired.' He had said and he ushered Flo out.

Two weeks later she was dead.

Mr Trevern kept Florence locked in her room for weeks as June turned to July, only letting her out to go to the studio to work and join Angel at meal times. She found a paradoxical satisfaction in her situation like putting on a familiar coat; she knew the texture and smell, the way the creases formed. The daily routine consumed her, any logic or pragmatism that might have unlocked the prison her father had inflicted on her, disappeared. She was in stasis. She had made a bid for freedom and failed and there was a conditioned part of her that always knew she would fail. She had been told it often enough. To make contact with Russell would destroy him. This way she could keep her secret love burning, pure and safe in a place her father could not touch. She loved Russell too much to put him in danger.

But as the days dragged on and there was no word from him she would try and catch Nan's eye as she served the dinner or padded around the kitchen hoping for a nod or a sign that a message had been sent. Nan carefully avoided her. The news of Mr Trevern's confrontation with Russell was common knowledge and she feared for them.

Finally Nan was passed a note. It came via a tanner's boy who had gone up to St Austell to see his granny. He had been told to hand it over 'with no other eyes upon it' so he knocked on Nan's door and furtively looked over his shoulder to the right and to the left before making her walk down a cut in some woods at the back of the row of cottages. She took the letter and then scolded him for reading it. He promised on his mother's life he hadn't opened it. In any case he couldn't read. He ran off and Nan put it in her dress pocket with a sense of dread.

The next evening after Flo, Angel and Mr Trevern arrived back from the studio Nan watched carefully, waiting for a chance to give the letter to Flo, but she was never alone with her for long enough. Every evening after dinner, Flo obediently went up to bed followed by her father who came down and put the bedroom key in a pewter dish on the hall table. Nan carried the letter for a week before she chose her moment. But she misjudged her employer. He was expecting contact to be made and he had been watching Nan like a hawk. She was the perfect conduit. What was it about her that infuriated him? He had never been able to fathom it. But now as he monitored her moods and movements he realised what it was. It wasn't just her dumb insolence, he'd got used to that, it was her spirit, her belief in her roots which gave her a strength that belied her servant status. In her sense of belonging there was a reserve which hid an unquenchable belief in their equality. To Nan they were all the same, they were Cornish. Class did not exist for her, they were one nation. Mr Trevern might pronounce 'pasty' with a long 'a' while she spoke it sharp and short, but what of it? For all his position and money they ate the same meal, cooked in the same way. It drove him wild that she would not defer to him. He watched her from his hiding place in the study. Through the partially closed door he could see her in the mirror take the key from the dish and turn the corner to the stairs. He would let her reach the landing before he chased after her.

Nan was sure Mr Trevern had gone out. She had heard the front door slam. She crept up the stairs, feeling her heart beating. A noise from below made her stop midway. She looked down into the well of the hall but she could see no one. She stopped outside Flo's door and whispered her name, there was no answer. She could hear a thud on the stairs and she quickly pushed the envelope under the door before facing Mr Trevern who was rushing towards her. He grabbed her wrist and pulled her along the landing and down the stairs. As she reached the bottom she stumbled and landed in a heap at his feet.

'Give it to me! Give it to me!'

She stood up and met his cold stare defiantly. Her lip trembled as she gave him the key.

'What message did you bring, for I shall search her room till I find it don't 'ee worry.'

'I only wanted to see if she needed company, sir.'

He came close to her face. She could smell his nervous breath, it was rancid.

'Alright then, what message were you to say to her. I know he has spoken to you. What plan does he have? To steal her away? Ha! Let him try!'

Nan looked him straight in the eye and said, 'I have not seen him' sir.'

Oddly he knew she was speaking the truth.

'So what would you want with a key eh? If not to go looking for our possessions to take?'

Nan was outraged, 'I do not want a thing from you. 'Tis an accusation I do deny.'

'Hiding is as bad as stealing and you know what the magistrate will do to that.'

''Tis you that is stealing. You are stealing that girl's life.'

Mr Trevern laughed loudly. He was relieved in a way. Now he could sack her without any repercussions. The gossip would be against her. She had tried to rob him. And he would not hesitate to prosecute her. Nan started to back away from him. She picked up her shawl.

'Your father I hear is getting old,' he said lightly, 'Mr Ellery tells me he's slow.'

Nan stopped. Fear in her face. There would be no work for Jack if he lost his job at the pits and Nan could not keep them. She would have no employment after tonight, she was sure of that. But she would not betray Flo. Loyalty was written across her face. She stared at Mr Trevern with hatred.

'I hope for your sake, Mr Trevern, the smell of burning fish is in your kitchen, for that is your only protection

179

against the evil spirits that will take you.'

Mr Trevern laughed again but something rumbled in him, he knew it was a curse and an uneasy look replaced his complacent grin.

'Be gone, I never want to see your empty face again.'

He raised his hand as if he was going to slap her. She ran down the back stairs to the servants' entrance and out into the road where she stopped to sob into her handkerchief.

Upstairs Flo ripped open her letter and read the verse of a poem. It said –

O the streams of Nantsian divide in two parts,
And rejoin as in dancing do lads their sweethearts.
So the streams, bright and shining, though parted in twain,
Reunite, intertwining, one thenceforth remain.

There was a space and then, 'I love you always' carefully written in small letters.

She smiled and kissed the paper. She felt loved and understood. Russell had recognised her creative soul. They drank from the same pool, shared equally a desire to express themselves, they both had natural, artistic talent. And theirs was a healthy love, not like her fathers, tainted with confused signals and a deal she could not honour. She felt comforted. He was close by and she was in his thoughts. One day they would be together.

She looked around the room for a place to hide the poem but she knew her father would be in the room in seconds to hunt the missive down. Reluctantly she began to tear it into tiny pieces. She crouched under the bed and pulled her pot towards her. He would never look in there. Tomorrow she could flush it away down the lavatory.

After he had searched her chest of drawers and wardrobe

and lifted the rug and made her get out of her bed while he pushed his hand under the mattress Mr Trevern smoothed his moustache and then his shirt before going back to his study. He felt satisfied. Maybe the girl had not lied. There was no message. He went to his desk and found a book hidden in a walnut compartment before settling down in his high backed chair. He began to flick through the pages until he found an envelope. He took out a letter and began to read it.

Nan never returned to Lemon Street as a servant. Mr Trevern employed a cook who came in daily and Nan immediately found a job in Webb's selling ladies gloves and hats on the strength of her previous employment with the Treverns. They gave her a smart dress to wear and paid her a good wage. Her family were full of pride; she had bettered herself. But she often gazed at Adam's chair rotting under the apple tree at the end of the garden. Flo cried when she heard that Nan had left but there was nothing she could do. Her father was obdurate and she had no bargaining power. She could only wait patiently for him to let her have more freedom.

Russell also waited. Every day he expected to be called to the engine room and be told to pick up his tools. But the call never came so he put his head down and worked extra hours, saving for his audition. His ambition still raged and his love for Florence was unchanged. He was desolate as he knew she would be. But once Nan stopped working in the house, means of communication became difficult. There was nothing either of them could do.

The strike dragged on and Mr Fairfax suggested they should increase the pressure and get to the core group, the brains as he saw it. The city remained charged with discord but visitors continued to arrive at the wooden railway terminus and the streets were packed.

23

I t had been a baking day and now it was a baking early evening on the quays. The windows of the houses shone with a red sunset and a few lingering holiday makers, the women clutching parasols for fear of burning on deck, were still boarding the paddle steamer *Lyonesse* for a late trip down to the Fal estuary. When they returned it would be night and the air would be thick with the smell of pigs. They had been herded defiantly into the middle of Boscawen Street in early August. The council were busy making new laws to have them removed; it was affecting trade.

The sun was lost behind the hills and a misty half light descended over Truro as John came out of the tavern where Bert Trevorrow did his fiddling. He headed for a narrow drang to relieve himself. His involvement with the strike had changed his life and as he let go a golden stream that bounced on the warm stones he thought about his life. He had made a decision to move away. Maybe go up to mighty Manchester. Learn to read if someone would help him. Dedicate his life to the trade union movement. Truro had become too small a stage. It was strange, he thought, how the familiar could be pushed so easily away by a small shift of emphasis, a word from a friend, a meeting with a stranger.

Routes were sometimes chosen in seconds. Although he had no time for fate and the predestined superstitions of his countrymen. Chances were given and you made the best of them. He wasn't like his fellow workers contented with their Sundays on the beach and their easy poaching from Kiggon pond for a freshwater supper. He had learnt it was ideas and action that mattered. He could change his life and the lives of others with the politics of the common man. He would leave soon. Perhaps tomorrow. He glanced down the alley to the gas-lit street and saw three men making their way towards him. He pulled his cap over his eyes and moved away from the wall. Two of them were abreast making it impossible for him to pass so he looked to the other exit but there were already two more men blocking the ark of light. John could feel the adrenaline pumping through his body. His fingers gripped the lump of lead he always kept in his pocket since the strike began.

He heard the sound of the wood rushing through the air before he felt it battering his face and he heard the pigs squealing in their pens. He was picked up from the ground and punched by a fist which bloodied his eye. He landed in the arms of one of the men and managed to register a scar running down the man's face before he was thrown to the ground and the kicking started. He struggled to protect himself by curling into a ball, holding his arms over his head but the attack was relentless. Boot. Scream. Another boot. Scream and another. After a while he ceased to know how many were crunching his broken body.

John's death took up a small paragraph on the back page of the *Royal Cornwall Gazette*. It said that the incident had occurred through drink and the desperate politics of the strikers. There was a leader article on the front page which said, 'The clay district of Cornwall is in a state of chaos. Men who have been described as one of the finest types in England have yielded to the screeching wild-cat talk of certain individuals who are apparently seeking their own aggrandisement and self-preservation and now have been led around the district more after the style of sheep going to slaughter than Englishmen and above all Cornishmen possessed of grit and commonsense.' More letters were written demanding the mayor rid the city of the plague of the trade unions and the shareholders eating their beef dinners in the Royal Hotel were euphoric. The rebellion would be over. We need one more headline Mr Fairfax said.

Russell mourned his friend and suffered deeply. He was tormented with not having healed the division between them and at John's funeral in the small Methodist chapel he sang 'Abide with Me' with such emotion that John's friends and relatives were inconsolable.

Mr Ellery crept into the service and sat at the back to pay his respects. Not only had he paid for the refreshments but he had bought the headstone as well. Guilt weighed heavily on him.

A few days later he was having a dinner with his wife when an explosion sent glass and debris flying across the tablecloth. He rushed Mrs Ellery upstairs and squashed her into a cupboard before going back to find out what had happened. The smashed window was glowing with flames. The curtains were shrivelling up to the pelmet and pools of fire burned the carpet making a trail to the edge of the mantelpiece. Neighbours were already in the garden with buckets shouting for him to help. They made a water chain to the pump in the road while Mr Ellery ran startled, puffing backwards and forwards to the kitchen where he had water on tap. Afterwards Mrs Ellery in a high state of nervousness demanded to be driven to her sister's at St Blazey. When they arrived she told him to leave. She wanted to be on her own with her family. He returned depressed to the wet and burnt out carcass of his dining room and wandered forlornly from room to room. They had been lucky. The whole house could have gone up and they could have been burnt alive.

The next day he cornered Mr Trevern outside his studio in an apoplectic rage.

'This time it's gone too far, Quentin, who the hell told them to go round causing explosions to my house?'

Mr Trevern looked to see if anyone was watching them before he spoke.

'I have no idea, James; it appears they got it wrong.'

'Do 'ee think I don't know that! But they chose my house, 'tis all I've worked for and I've a fireplace in every room mind. Mrs Ellery is shocked, Quentin, she's staying at her sister's. But for how long? I'll never find another woman. My hair is dropping out with worry and there's no attraction in a bald-headed man with no money. And now the police are round asking questions,' he raised his voice and clung to Mr Trevern's arm, 'the bloody police on our backs. What else will they find out eh? I'm not one to rattle the bucket and run, Quentin, I haven't got the nerves for it. And don't you forget we've blood on our hands'

Mr Trevern looked into the perspiring face of Mr Ellery and smelt his fear.

'For Lord's sake keep your mouth shut, James. After this they will be back to work before you know it and then it will be whacks of money for all of us.' He straightened Mr Ellery's tie, 'I'm sorry for your house. 'Tis not right and someone will be charged. You wait and see.'

Mr Ellery was placated. If he could have a head on the

block it would make the cost of re-building easier. And it could have been worse. The dynamite hadn't been prepared correctly. They were amateurs. The irony was he had paid them to do it.

24

The August sun was so hot it melted the tar pasted over the slate roofs of the houses. Sailors said it was like Marseilles. On the other side of the river the heat penetrated the dense broccoli woods and lit up the coves where rotting, upturned boats lay forgotten on the tidal mud. Truro almost sank with tourists. The traders were content.

Russell had saved enough for his fare aboard a cargo ship to London. It was cheaper than the train and he needed every penny. His audition wasn't scheduled for a few weeks and he would have to find a temporary job and lodgings when he arrived. He had no misgivings about passing the audition but he had to ask Flo if she would join him. He couldn't leave her behind. He trailed her back to Lemon Street from the studio each night. Most evenings she was with her father.

Just before closing time Flo left the studio alone. Russell followed her to Griffiths' bookshop and waited patiently under the green awning shading the pavement from the heat. As she came out he grabbed her and placed her with her back against the window protecting her with his body in case any one recognised them.

She started to shake and after he had kissed her cheeks

and eyes and lips she shrank into his arms.

'Oh, Flo,' he said and he looked over his shoulder towards the studio, 'we've not time but will you come with me? To London for I am to be gone soon.'

Her helplessness was too much and he held her again.

Finally when she had stopped shaking she said, 'It is Angel. You understand?'

He tipped her chin so he could look into her eyes, 'Will you meet me again and let me persuade you? Will you?'

Flo nodded, 'I will try. Be here tomorrow at this time and now I must go for your life would not be worth living if he finds us. Russell...'

'Yes?'

'I'm sorry about John.'

She kissed her fingers and put them to his cheek and he told her he loved her before walking away

Flo had a feeling it might be the last time she would see him and she wanted to call out and tell him she would run away with him but she could hear Mr Griffiths piling books behind the shop counter. Russell turned and waved.

Superintendent Woolcock felt proud. He believed that he and his five-man team had single-handed stopped the strike. He had been up to the pits and addressed the small group of pickets with great force and confidence.

'An assembly of this kind is unlawful,' he said through a megaphone, 'there are people who may recognise you and if your names are given you'll be in a lot of trouble. I don't want you to get into trouble, so I'm telling you this warning. This has been going on too long and the death of one of your own is something terrible. It's time you went about your honest business.'

His men had been impressed with his speech and told him so later that evening over a pint. The relief they felt as the workers started to break up and go through the gates could not be measured. Both sides had lived in daily fear of their lives. The small wooden cross placed on the roadside in John's memory was piled high with flowers.

The meeting with the shareholders had been planned after Mr Ellery's house was blown up. The superintendent took two of his policemen with him.

Mr Woolcock saluted and the other two tipped their hats as they came into the oak room. Woolcock had been in the army and ran a tight ship.

'Would you like to sit down, gentlemen?' Mr Fairfax asked.

'Er, no thank you sir, not at this time. I think we should get on with the business. I am pleased to say I have made a girt progress in this area and I have upon me the names of the troublemakers. There's warrants out for their arrests.'

Mr Ellery tapped the table nervously as Mr Fairfax dragged on his cigar. There was no need to worry, the scar-faced man and his cronies were half way to the Indies by now.

'And I can guarantee we'll get the man that caused the fire at your house, sir.'

'A shocking event, it's put a blight on this new city that won't be forgotten in a long time,' said Mr Pasco shaking his head. He offered the policemen a saffron bun. One of the young lads crammed it in his mouth.

'I've a hole where my best room was … I've a fireplace in every room mind,' muttered Mr Ellery. He looked a bit deranged.

'You're sweating like a bull, James,' Mr Parr said under his breath.

'Have you got the list of perpetrators with you?' Mr Trevern held out his hand to Mr Woolcock.

'Here you are, sir. After much asking about. This is the complete and full list of names who subverted to the trade unionists.'

Mr Trevern scanned down the list, 'But you've a name missing here.'

'Really, sir, forgive me, I assure you we have been very thorough.' The superintendent was affronted and pulled himself into a parade position.

'You're three scats behind superintendent. This is the name you need. He'll be the villain behind your fire, James, just you wait and see,' and Mr Trevern took out a pencil. He returned the list to Mr Woolcock.

'Russell Bell,' the policeman read, 'I shall send my men to bring him in toute suite.'

The young trainees were commanded out of the room. Mr Pasco was worried.

'Are you sure, Quentin?'

'As sure as the nose on my face, Alfred.'

A feeling of pure peace swept through Mr Trevern as he sat back in his chair. With any luck the magistrates would send his daughter's defiler to Bodmin for a long stretch and by the time he came out he'd be ruined and she would want nothing more to do with him.

She waited outside the bookshop for as long as she could; until Mr Griffiths came out and asked her if she needed any more books as he was closing the shop.

'I shall be bringing in the cover directly, Miss Trevern.'

Flo's face was a worry and Mr Griffiths thought it best to leave her for a few minutes. He had some costing to do. Let her enjoy her people-watching from the safety of his doorway.

She heard the police whistles and the shouts of the constables as they came running around the corner from the Municipal Buildings. They charged down Boscawen Street pushing holidaymakers and women with prams out of the way. The excitement brought shopkeepers to their doors and a group of young boys ran after the police throwing their caps in the air.

'He was just here,' a policeman yelled.

'He's in River Street. That way.'

Mr Griffiths was beside Flo in seconds scratching his head.

'They've got one of them.'

'Who is it?' said Flo her heart sinking.

'It isn't for me to say, miss, but I know they were after the man who caused explosions. And let's hope they've caught the one that smashed that poor boy to pieces.'

Flo saw Russell clearly. He was at the top of the city dodging through washing hung out to dry in the back yards of the cottages. He leapt over a wall and ran for his life across scrubland towards the woods. As usual, her premonition had been right.

25

The emptiness, the everlasting emptiness. A void. A vacuum that only he could fill and the light that had disappeared ceased to illuminate any beauty around her. A dull nothingness that colonised the pit of her stomach until her gut could stand it no longer and pushed upwards in a spontaneous contraction seeking relief from the tension. It burst out of her with wracking sobs that contorted her body bringing her to her knees, turning her head backwards and forwards in a dreadful seizure to rid the pain that trapped every muscle; the loss of him and the grief of love sickness for which only time was the cure. It was a sickness alright or an infestation by a spriggan. It slept in her chest, lounging heavy on her heart. Unfolding its legs with a grin, kicking at her throat until the tears came again and again just when she thought she had control of it. No said the evil one. I've still got you. He's gone. He will not to be yours and he's gone. She heard her heart break with the weight of it. Night after night deep into the stillness with no hope of relief except the sharpness of dawn and the cock crowing. Maybe a brief respite as she rose and washed and reached out to choose her dress, but then the spriggan woke too and mocked her, stretching its arms it hit her hard in the viscera and she felt the rawness of Russell's going as if it were yesterday.

Angel had grown silent. Her sister had retreated into her own world and she could not reach her. Nan had gone and there was no one to take care of her except her father. So she obeyed his demands. She was tired of his tickling games but he always persuaded her into them. Sometimes he touched her in a place that instinctively she knew was wrong, his fingers would tickle between her legs as he told her he loved her. But it wasn't unpleasant and now that Flo was giving her no affection, it was a sort of comfort.

Pushing the boundaries was unplanned for Mr Trevern. Touching Angel was spontaneous and often when Flo returned home Angel would be sitting on his lap, clinging to him as he cuddled her. It seemed as natural as the seasons to go from the emotional to the physical and in his room after laying one of his wife's dresses under the quilt beside him, he would pleasure himself. But after a while masturbation ceased to satisfy him and he began to plan what he would do to Angel. He was surprised at the thrill it gave him, the anticipation, the expectation; this afternoon will be the afternoon when I can investigate her body further, this evening is when I can ask her to touch my erection.

But he never did. And as late summer turned to autumn and the wet hills drained into the rivers covering the dips of summer mud, the closed world in which they lived turned progressively inwards.

The great sprawling metropolis that was London was a shock for Russell. The wide, dirty river with its cargo ships packed side by side, the miles of warehouses, the thousands of dockers employed, the slaughterhouses, the gas works, the fisheries and tanneries spewing poison into the water made Truro seem like an unimportant speck on the face of commerce. He watched gallons of sewage and toxic waste pour into the Thames at Barking during high tide and wondered what it must have been like before the sewers were built, when the faecal matter went down with the ebbing tide only to come back as the tide returned. Although it was much cleaner now thanks to Disraeli giving the Metropolitan Water Board money to clean up the portion of the Thames that ran below parliament, Russell quickly learnt you only drank beer in London, typhoid was but a sip away. But he had what he had yearned for back in the clay pits. He could walk down a street where no one knew his name and neither did they care. The heaving push for survival inflicted a selfishness he was not used to and often he felt lonely. He was a visitor to a strange land with no references.

He decided to be practical. After his audition his job at the Opera Comique was guaranteed. He was to take over from one of the chorus in the *Pirates of Penzance* who had broken an ankle falling down a flight of draughty stairs that led to the stalls. He had a month before he started. He found a job working in a stable for a Hansom cab owner and slept uncomfortably on a platform above the horses. But after pickpockets singled him out as a bumpkin, and robbed him of his pay on an omnibus negotiating traffic in Oxford Street, he was forced to ask for an advance from the company. The board realised he was a talented boy who needed support and he found better rooms near the theatre. He was still amongst the villains and prostitutes but at least the activity of the boats outside his attic window had echoes.

His pulse was racing as he made his way through the maze of slums surrounding the theatre on the East Strand for his first day's rehearsal. Singing with the Truro amateurs was a world away from performing to Arthur Sullivan, a tough overseer.

The company manager told him to watch from the wings to introduce him to the moves in the show. He knew the music well and hummed along under his breath as the singers waited, chatting to each other before making their entrances

'The name's Danny Fisher, Cornish, how you doing?' A slap on the back made him turn and a well built man with a white plume across his black hair like a badger extended a welcoming hand.

'Russell Bell, I am pleased to meet 'ee'

'Pleased to meet 'ee ay?' Danny laughed at Russell's West Country accent, 'Are you settling in?'

'I can't believe I'm here really.'

'You'll get over it, especially when 'Sir' has words for you.' Danny nodded his head towards the composer in the front row. Russell stared at the celebrity in awe.

After Russell had sung his part and met with overwhelming approval from the company, Danny showed him to a pub in Drury Lane. They pushed their way through the closely, packed tables and Danny said hello to various people, a stage hand, a ballet dancer and an actor in a top hat who looked like a woman.

Danny caught the expression on Russell's face. 'Yes. Be not afraid. He's a she. It's a good act though, she's going to be a star.'

They both leaned against the bar. Russell had his music stuffed in his jacket pocket.

'Your first time in London?'

'That's the case, arrived a few weeks ago. 'Tis awful different up here.'

'Can't wait to get out, mate,' said Danny beckoning the

barman over, 'damn, filthy city isn't good for the chords. But *Pirates* is a big success, bigger than *Pinafore* and I reckon it's going to New York again, I'll be the first on the boat. I've heard those American girls know how to give you a bit of what you fancy.'

His laugh was a low, infectious gurgle. No wonder Danny was such a popular member of the D'Oyly Carte.

A shadow passed across Russell's face, 'Ah my intentions are elsewhere.'

'I'm not talking about love, Cornish, just a bit of hokey pokey.'

The barman finally came over.

'Two pints of ale my good man.'

'Bloody singers, iron hoofs the lot of you.'

'Now is that a way to speak to one of your regular customers.'

The barman poured beer into glasses, 'Bloody gipsies.'

'He's having a joke, I owe him,' explained Danny but Russell read the barman differently and for the first time heard the prejudice against theatricals.

'So you were in a spot of trouble?'

'I can't go back, put it like that. Fact is I left something important down there.'

'Get it sent up by train, it's easy, Royal Mail.'

Russell paused, contemplating the suggestion.

'Be mighty uncomfortable for her. Travelling by freight.'

Flo waited every day but she did not hear from Russell and the hopelessness of her situation hit her. The longing that had now become a kind of drug was an impossible habit to give up. It would drive her to read and re-read the same piece of poetry until the writing became a doomed lament.

She slept with Russell's photo underneath her pillow, waking through the night to touch his face. She knew each contour, each line, the look in his eyes haunted her. Sometimes she could see him as he moved on top of her. But she soon realised she had worn the memories dry. She searched to make them more acute, more immediate. She re-examined their walks, the places where they had met, the words they had said to each other. In her need for him, she put more meaning into each remembered encounter as if they were a scene in a play where the author already knew the ending and was carefully crafting his story with building blocks. But she knew real life was not a play, there was no shape to her tale. Each meeting had been random like the wild flowers in the fields where they had made love; the seeds grew where they landed with no thought to the denouement. She had lost her gift of second sight; love seemed to have confused her so she clung to every possibility. He would come back. How could he forget her? They had destiny between them. And then in the early hours of morning she saw him with someone else, holding another woman, kissing her, smelling her hair and she hated him; hated him for leaving with so many promises, hated him for pursuing her and hated him for his ambition. And so the endless cycle continued until she made herself ill and the cook had to come with soup in the afternoon while she lay in bed. Her father paid for the doctor to examine her. He pronounced her weary and recommended her father stop her duties in the studio and allow her to walk in the fresh air. So she walked. She walked in the winds that blew up from the sea blowing the purple leaves from the trees. She walked in the rain until her tears fused with the drops and plastered her wet hair to her face. And she walked in their fields where the memories stalked her like a faithful dog, snugging down beside her when she lay in the dying grass and following on her heels to the river where she looked longingly into the water for deliverance from her malaise. Nan knew Russell had left without a word and she worried for Flo. She met up with her whenever she could, although much of her time was taken up with courting a Thomas boy, one of the butcher's sons from Ferris Town. He had become besotted with her wide hands and hips and imagined her behind the counter heaving carcasses for him to split. They could have a prosperous life, as he was to inherit a farm from an uncle, if she agreed to marry him. But she hadn't said yes.

Flo leaned on Nan as her equal and Nan listened to Flo's outpourings patiently, rarely judging but always there, as only a good friend could be.

Eventually the longing dulled. Like any disease it peaked and the body needed to heal itself. Enough it said, life is wanting you back. She turned her face to the sun and breathed it in and the evil creature that inhabited her shrank into the shadows. Nan felt comforted that her face had colour again. Her worst fears that Flo might have died of a broken heart were expelled. She held Flo's hand and the two women walked to the woods above the clear river and picked blackberries.

But in truth, in the emptiness of the early morning, Flo still waited.

Angel was wearing a sailor's costume, the striped trousers over black stockings stopped at her knees. On her head was a panama hat and a wide black sash was tied around her waist. She posed in front of a misty, painted forest with one foot on a wooden trellis, her arm leaning on her leg, her hand curled against her cheek. The position was childlike but attractive. Mr Trevern knew his business. He sold these postcards by the hundreds to mothers and grandmothers and sweethearts.

'No, don't move.' Mr Trevern appeared from behind the camera and fiddled with the bow on the ribbon. He was nervous, almost excited, 'You're doing well.'

'Papa, I want to stop now. These trousers are hurting me round here.' She stretched the material trying to make them bigger. The thought of it chaffing her soft parts aroused him.

'Just one more, one more, my handsome,' he produced a lollipop from his pocket, 'and after the photo look, you can have this.'

Angel wanted to go home. She shouted loudly at him.

'This is uncomfortable! Papa!'

He realised she would cry any second and it always upset him when she cried. He watched her take off her jacket. He wanted to help her but he had only ever undressed her top clothes before, on the beach so she could play in the sand in her petticoats, or removing her overcoat coming into the house. It was Florence's job to get her ready in the mornings and give her a bath at night. Bathing had become easier since he had installed a new gas geyser decorated with a marble effect. He was very proud of it and Angel had a bath most evenings. But he would no more dream of opening the door to make sure the water was the right temperature or wrap a towel around her to rub her dry than sell his shares in China Clay. This morning it was Florence who had squeezed Angel into the sailor's suit exclaiming how much she had grown.

Mr Trevern picked up the jacket Angel had thrown on the ground. The little girl was struggling with the trousers. He knelt beside her his hands shaking as he undid the buttons. He waited for a second, a thought concentrating his mind. What if he was caught? What would people think? Everyone knew incest was pushed under the carpet. The nature of the act was not something that was spoken of in public; it carried its own secrecy. You could see the result in the faces of the mentally ill at Bodmin jail and the occasional idiot protected by family, peering over a country wall. But surely the feeling he had for Angel was different, it was only love? He had no wish to harm her. You could not be incestuous with a young child.

Angel held onto his shoulders as she stepped out of the uniform and stood in her underclothes, perfect in her innocence. He took off her hat releasing her golden hair onto her shoulders.

'Thank you, Papa,' she said and she smiled, her face lighting up with relief.

He had an overwhelming desire to hug her, to hold her close and he drew her to him burying his nose between her legs, breathing in her scent like a man gasping for water in the desert.

The door to the studio opened. Flo quickly took Angel by the hand and walked her out of the room.

Mr Trevern remained on his knees his head bowed as he was to do later in the aisle of the half-demolished church, praying inside his head for deliverance. Most people were there to celebrate the last Sunday service in the old St Mary's before the building of the cathedral started. It was overflowing.

Later that night Mr Trevern heard the sound of Angel's bed being dragged across the landing to Florence's room.

26

The sight of her father with his face pushed into Angel's crotch shocked Flo into action. Her suspicions were confirmed. He was losing control of his senses. What she had witnessed was unsavoury and unnatural and there was no other option but to take Angel as far away from him as possible.

He often gave Flo money for books and clothes and she began to store it in a locked box under her bed. She formulated a plan to leave the house and Angel and she would catch a train to London. Once there, she would find a reputable lodging house and begin her search for Russell, starting with the theatres. After they were married she would find a job as a governess to support them all. She could teach Greek history and poetry. She had the manners to show she came from a good family.

Her plan was to ask her father if she and her sister could take food and linen to Williams' almshouses in Pydar Street. It was a gesture Mr Trevern would appreciate. He liked the family to be seen as philanthropic and it would be an education for Angel to learn how the city cared for its old people. From the alms house they would not return home but make their way to the station. But eventually a better opportunity for escape was presented to her.

Her father had been given the plum job of photographing the building of the cathedral. It had been a political choice. There was no one else considered by the council. He announced his news at breakfast after telling Angel to stop chattering.

'Papa's got a big day. I am helping to make history and let me say this, my pictures will be printed in books for years to come. My name will live on. Something for you both to be proud of. I am honoured that they have asked me.'

Angel had clapped him and Flo congratulated him before whisking Angel away to clean her teeth. It was a full-time job watching over her sister.

Every day Flo helped him pack a cart with equipment and he would drive it to High Cross and park beside the horse buses. Will Lander, a young steeple jack he employed helped him unload. He would then decide what angle to photograph the building work from and which of the scaffolds to use. He had to be careful not to get in the way of the stone masons and often he was only two steps behind them, high up on the ladders for hours, away from the house all day and well into the evening. Florence marked a date on her calendar and checked the timetable.

Autumn brought a white rain sweeping down the valley bleaching the views and fogging the river, although there was still heat trapped in the granite hedgerows and the combination produced a sub-tropical climate where exotic plants could survive most winters. Out at Probus a banana tree was said to be flourishing.

Flo hurried Angel to the front door where there were two bags and a basket on the floor. Angel was moaning.

'Don't take on so my dear,' said Flo, 'you can't bring all your dolls but when we get to London I shall make you another like you've never seen before.'

'Like a piskie?' asked Angel.

'With the waistcoat and shoes.'

Flo picked up the luggage and basket filled with saffron cake, lemonade and cheese. It would take twelve hours to reach London and there were no refreshments on the train.

They walked to the station and arrived early. Flo knew they would have hours to wait for the train, but she needed to leave the house as soon as Mr Trevern had gone to work. If he returned unexpectedly he would assume Florence had taken Angel for a walk and wouldn't search for them until it was too late. She had bought the tickets and she prayed nothing would go wrong. They found the brown and cream waiting room with an oversized oval clock above a sooty fireplace and settled into a corner. She could hear the driver of Lean's van, a horse-drawn box on wheels that transported goods from the station talking to his horse, asking it to reverse. She brought out a book. She would read to Angel to pass the time.

A few hours later the train noisily arrived and the station was packed with people, almost without Flo realising.

'Stay close to me,' said Flo as she dodged the crowds struggling with their baggage. She found an empty carriage and lifted Angel into it.

'We have more time to wait my sweet, but we will find a game to play.'

From behind she heard a voice she recognised. It was Mrs Frith.

'Florence Trevern, and where you off to 'en.'

The surprise in Mrs Frith's voice made Flo flush and she quickly stepped into the carriage. But Mrs Frith was persistent. She stuck her head through the open window.

'Goin' for an outing? 'Tis the middle of the week?'

'We...we're up to St Austell, Mrs Frith.'

The old woman leant further in and noticed the luggage.

'Seems to me you're going for more 'n a day. More like a week.'

'We're staying with – with a friend of Mr Pasco's. There is a party and a marquee for the children with a sugar fountain.'

Mrs Frith seemed satisfied with the answer. She knocked her hat askew as she pulled her head back.

'Well you give my regards to that dashing father of yours, I shall see you directly.'

'Got the backside of a camel,' thought the guard in his peaked hat as he passed behind her. He was off to have a meal. He had a couple of hours before the freight trucks were loaded and the great engine turned its wheels again for the long haul to the metropolis.

'Damn,' Flo sighed.

'Damn,' said Angel.

Flo smiled and put an arm round her. She thought of Russell and hoped he would be happy when he saw them. Only for a second did she have misgivings and the spectre of another woman brushed her shoulder.

Mr Trevern looked dishevelled. His usually manicured nails were dirty and he had forgotten to smooth his hair. It had been a rough crossing from night to morning as if he had lived and died in an infernal, watery waste where a demonic Poseidon tortured him with memories.

As he greeted Will Lander his hand shook.

'Perfect day for it Will.'

'I've rigged a platform up there for 'ee sir. I do hope you can climb it, but if you can't, I'll give you a hand.'

Mr Trevern looked up to the second tier of scaffolding.

The first stages of the building had progressed rapidly. The walls were already fifteen feet high. It would rise from its foundations, hemmed in by shops and houses, to two hundred and fifty gothic feet and it would take thirty years to complete. Only John Pearson the architect could visualise his spires and porches adorned with statues of past bishops.

Mr Trevern passed the camera to Will and climbed up the ladder gripping the top rung before heaving himself onto the first platform a few feet above the ground. The sheer granite blocks rose upwards towards a grey sky where the gulls had already found a perch and started their endless daily screeching to protect the new territory.

The second ladder leant against the next scaffold at the top and Will was up it like a monkey, carrying the camera.

'Here, sir,' and he helped the older man find his feet. From below, the site manager shaded his eyes to look up at them.

'Morning, Mr Trevern, is the boy doing alright for you?'

'Very good, Mr Jones, no complaints.'

'Well you can cuff him if he doesn't comply with your wishes.'

'I shall push 'ee off if you do,' said Will joining in the banter.

Can you put the tripod in the basket for us,' shouted Mr Trevern.

Will slowly winched up the basket on a pulley attached to a upright post. It swung precariously in the air.

'This is a good view,' said Mr Trevern turning ninety degrees to look for the light. The two men peered down at a rough, dirt track that ran through the middle of the site where navvies cut and worked the slabs. Soon the craftsmen would be called in to shape arches and pillars and create the rose window that was to be part of the west front.

The wind was blowing stronger and although the rain had stopped, the narrow piece of wood on which they were standing was slippery. Mr Trevern extended the legs of the tripod and placed them firmly on the platform as Will passed him the camera. They moved carefully like two divers under water engaged in a dance, both of them knowing the steps but taking time to execute them. Mr Trevern screwed the camera in place.

A man wandered around the corner from the other side of the scaffold wheeling a barrow.

'Tell him to stop Will and look this way.'

The young man squeezed past the camera and holding on to a rope that acted as a rail, he called out to the stone mason. The workman acknowledged Mr Trevern. They had been told of the project and there wasn't one of them that did not appreciate a break for a few minutes while the shutter clicked.

'Now come here and help me.'

He found a rag in his pocket and gave it to Will, 'Can you rub that smudge out, I can't seem to reach it. There. No, to your left. Yes that's it, give it a clean.'

He scrutinized the lens again. The light was not so good today, it was going to be a challenge and there was still a speck of dust in the top right hand corner of the frame.

'Has that done it, sir?' asked Will as he squeezed back beside Mr Trevern with the piece of cloth.

'Bugger me if it hasn't, Will, here give me that. I know exactly where is it is.'

He leant around the camera and tried to reach the lens but his foot slid beneath him and he lurched forward knocking the camera and tripod onto the platform. Will shouted and caught it as it teetered towards the edge.

'Sir,' said Will pleased with himself, 'I've got the camera,' and he dragged the equipment back to safety.

Mr Trevern had put his hand on the rope to save himself and as he turned to check he hadn't lost the camera it snapped and hung blowing in the wind.

There was a moment frozen in time where Will, the camera, the stone mason's face full of shock, the wall of the cathedral and the sky now flecked with blue, turned upside down in a rotating vision spinning away from him. Strangely as he fell, he felt no fear, just disgust for allowing the accident to happen. The ground came up to meet him and then mercifully there was nothing.

Russell was finding rehearsals tough. Because of his good looks and vocal quality they had decided to make him understudy George Tunbridge in a curtain-raiser to the *Pirates of Penzance* called *In the Sulks*. When the show finished he would rush back to the dressing room where he had just enough time for a quick change into his pirates costume complete with tufted, hairy eyebrows, wig and beard before he sprinted on for the overture.

In the Sulks was a light piece and had not been written by the masters. Russell found the music by Alfred Cellier trite and uninspiring. He wanted to move up the ranks of chorus and maybe get a chance to play Frederick, the leading juvenile. But as the company was going on tour with the curtain-raiser at the end of the year it meant his contract was guaranteed. He didn't grumble too much, at least there was a strong possibility he would go on for George Tunbridge who was known to enjoy the odd glass of wine between shows and be completely incoherent at the beginners' call and as his new friends kept telling him, he had a lot to learn about his craft. He really saw Gilbert and Sullivan as a stepping stone in his career. His heart still lay with Verdi and La Scala.

The other understudy in the show was a soprano called Ellen Barsley and Russell quickly established a friendship. He had never met a woman like her before. She was Glaswegian, witty and political, not out to snare a rich husband like many of the other flirty singers in the chorus. Independence shone out of her.

After the demanding days rehearsing and playing she would join Russell and Danny in the hazy atmosphere of the Opera Tavern, newly built the year before on the wave of the big pub boom. They would sit in the clear unsooted windows and Ellen would talk about her new friend William Morris.

'Where did you meet him?' asked Russell, impressed with her connections.

'I heard him speak at a meeting for the Women's Protective League, he was seconding a motion for woman's rights. He's a great man. He believes no one, not even the poorest worker in the land should live without art and beauty.'

Danny shovelled a piece of pie in his mouth. He had bought it in Covent Garden market and carried it over to be heated up behind the bar, a service most pubs provided in London.

'That's daft, I can't afford a painting. Do you think that man there can buy a work of art?' He pointed through the window to a hawker selling newspapers under a gas light, 'I don't think so!'

'I am sure Mr Morris does not mean that beauty only exists in something manufactured like a picture, only a simpleton would imagine that to be the case.'

Russell lifted his eyebrows at Danny who snorted. He was

used to Ellen's thinly veiled attacks.

'He means socialism is not only about struggle but it should give you sensual fulfilment and hope. He says, when there is a serious strike of workman against the poisoning of the air with smoke, and the waters with filth, art is getting on indeed. Oh how he can explain things.'

'Pah,' said Danny waving her aside with a dismissive gesture, 'Anarchists, Fabians, Socialists, Socialist Unionists, there's too many of them, 'as far as I can see they all shout their heads off to the labourers who listen politely but only want the Trade Unions and a riot. Most of them are ignorant anyway. What do you think Russell?'

How Russell wished John was sitting opposite him drinking in the debate.

'I think the answer, maybe the answer is education?'

'That's the most sensible thing that's been said here tonight,' said Danny lifting his glass and toasting his new friend.

'Up to a point he is right,' agreed Ellen, her intelligent eyes scanning Russell's face, hoping to lure him into her camp, 'but the death of the whole bourgeois system is the only answer. For the last thirty years capitalism has been living in a world of growing markets and great profits, I mean even an idiot could make a splendid profit these days.'

'But that's good, Ellen, that's what we all want. Isn't that so Cornish?'

Russell nodded but he was thinking of Florence and her eye for objects and shapes.

'William Morris said 'the test of the realisation of socialism will be the abolition of property.'

'No! No! Now that's going too far,' Danny was on his feet. Russell couldn't decide if he was serious or acting.

'Does not your Mr Morris live in a nice house? Is he not

a rich man? He likes to call himself an artisan but in truth he's a ponce, a philistine, preaching to those less well off than he. No one wants to be bullied into a modern world.'

Ellen was angry and she too was on her feet, jabbing a finger at Danny.

'Just because the government saw fit to build eighty two miles of sewers doesn't mean the poor are lifted out of their poverty. There's work to be done, Danny boy. Not everyone has the gifts that we have. Very few can work and have the pleasure of it like us. We're the lucky ones, most of the population need to be helped out of degradation. It is industry that has caused this chaos. London is a symbol of the awful individualism that is spreading in the world.' And she stormed out.

Danny looked despairingly at Russell and then his face creased into a huge grin. He knew they would make up tomorrow before the next show with a hug in the wings and some mumbled apologies.

'Fancy another?'

Russell said, 'Of course, I'm thirsty as a gull.'

'As a gull ay?' said Danny and took their glasses to the bar.

The idea that he now belonged to an elite class, a group of people who actually enjoyed the work for which they were paid had never struck Russell before. A part of him was still in the pits, his face and hands raw with clay. Singing was always a hobby, it wasn't real work. But he was changing. He had learnt to forget himself in a part and he soon discovered it was the perfect way to avoid reality, the theatre was an escape as potent as opium. He was submerged in it and all its influences with its unconventional life style and its own conventional rules and he realised only by the grace of God had he got out.

27

Flo had been playing 'Ho, Ho' with Angel while they waited for the train to leave. A game which involved Angel doing everything she could to make her sister laugh. Florence eventually gave in as Angel expertly mimicked a sailor they had once seen with a wooden leg who rose up and down as he walked. Later they heard that the leg had fallen off and rolled past the Ship Inn to the Malpas ferry slip. The poor man had followed hopping all the way but it was too late to rescue it. It was last seen on its way to Pendennis point with a black chough at the helm. However unfortunate, the incident made Flo laugh and she laughed until tears came streaming down her face and her ribs ached.

'No more, no more,' she spluttered and they both burst out again rolling on the seats together.

The door opened and a smartly dressed business man from London with an umbrella and top hat settled into a seat opposite and brought out a newspaper. Flo and Angel quietened down and resumed their reading. Occasionally he would peer over his glasses at them and smile.

Outside last minute passengers piled into the train with crying babies, luggage and food. A few were only going one stop and a bleating lamb was picked up and shoved under a seat. The guard walked along the carriages banging the doors making sure they were shut and Angel leaned out the window as the engine of the Great Western Railway shot steam, white into the slate sky.

'Sit down, Angel, we'll be off in a minute.'

The man smiled and lowered his paper, 'Going to London?'

'Yes, I'm afraid she is full of fun. It is her first time,' Flo paused as a whistle blew and she tried to stop Angel bouncing on her seat and then added, 'and mine.'

'I see. Well at Paddington station you won't see cows in the field next to the platform like you do here. You must look up at the roof when we arrive. It is a feat of great architecture that has to be seen. A marvel of engineering. And we have the railway that goes under the ground too. Called the Metropolitan Railway.'

'Yes, we will be going on it I am sure. Again I am afraid to say, for the first time.' Florence dreaded it. To travel on a small train deep in a tunnel which ran under roads and houses seemed like entering Hades.

'And to which part of London will your journey end?'

'I...I'm not sure, I do have a friend but – 'Flo realised she was not sounding confident and pulled herself together. She finally came up with an area where a bookshop was located that had sent her copies of Robert Browning's poetry.

'South Kensington.'

The man had smiled knowingly and searched in his jacket pocket.

'If you need any help, here's my card, I would be happy to be of service. And in the meantime we have a long journey ahead so may I introduce myself. Samuel Saunders.'

Flo thanked him and told him their names. The card said, 'J.M. Saunders, manufacturer of fine woollen carpets and materials.' He was probably down to do trade with the mill above the town.

Another whistle blew. Angel went to the window again and nearly lost her footing as the carriages started pulling out of the station.

Then an odd thing happened. Flo remembered that Angel suddenly looked worried as she turned to her sister for an explanation. Two policemen came charging down the platform waving to the guard who kept blowing his whistle. The train noisily came to a halt. The driver, a red bandanna around his head, his face an oily black, yelled angrily to the guard above the sound of hissing steam. The train was almost out of the station. It was only the last few carriages that were parallel to the platform.

'Dearie me, the driver will be cross,' said Mr Saunders, 'it had better be a good reason for stopping, he has a schedule to keep and this delay means he'll have to work overtime going through Devon to make up the time.'

The policemen arrived at the carriage behind them.

'Probably a member of staff needs a ride to Plymouth,' Mr Saunders joked

'There they are.' One of the policemen shouted as he spotted Angel and they were with them in seconds.

'I'm afraid you will have to get off the train, miss. There has been a terrible accident.'

Mr Saunders looked concerned and immediately took on the role of protector.

'Are you sure, constable?' He said, 'You don't want to go upsetting these ladies for no good reason.'

'You be Florence Trevern?'

'Yes,' Flo said. Her mouth was dry. Of course her father would hunt them down. Why did she think she could run away without the whole town hearing about it. Mrs Frith, she thought. She would have told him where they were.

'Well,' tis your father. He's had a nasty fall.'

She picked up their bags before thanking Mr Saunders for his kindness. She saw disappointment in his eyes as if he was looking forward to her conversation and company.

'You have my card. If ever you are in London – and also I visit Cornwall often, please do not hesitate to...' and he placed a hand on hers, 'I do hope your father is not hurt.'

But he was hurt. Initially a vague thought had passed through her mind as she searched the bland face of the policeman that maybe her father was dead. And in those few seconds a path opened up with possibilities beyond imagination. Even after they arrived back at Lemon Street and she saw him lying on the sofa attended by a doctor and nurse, a shadow of the idea lingered and mixed with her concern for him.

In fact for such an awkward fall he was not hurt badly. Mr Jones and Will said he had the luck of the pixies, he should be dead, but he had been saved by a pile of straw used to clad stones during transportation. The doctor diagnosed he had a broken foot, his hip was severely bruised and he had concussion. He needed herbal teas for shock and laxatives to cleanse the system. He was not to be moved. So a bed was brought into the study to make it easier for Florence to look after him. He refused a full-time nurse or anyone else fussing over him and convinced the doctor his daughter was quite able to care for him. His anger had returned and he cussed and grumped at his bad luck. The only thing that made him feel better was the knowledge he had taken enough photos of the fledgling cathedral to warrant an entry in the local, history books.

Every day as Florence brought him food and helped him sit against the plumped pillows, he stared at her coldly waiting for an explanation. They had not talked about her run to the station and it simmered between them.

Finally one afternoon he said weakly, 'Come and sit beside me, Florence.'

She drew up a chair beside his bed after removing his tray of stew and dumplings which were half eaten.

'What were you thinking of, maid? Trying to go away like that? Maybe it is your duty to tell me? Maybe you could offer an excuse? A reason? For I harbour these thoughts during the long hours of recuperation that do me no good. Ay? Can you explain? I see you won't answer. I just thank you for returning to look after me. For I don't know what I'd do without you.'

'I'm sure you would have done well without me, Father. The doctor says you will be walking soon, it's shock that has taken you.'

'You belong here, Florence. In Cornwall. It's terrible hard for one of us to fit up country. We're a different race, see. Different way of thinking. You belong down here near me. But now it's alright because even in your weakest moment you could never leave me while I'm an invalid.'

His watery eyes bore into her. She couldn't avoid the confrontation any longer.

'There are...many reasons why I...wished to leave,' she said finally, 'I do not want to say what they were. Only...I found Russell Bell and I love him, Father. I shall stay and care for you, it's my duty, but you must understand, if he comes back for me, I shall be married.'

Mr Trevern smoothed the sheet. Some crumbs of bread sprinkled the eiderdown and he flicked them to the carpet.

'He will never be back for you, he's gone. That sort never comes back. Never. He's off with the pomping folk, blazing his own path.'

Flo picked up the tray. She couldn't bear to see the triumph in his face. Luckily Angel called from her bedroom.

'I must go, Father.'

'I don't know why you don't let that little girl come and see me? She cheers my heart. It will help me to get on my feet again?'

'I will bring her later to say goodnight.'

After she took the tray to the kitchen, she returned to empty his pot into the water closet and give him his opiate medicine. She went up to her room and found the photo of Russell under her pillow. It was beginning to fade although she had been careful to set it well. She ran her fingers round the outline of his lips and sent her thoughts to him, hoping they were strong enough to reach above the London din.

Most of the time Flo kept Angel busy with lessons and walks and teaching her the piano, ever watchful of leaving her in her father's presence. Flo impressed on her sister that their father was gravely ill and needed to be quiet. The sound of his cries as he attempted to move his shattered foot was enough to convince Angel to leave him alone. But it was no way for them to live. To be his jailer. To keep him from the one thing he desired and he turned on Florence. Any mistake she made he ridiculed or criticised. With uncanny accuracy he could wound her. Often when she was least expecting an ambush, he would sense when her mood had lifted and bring her down with a casual swipe. Her photography was bad, her looks were plain, no one would love her, she would achieve nothing, she was lucky to have him keep her.

His grumbling became unhealthy, he enjoyed it, often hooting with laughter after a particular attack on a friend or neighbour who had been kind enough to visit. Only Mr Pasco took the trouble to ask how Flo was coping. He had heard the story she told Mrs Frith, that they were off to visit a non-existent friend of his in St Austell and he had kept quiet. He assured Flo her secret was safe with him. He was sensitive enough not ask where they were going, although he knew the answer. Only the week before he had told the Police Chief that Russell Bell had not joined the strikers. He had his work slips from Mr Ellery to prove it. Her father made fun of him. The Royal Hotel was little more than a den of vice and the Opera Society was a joke worth knowing.

'The man do talk and talk. Quietness is the best noise as Uncle Johnny said when he knocked down his wife.' And he coughed as he tried to eat a piece of saffron cake Mrs Frith had brought him.

Flo supposed that his need to criticise others was to build himself up after his fall. But only he knew it came from fear; the fear his daughters would leave him as his wife had done; the fear that Florence would remember what had happened that night on the river bank. All his bravura was a sham. Deep inside, he was a small boy watching the colossal waves of the ocean crash into the rocks at Land's End. A small, frightened boy who had turned into a bully but hadn't meant to. And even though he lay on his sick bed unable to move, he still longed for Angel.

He would catch tempting glimpses of her skipping past, a flash of blue skirt and blonde curls like a mix on his palette. She would peer around the door, her soft cheeks pressed into the wood as he enticed her closer, whispering so Flo could not hear. Sometimes she would respond and creep in, a naughty grin on her face, complicit in their private game. He would give her chocolate that Mrs Parr had left or a sugared grape brought in by Mr Fairfax.

'Now you mustn't tell your sister,' he would say, 'she'll have me hung.' And Angel would look grave and promise, firmly crossing her heart and pretending to cut her wrists. He asked for a kiss and she would climb on the bed beside him and put her head on his chest before pressing her wet lips against his.

'You're my special girl,' he murmured.

Flo's night terrors grew. The apparition of her father loomed larger and more grotesque until he transformed into a monstrous gorgon with many arms and each arm held a sword that cut and swathed the boiling water. Isolated in the flow, he searched beneath the surface, dipping into the murky depths as a cry of utter desolation rang through the disproportionate shapes of her nightmare valley. Once in the half awake, half asleep reverie of early morning, another memory of her mother emerged. She heard her parents in their bedroom arguing, her father's raised voice above her mother's insistent tone. The sound of a slap like a wet rag on the stone kitchen floor. She stumbled out of bed and looked through the half-open doorway. They were struggling like two rams, pushing backwards and forwards across the room in a strange, naked wrestling match. Her father had one of her mother's stockings around her neck and he was pulling her towards him. She could see the bright, red marks where the cotton had cut into her flesh. Flo called out and they stopped. Her mother came over and wiped her tears away with her hand.

'It was only a rehearsal,' her mother said trying to sooth her.

'Yes, of course,' her father agreed as he quickly pulled on his dressing gown, 'you know I am to be in the opera show this year and I couldn't for the life of me learn the steps. Got feet like half crown shovels. Ha!' And he did a little shuffle.

Her mother took her back to bed and told her not to worry. But she had always known it was a cover-up.

28

Adam couldn't remember what time or day the sergeant major arrived. He barely heard the pounding and the door being kicked in by two army cadets, wood splintering across the room. He was told later that he had been lying unconscious in a pool of blood and vomit. They poured a bucket of cold water over him and dragged him to a pony and trap. He was driven to Back Quay on a balmy evening and carried past staring tourists to a topsail schooner called *The Lady Ebrington* where he was handed over to a midshipman. Still unconscious, he was thrown onto a narrow bed in a steerage cabin to sleep on the long journey. As he woke through the nights, raving and shouting, they fed him laudanum to keep him quiet. Frequently the captain had to apologise to other passengers about the noise and often they had to tie him to his bed.

He was lucky. Private Wassail had been looking for him. He had collected his VC from the Queen and hoped he might have heard from Adam; a congratulations maybe, a message of gratitude. But nothing came. So it was with a mixture of annoyance and curiosity he made the effort and managed to track him down. A letter came back from the Captain of the Duke of Cornwall's Light Infantry explaining Adam's situation. There was a P.S. at the end which read, 'I gather from my informants that this man is a trouble maker and suggest you do not endeavour to meet with him as he appears to have succumbed to the perils of alcohol.'

Private Wassail felt sad. Their shared history was also the history of Rorke's Drift and the terrible post trauma of the fight. He hadn't saved a life to have it lost a year later. Before he returned to his regiment he arranged for Adam to be sent to the military hospital at Netley. He would try and visit him on his next leave.

They arrived at Southampton on a depressing morning on a flat sea and Adam was helped from his stinking cabin onto the deck. He looked along the endless length of pier, constructed especially for the hospital boats, watching patients being unloaded onto stretchers and wondered where he was. He made no fuss as he was lifted into a wheelchair by a couple of orderlies and even managed to say goodbye to the captain who couldn't wait to get rid of him. He was hurried up the pier and put in an ambulance wagon along with twenty other men.

Even for the very sick, none of them would ever forget their first sight of the Victoria Hospital. It had been built by royal command to cope with the casualties of the Crimea War and was rapidly becoming a centre of medical advancement. The three rectangular buildings, each with its own bell-turret and cupola, shared one imposing façade a quarter of a mile long filled with hundreds of windows set in pristine granite. It housed one hundred and thirty eight wards in which there were a thousand beds. The locals were extremely proud of it and families would picnic in the spacious grounds on Sundays and on funeral days, visit the tiny chapel to bury their soldier relatives in the graveyard. It was magnificent. The biggest military hospital ever built in the world.

Adam was met at the main entrance by the superintendent Mrs Jane Drebble. She asked the orderlies to wheel him to her rooms and as they set off down the long corridor passing soft-footed nurses, padding up and down pushing trolleys, Adam had yelled obscenities at them.

One of the orderlies wrapped him on the knuckles with a stick, 'Not in here,' he said.

'Please have respect William,' said Mrs Drebble with compassion, 'you cannot imagine what this poor man has been through.'

Chastened, William apologised and left them alone in the comfortably furnished room with a high, stucco ceiling and a Lincrusta embossed wall covering.

She had personally promised Private Wassaill she would keep an eye out for Adam but when she saw him she rather regretted having done so. Adam was more of a wreck than she expected. His face was red-veined from drink and she spotted immediately he was in the first stages of addiction withdrawal, he could barely string two words together. His legs were a terrible mess. She found cuts and bruises and blisters filled with a foul smelling, brown fluid. She was not sure where to send him first. The surgical ward or the asylum wing.

'I too was there, Adam, in Africa,' she said.

Adam had looked up at her pathetically from his chair and met her kind eyes.

'Isandlewana?'

'No, not there, but at Pietermaritzburg and Addington. In Natal.'

'A nurse?'

'Yes, the wounds were horrific, the worst I've ever seen. Do you have dreams?'

Adam's fists waved in the air but no words came out of

his spittle-caked mouth. Eventually he let out a small cry for help. Jane Drebble put her hand on his shoulder.

'I have dreams, Adam. Bad ones. And sometimes the sights return to haunt me. Is it like that for you?'

Adam nodded, perspiration trickling down the side of his face and then he shouted at her cantankerously, asking for a beer.

'Be quiet now. We will do our best for you. You must be seen by our surgeon.'

She rang a bell on her desk and William returned.

'Take him to registration. I think you will have to write it down for him. We know his name. It's Adam Pollard. But age and date of birth, I doubt he will remember. Take him to ward twenty and make sure Nurse Stewart cares for him.'

'He was given this on the boat from Cornwall, mam. Shall I arrange for more?' William held up the bottle of laudanum.

'Good heavens no, what are you thinking of? It's a mixture of opium and alcohol, man. We don't want to give him another addiction.'

William sighed. He knew it meant a busy few weeks and the strait jacket. Adam wouldn't last long on the surgical ward. And he was right.

After he was tucked in a bed between white starched sheets, the surgeon arrived in his frock coat. Adam threw up in a bowl as the surgeon examined him. Student doctors stood in a circle, peering over each other with notebooks and pencils in their hands.

The surgeon began his diagnosis in a weary, educated voice, 'His fever is moderate but will increase if this condition is allowed to continue. If you touch his skin here lightly you will have a crackling sensation. It's a kind of gas produced by the infection. At the same time the blood is leaking out of his vessels. His heartbeats are rapid. He also must be in severe pain but as I understand it, this patient has an addiction to alcohol and won't have been feeling much. Understandable poor chap, but it's an ignorant reaction to dealing with his condition. As you can see the area around the blisters is quite pale and it's important we amputate before the skin becomes dark red or purple. This can happen sometimes before your eyes as the symptoms suddenly worsen.'

The surgeon touched Adam's feet and then his hands 'One last thing to remember is the coldness of the extremities. Luckily he's not bright yellow yet. Believe me I've seen the entire body infected from one single wound. Nurse?'

Nurse Stewart hovered beside him, waiting subserviently.

'Make this patient ready for the operating theatre. I doubt he'll make it. But we can but try.'

The mist came and went. Sometimes there was light but mostly it was dark. And then the darkness cleared and surreptitiously divided into day and night. For a second as he woke there was no pain. A glorious valley of comfort. But as the morning passed he climbed a never-ending mountain which peaked and troughed always returning him to a higher level. His desperate cries brought the nurses running with more dressings of wet carbolic acid and iodine. Often when he was delirious and begging for morphine the duty nurse would only open the window. Fresh air was believed to be restorative. In the afternoons the surgeon arrived and re-screwed the brass tourniquet on his seeping stump. He lay watching the clock on the wall, steeling himself for the night which spanned a year, as he counted the hours until

Nurse Stewart put another dose of the precious drug to his lips. He began to number the different highs of pain from one to ten in the hope of more valleys. If it was a five followed by four maybe there might be a three. But usually by morning he was writhing in a numerical mess with ten shrieking inside his head. Sometimes in an opium-fuelled dream the bogey man appeared. An Africa warrior in full ceremonial dress, tufts of feathers foot high on his head like a strange palm that had taken root, his penis hanging down on his naked body, a zebra-hide shield held to protect his heart. The African grinned like a creature from Hades and he shrieked with fear. Sam came running to pin him to his bed and more morphine was administered against Jane Drebble's instructions

Jessie Stewart watched him with a worried look on her face. She hated knowing a patient could die. She had become a nurse to save lives. She certainly was not going to see Adam go on her watch.

'Adam,' she said softly in his ear, 'drink some of this water.'

She lifted his head towards the beaker and he managed a few sips. His face, already drawn when he arrived had taken on the shape of a skull, the skin barely covering the bones, his teeth jutting forward, his eyes lost in their sockets, he would have been left for dead on the battlefield. He began a ranting, roving speech, picking words randomly which seemed to have no meaning except to him as he nodded and answered his own thoughts. He reminded Jessie of the patients in D-wing. She had only been through the double locked doors once to help with an inmate who had harmed himself – they would slash their wrists with anything they could get their hands on – but it was enough to show her the tragedy of mental illness. Jessie hoped Adam would not end up behind the bars, but she didn't hold out much hope. Already Mrs Drebble was in consultation to discover if they could give him the same standard of post-operative care under lock and key. He was disturbing the recovery of other patients.

'Adam, tell me, what is your name?'

Jessie's face blurred as he tried to focus. He knew her name. He had heard the matron calling her and the surgeon ticking her off for a bedpan she should have emptied. But he wasn't sure who he was. There was something missing in him or was it outside him? He felt with his hand where his leg should be.

'Is...there...gone?'

"Yes, Adam, we have told you, you were very, very ill. In order to save your life Professor Lennox had to make an amputation.'

'Am...pu..shun. Here!'

She was unsure what he meant so she said, 'Yes, we did the operation here.'

'No! Here!'

She leant into him and he snatched a handful of her hair pulling it out from her nurse's hat until she squealed.

'Got you.'

Jessie twisted her head as she tried to release herself from Adam's grip but surprisingly he was strong enough to hang on to her. William made his way purposefully down the long line of beds and roughly prised Adam's fingers away.

'It can't go on, I've got to report him,' he pointed at Adam, 'and you can shut up you bastard.'

Jessie was a tough girl but the viciousness of Adam's attack had shaken her and she allowed William to steer her back to the nurses' rest room. He made her a cup of tea and sterilised her arm where Adam had inadvertently scratched her.

'If he's not turned mad now, I can tell you this, when he comes off the morphine he soon will be. If you don't go to see Mrs Drebble about it, I will.'

Later that day Jessie waited outside the Superintendent's office straightening her grey dress and scarlet cape before knocking.

'Come,' said Mrs. Drebble, 'oh Jessie it's you and how can I help you?'

Jessie looked embarrassed. It wasn't in her nature to tell tales.

'It's about a patient, mam.'

'Ah. And I think I know who it is.'

'He is extremely difficult. I am doing my best but he can be violent and today …' She touched the bandage on her arm.

'I see.'

'I wish to be transferred to another ward if it is possible?'

Jane Drebble looked at the strong girl in front of her. She was made for the job. She didn't want to lose her.

'You have my sympathies nurse, but I chose you to care for this particular case because…' the Superintendent paused and looked across at a tiny carved cross propped up on the mantelpiece given to her by a rehabilitated patient, 'because, I recognise in you, something of myself.'

Jessie felt flattered. She sat down as the older women gestured to a chair.

'As you know, I worked in the hospital tents in Africa and I may say, some of the sights were unspeakable. It took all my resolve to cope with the severity of the maimed and wounded. Men were driven to extremes of human nature and perhaps, forgive me if I'm telling you what you have already understood, but perhaps, recovery is not only physical, but spiritual too. I saw many men in the Zulu wars with the same pathology as Mr Pollard and sadly I do not know how many of them are alive today. The memories of war are never forgotten. You can't wipe them away. You just hope you can learn to live with them. Unfortunately most soldiers never discover how to do it.'

'Please, mam, I don't wish to contradict you but I believe Mr Pollard's mind has turned. And I fear there is no hope for him.'

'Mmm.' Jane Drebble rose from her chair and reached for a newspaper from a pile on a shelf behind her. She found the page she was looking for and gave it to the young nurse.

'Just before you started working at this hospital, we had a soldier here called Private Frederick Hitch. I'm sure you remember that the Queen arrived to give him his Victoria Cross?'

Nurse Stewart examined the photo in the paper.

'Yes, I have heard about it. She visited many of the wards.'

'He received his honour graciously, but after all the fuss and pomp and the entourage left, he said to me, "What was all that about?" Can you imagine? The poor man was so traumatised he had no notion of what it meant. He was one of a few survivors from the awful massacre at the Drift. His bravery took my breath away. It took months for him to recover. But he did recover and he walked out of here a new man. Now we have a chance to save another. It is a gift, Jessie. We are not only repairing his body, I hope and pray we can restore his mind too. I am sure, underneath, he is a good person. Shall we try and discover who he is?'

She took Jessie's hand in hers. 'I have enormous faith in you, I knew, out of all my staff, you were the one for this job. I am certain you have the strength to withstand the terrible conditions we observe in our patients. I know you have an exciting future ahead of you.'

Jessie flushed with pride. She shifted slightly from one foot to the other.

'Forgive me, matron. Of course, I will endeavour to do my best as always. Thank you for listening to my grievance. It seems so inappropriate now. I have been foolish.'

'Should you return to your ward now?'

'Oh yes, yes. And thank you. For reaffirming our purpose in being here.'

Mrs Drebble smiled to herself as Jessie closed the door. She went to the window and gazed out at the delicately sculptured war memorial set on a grassy mound in the middle of the sweeping lawns. Most of the wards faced north-east, away from the sun, looking over the vast, coal bunkers needed to fire the boilers. How much better it would have been if Florence Nightingale had helped design the hospital as the Queen had wanted. She would have given the sick a more pleasant view.

From that moment, Jessie Stewart made Adam her reason for getting up in the morning. She was there when they transferred him to a special ward in D-wing and she was there in the middle of the night to hold his hand during the weeks of battle to maintain his sanity. She wheeled him in to see the Phrenology Professor who examined his head for lumps and bumps to try and identify his temperament and after it was decided he was suffering from neurasthenia and should have treatment from the new electro-medical machine, she promised she would ask if she could be allowed to stay in the room. As it happened, they needed a nurse present. She watched them attach the electrodes to the skin on the back of his neck and she jumped with him, as the shock vibrated through his body. Afterwards he lay on the bed in a deep sleep. For the first time in months she felt he might have had some peace. He was still prone to talking to himself and to bouts of anger and to screaming from a ghostly pain where his leg had been severed, but Jessie's care and attention went a long way to helping him. His neurasthenia was only a temporary condition, so the professor had said, and she prayed he would make a full recovery.

The winter weather hit the south coast with icy gales that whistled around the hospital corners and down the draughty corridors. Jessie wheeled Adam along a path to the great, wrought iron gates at the entrance to the hospital. She had tucked a tartan rug over his lap and rammed a cap on his head which made his ears stick out. He rubbed his hands and enjoyed the cold air on his cheeks. He didn't mind winter coming. The swirling leaves dancing in irregular patterns across the grass gave him a sense that he was alive.

'You see, Adam, there's the world out there, through those gates. And you should be living in it.'

'Oh, Jessie, 'tis a grand idea. But I don't know yet.'

'No, not yet. But in a few months' time. And there are many jobs you can do. You can go for training to learn how to make things. I shall find out more for you. I believe there is a factory that employs veterans near here.'

'So you don't want me to leave then?'

Jessie noticed the twinkle in his eye. She was used to his flirting and she didn't mind. She was fond of him. Not in any romantic way, they were just good friends.

She faced the wheelchair toward the hospital and they headed back on a path which took them around the perimeter of the grounds.

'Tell us the story of the ghost, Jessie?'

'And where have you heard that from?'

'You can't be in this place for long and not hear of it.'

'I think it is a bag of nonsense.'

'Go on with 'ee.'

She stopped and hid his freezing hands beneath the blanket.

'Well apparently there was a nurse who fell hopelessly in love with a patient. But she found out he was seeing another woman.'

'He can't have been so poorly then,' joked Adam.

'No I suppose not, maybe he escaped at night. Anyway the nurse found out and murdered him and then one day she overdosed on morphine and killed herself. And ever since, she has been walking the wards searching for him. One of the student nurses is adamant she has seen her. But I think the night watch brings visions and strange shadows. It's easy to imagine ghosts.'

''Tis a sad tale. Better watch myself with you.'

'And what are you suggesting?'

'You know you love me really.'

'You are extremely naughty, Mr Pollard.'

It did him good to hear her joke with him and so he carried on.

'I'm not so incapacitated that I don't see how attractive you are, Miss Stewart.'

'Now, now, Mr Pollard.'

He chuckled and tried to make the wheels go faster with his hands, making her walk quickly to keep up with him.

'Now you stop now, you'll be falling out if you're not careful.'

'Give us a kiss, Jessie.'

She threw her head back and laughed and to Adam it was a miracle that he enjoyed it so much.

As Jessie struggled with the wheelchair through one of

the many back doors William came rushing towards them.

'He's got a visitor, I'll take him.'

Adam looked amazed but Jessie smiled and said goodbye before removing her cloak. He could hear the squish of her heavy shoes on the linoleum floor as she went to the nurses' room.

'Well, here we are,' said Mrs Drebble as Adam was pushed into her study. To begin with, the direct light coming through the window hid the fact that another person was sitting in the corner. But as his eyes became accustomed he could see clearly it was Nan.

'We'll go out, William, and give Mr Pollard and Miss Peters some privacy.'

The door closed and there was an uncomfortable silence. Nan was exhausted. The trip had taken days. She had bought a steerage passage and like Adam come all the way from Truro by boat. It was the first time she had been out of Cornwall and she decided it would be her last. Southampton was too flat and the surrounding coastline too uninteresting. The quays were swamped with the military and the navy and she didn't like the way they looked at her. She couldn't wait to get to the hospital to meet Adam.

'Would you like to sit by the fire, Nan?'

Adam was the first to speak. She said thank you and settled into a high backed chair with relief.

'Well, I wanted to come and see you Adam. Are 'ee alright 'en?'

He was embarrassed. The gap between them was immense. Recently he had been feeling much more like the man he had been before Africa, although he knew he couldn't be the same. Too much had happened

'It was hard, Nan, but I don't do the drinking any more. Not a drop. Anyway...' he gave her a wry smile, '...they don't

233

give it to me.'

'Good,' answered Nan, 'very wise.'

'Look, Nan.'

'Adam I have…'

They both spoke at the same time.

'You say first, Adam.'

He noticed, as if for the first time, the curves of her body and the old attraction came over him. Her eyes were always honest and direct.

'Nan there is so much for me to say to you I don't know where I should begin.'

'Oh, Adam I…'

'No, let me finish. I was not…not right when I came back and I am ashamed of myself. Some days I have hardly wanted to wake for remembering my bad behaviour, and not just to you. But the clever doctors here make me talk and do you know, Nan, I would never have believed it, but I think my mind is cured from gabbling! I have learnt that I was suffering in my head, Nan. From being in the fight. I had shock see and it disturbed me into drinking. It was not my fault, so they tell me. My will was broken. I'm not saying I don't sometimes think about a drink, but I believe the addiction has gone away. I have to be proper vigilant. But I am doing well.'

Nan was riveted. His anxious face was red on one side where the coals from the fire had warmed it.

'Nan, allow me to say, it is awful the weight of guilt I have when I think of you and I'm sorry. I'm sorry.'

Unexpectedly he started to cry. Nan could see how weak he was, but there was also a clarity in his face as if all his pain and worries had been drained from him. She stared into the flames before choosing her words carefully.

'Adam, you were the only one for me. From when we

were at school. Remember?'

He smiled and brought out a hankie from his coat pocket. He blew his nose loudly.

'You were my best girl.'

'And you were my prince. And we had some fun courting. Oh I never imagined I would be with any one else. But Adam…I am…I am with someone else and we are to be wed. And I've made this journey to tell you myself.'

Adam's face didn't move. He was surprised how this news didn't hurt. He realised he never thought she would come back to him and neither had he any intention of returning to Cornwall. He had stepped through an invisible door to another life and was reinventing himself. He was happy to leave the past where it was. But he needed something from her before she left.

'Congratulations, I hope he is a good man who will look after 'ee.'

'Yes, yes, he is.' She looked down at the floor, her feelings in turmoil.

'Nan can I ask you to…'

'Of course, Adam, what ever I can do to help you?' said Nan quickly.

'Do you forgive me, Nan? I very much need you to forgive me.'

She went over to him and knelt on her knees on the floor, putting her head in his lap. He gently stroked her hair.

'Adam, I shall always love you, always. I do forgive you with all my heart.'

There was a knock and Jessie poked her head around the door then quickly ducked away as she took in the scene. They heard her raised voice.

'Mr Pollard, I have to take you for your hydro treatment.'

'Miss Peters will bring me,' said Adam.

Nan was wet-eyed as she kissed Adam's hand before getting up. She held the handles of the wheelchair and pushed him into the corridor.

'Finally got to take you somewhere, Adam.'

He nodded.

'Which way?'

'Left and all the way to the end.'

'That seems like a long way.'

Adam suddenly felt cheerful. He pretended to crack a whip.

'It's not, when you know where you are going.'

29

ngel was happy she was back in her own bedroom, but today she had arranged her dolls on Flo's bed. They were visiting for morning tea and she had carefully placed a toy cup and saucer before each doll. Tamasin had a piece of figgy cake because she was her favourite. She lifted a teapot from the bedside table and poured water into the cups.

'It is very good of you all to be here today,' she said in what she assumed to be an aristocratic accent, 'and we have a visitor.'

One of the dolls toppled over as she searched under Flo's pillow, 'Here we are, Mr Russell Bell, famous opera singer, curtsy for the gentleman.' She bent each doll from the waist, except the old, wooden ones, who lay flat on their stomachs.'

'How nice to meet you, Mr Bell,' she spoke in a high squeaky voice.

'And would you like some tea, Mr Bell?'

'I am grateful for your kindness, Miss Trevern. And may I say how pretty you are.'

'Oh ho ho, Mr Bell you make me proper shy.'

'You are special, Miss Trevern.'

'I am afraid that is true, Mr Bell.' She showed the photo

of Russell to the dolls.

'Now which one of these lovely maids would you choose to kiss?'

She revolved the photo around the circle until it faced her.

'Well, Miss Trevern, I do believe it's you.'

'You can't have me for I am promised to my papa. He is my boyfriend and he makes me feel nice. '

'Just one kiss.'

Angel brought the photo to her mouth, 'You are a naughty, naughty boy and even though you've asked me, I will not kiss you any more.'

She tucked the picture of Russell in her apron pocket and collected up the tea party to take back to her bedroom.

In the evening Angel tried to copy Flo as she made pasties, dipping her fingers in a bowl of flour and sprinkling it over her own square of pastry. Flo methodically rolled the rolling pin while keeping an eye on her father who was dozing by the stove, a carved walking stick leaning against the back of his rocking chair. Earlier he had asked the doctor if he could try and walk. The doctor who was older than his patient by at least ten years had demanded Florence help him. Between the two of them, they had shoved and carried Mr Trevern complaining to the kitchen, much to Flo's annoyance. She did not look forward to getting him back to his bed on her own.

The rain beat solidly against the window as it had done for weeks and in the silence punctured intermittently by her father's snores, Flo could hear water pouring off the roof and overflowing into the butt in the garden, great puddles were forming and seeping into the foundations of the house.

Angel banged down her rolling pin.

'I can't do it.'

'Be quiet!' said Flo and she looked towards Mr Trevern who was mid-snore as he sucked in ripples of air.

Angel left the kitchen table and went over to the window. Everything was drenched with the sound of water. The hens looked permanently bewildered as they poked their heads out of their coop, droplets of rain trapped in their head feathers. She wanted her father to take her out to feed them. She fished the picture of Russell from her pocket. She had forgotten to put it back but she would have time before Flo noticed it was gone.

From his chair Mr Trevern stirred drowsily and fixed his eyes on Angel.

'What you got there my cheild?'

Angel's expression was an open face of guilt as her sister saw the photo she was holding in her hand.

'Bring it here, my treasure,' her father demanded.

Angel hesitated as Flo glared at her

'It's mine, Father,' Flo said quickly.

'Give it to me Angel, do as you're told.'

Flo tried to snatch it out of Angel's hand but was too late. Her father barely glanced at it before casually leaning over to the stove and throwing it on the coals. The photo burned slowly, the chemicals on the treated paper flaring sporadically with a radiant, blue flame. Flo's face was white with anger. Not because she had lost the photo, she still had the negative and as she was alone so often in the studio doing her father's job, she had time to make another print. No, it was not the loss of the photo that was upsetting, it was the pleasure her father had in hurting her, the look of satisfaction as he poked the stove, grunting as he leant forward to make sure the pieces would disappear into the sooty wasteland of the chimney. It was tinged with such malice that it made her hate him.

She ran out of the kitchen. She reached the top of the stairs and heard Angel following her.

'You didn't have to give it to him.'

'He made me, Flo.'

'It was my private property, it belonged to me. You had no right to take it.'

Flo slammed her bedroom door leaving Angel outside.

'You keep away from me,' shouted Flo through the door.

Angel sat on the run of carpet on the landing snuffling and tapping but Flo ignored her.

From below their father called, 'Come down to me Angel, come here my bird.'

But Angel didn't move. Eventually she fell asleep lying with her thumb in her mouth, her face splashed with dirty smudges from crying.

Mr Trevern waited in the darkening kitchen for Florence to come. He couldn't reach the matches to light a candle and he was exhausted from calling for help. An aching fatigue had crept over him. It was lucky his medicine was within reach and he downed half a bottle to help him sleep. A dreamy sensation from the opium flowed over him and his mind drifted to Angel. He had been imagining the sexual act with her for quite some time now. He felt as long as the fantasies remained in his head he would not be violating her and he managed to convince himself that the erotic imaginings were not wrong. In fact they were, in some ways, normal. He had no intention of acting out what he wanted to do; the thoughts were just a prequel to him masturbating and sometimes he had to admit Angel transformed into his wife so that the two merged in a sexual blurring, like throwing a slick of colour into a jar of water and watching the thread, pale. As long as he didn't touch her in those forbidden places where he wanted to touch her. As long as he didn't insert his finger inside her or examine between her small buttocks or ask her to feel him. As long as he didn't cross those bridges he could live with himself, because if he allowed it to happen, if he went further and persuaded her to take him in her mouth or find out if it was possible to have intercourse with her, he knew he could never live with the shame. But he was an addict. After each orgasm he plummeted to even greater depths of guilt which in turn created the link to start the cycle over again. The fact that he had not transgressed, that the signals on the line were down preventing him from travelling further, gave him permission to indulge the fantasy. The challenge was to keep his eye on the signal and every time Angel climbed into his lap and curled against him lovingly, as he felt the erotic feeling swell his body and he saw the white cross of wood going up to let him pass, with a loud clang of a bell he had to fight his need.

Sometimes he searched his past to make his behaviour accountable. Was it enough reason that his wife had died? His childhood had been no different to anyone else's. They had struggled, but there was always food on the table. His mother's love had been unconditional. His father was harsh when he beat him but encouraged his ambitions. Only the one time, the afternoon forged in his memory, when on a visit to St Ives a powerful swell had picked him up with a giant's hand and slammed him hard onto the sand. Choking for breath he had crawled away and sat watching the spray lift from the breakers blown backwards by the wind, the navy blue waves booming in his ears.

A fisherman had seen him nearly drown and run down and scooped him up taking him back to his boatshed where he had made him tea. The man's hands were stuck with scales and pin-cushioned with scars from hooks and as he rubbed him dry, he briefly touched his penis. He remembered it as a warm, comforting feeling combined with the salty smell of the sea and oil from the nets hanging across the wooden beams. His mother came looking for him and took him away, accusing the fisherman of kidnap and threatening him with the local magistrate. Could this experience be pricking him with devils? Persuading him into wrongdoing?

He was barely conscious when Florence came down the stairs and helped him limp to his bed. He remembered apologising for burning her photo and begging her forgiveness but he hardly noticed her steely face.

It rained for days and still Flo refused to talk to Angel. She neither smiled nor frowned. She was like the glassy-eyed fish lying on the quayside, blood dripping from their open mouths. Nothing could touch her. Not even her love for her sister broke the icy film of control she developed to cope with her life in Lemon Street. She had finally realised she would never be able to please her father. Even if she tried her whole life she would never receive the kind of support she needed from him. So she gave up. She ran the house, bathed him, changed his bandages, helped him walk a little further each day and took him to the water closet with a passive containment. She went out covered with a cloak after her father had spotted a dead hen lying flattened in the mud by the downpour.

'My poor bird,' her father said with tears in his eyes as he watched her burying it through the kitchen window, 'I couldn't do a thing for you. I tried to save you but you'd gone too far and there was nothing that I could do. Nothing.'

Angel had been upset too. The hen was her favourite.

And it continued to rain. Shopkeepers piled sacks against doorways and worried faces pressed against windows. Every day the town waited for the tide to come in.

Three weeks after the rain started Flo locked her bedroom door after putting Angel to bed. Her father had been particularly demanding and she needed solitude. She slept badly, aware of the thunder echoing outside and the lightning briefly illuminating the room but she didn't hear Angel call. Angel begged to be let in. She banged on the door and whimpered as rolls of thunder shook the house but Flo pulled the pillow over her head. The small girl waited on the landing, hugging her doll. Downstairs, through the half-opened door she could see a light in her father's study. She crouched on the floor and peered through the banisters, two round eyes wide with fear. Her father couldn't come to her even if she shouted; the stairs were too difficult for him to climb. A flash of lightening hit a tree next door sending Angel running down the stairs. She burst into his study. He looked up over his glasses and put his book on the table beside his medicine.

'What's the matter my cheild?'

'I'm frightened, I don't like it and Flo won't talk to me. Please, Papa, can I be in your bed?' She whimpered.

'Of course you can, my cherub. Stop your crying now. Come here, come to Papa.'

He took her in his arms.

'There, there, 'tis nothing to be afraid of. Only a bit of thunder. He'll be gone directly and he'll take his Mrs Lightning with him. Papa will give you medicine to help you sleep and when you wake, will all be done and dusted.'

He reached over and found the bottle. 'Open your mouth

while I put a few drops for you.'

Angel made a face as she tasted the sour liquid.

'It's nasty, Papa.'

'You swallow and I've got a fig you can have.'

Angel, calmer now, munched on the treat and dropped off to sleep.

Mr Trevern watched her thick, blond lashes flickering. Her downy skin was like a peach ready to eat. The moment had been given to him. He had no idea she would be in his bed this night, so passive, so golden in the lamp glow. His arousal was a given. He put his hand between his legs to feel his hardness, the wet tip pressing against his night shirt. He picked up her hand and let it flop on the mattress. She was deep in a drug-induced sleep.

A strange force came over him, as if his mind was invaded. A voice was speaking to him, 'You must do this. You have permission. It has been sent to you.' He kissed her on the mouth. He moved her clothes up to her waist to reveal her naked body and gently rubbed her vagina as he touched himself. At the back of his mind he believed it might be soothing for her, calm her fear of thunderstorms, make her feel safe. This was their little secret, as if they had witnessed a murder together and they would keep it between them forever. But there was confusion. He also hoped she would be enjoying it as much as he was. He felt a surge of love as he inserted his finger in her opening and to his surprise it was moist. The signal on the line came up and a deep sense of contentment spread over him as he penetrated her.

30

Tonight there was a party after the seven o'clock show at George Tunbridge's house in Holloway and Russell and Danny pushed their way through a group of fans at the stage door, all of them wanting to make contact with their favourite pirate. Ellen came running down the stairs, the remains of her stage make-up still on her face and they leapt aboard an omnibus, the post-show, adrenaline high racing in their systems. The horses pulled away and the coachman negotiated the busy traffic in the Strand. Even at this time of night London was busy.

It was chilly on the top deck and Russell wrapped his new coat around him. He had fancied a floppy hat in Dickens and Jones to complete the look, but it was too expensive. It would have to wait until next month. He had to compete with Danny who had a certain élan and was, by all accounts, a snappy dresser.

As a light drizzle fell coating the surface of the road in a thin layer of ice, they gossiped about the mistakes in the show and the high standards Gilbert demanded from his company. He was known to be influenced by a theatrical genius called Tom Robertson, the man who created cup and saucer realism. Gilbert wanted truth in his productions and an unusual level of reality in his sets and costume. And also from his actors. He had a reputation as a man to be feared and if he didn't get what he wanted he became angry and confrontational. Only last week, they heard one of the principals had bopped him on the nose.

'Let him come on to me and he'll know what it's about,' said Danny, his hand in a fist.

'He is brilliant though.' Ellen usually took an opposing view to Danny, it was habit and part of their friendship, 'I know he's bombastic but his irony and parody! Those rhymes and puns, it's marvellously intelligent surely?'

'I think it's funny, how he behaves with Mr Sullivan,' Russell said, ' they are so different. One of them sour as a sab, the other looking like a tooth drawer.'

Danny and Ellen laughed. They loved Russell's expressions, they found them poetical, although they were frequently baffled by what they meant.

'I've heard,' said Ellen, 'Monsieur D'Oyly bags is building a new theatre next year, we'll be on the move.'

'This is where we get off,' yelled Danny and they descended the iron staircase onto a street of recently built houses.

Holloway was known as the new suburbia. A place of clerks and managers who travelled every day to work in the city. Rows of terraced houses with curtains drawn protectively across their kingdoms. Respectability was the key word in this part of town. In some ways it was an unusual place for George Tunbridge to live, but in fact it was what all actors of a certain age craved. Security and a knighthood. And Mrs Tunbridge had little time for the theatre, the make-up and smoke girls with their sensuality so far from the femininity of most women were too much for her. It was surprising she had agreed to a party.

The house was tall with a small front garden and a hedge

behind a wrought iron fence. They could hear a piano playing in the front room. Mrs Tunbridge called it the 'morning room.' It was where she entertained neighbours hungry for stories of the theatre. They always went away disappointed.

George opened the door, a glass of soda water in his hand. He never drank at home.

'Welcome to my humble abode,' he said his arms outstretched. 'Go through, there's drinks and eats on the table. Mind the rug, don't drop anything, the wife, you know,' and he tapped the side of his nose with his index finger.

Forty people were crammed inside the small parlour, many from other companies playing in the West End; variety shows, straight plays, the ballet and artists from the community in West London. Mrs Tunbridge circled the room offering cake and a jug of beer, a look of superiority on her face as the bohemians invaded her buttoned-up existence.

A large woman dressed in a colourful kaftan and a turban called them over. Danny enveloped her.

'You were at least two octaves flat this afternoon, Clementine.'

'If I didn't have that stick of Brighton rock singing in my ear hole I might stand a chance. She's got two left feet and a face I'd like to ram into a lemon pie.'

Danny looked across at the slim Eliza with her hair loose on her shoulders, a cigarette between her rouged lips.

'Temper, temper, genius does what it must and talent does what it can.'

'I've always had a soft spot for you, Danny boy. Oh Danny boy …' Clementine began to sing.

Ellen took them to meet a young man with long, wavy

hair and a lily in his button hole.

'He is friends with Oscar Wilde, he's an aesthete too and a socialist,' whispered Ellen excitedly. 'You know Oscar well don't you, Henry?'

'I was at Magdalen with him, yes we were good friends, he was much maligned. They called him effeminate and a dandy. Most people found him immoral but I was drawn to him. He is down from Oxford and lecturing in London. His poetry is interesting, Greek inspired of course, have you read *Ravenna?*'

'I have to say,' said Danny, 'I've never heard of him.'

'He's written a play too, called *Vera*. It's peculiarly Russian in flavour, set in Siberia.' Henry smirked at the memory of some private joke. 'It was produced this year.'

'Does he like Mr Gilbert and Mr Sullivan?'

'Of course, we are friends with Mr Gilbert. I believe he is about to write a piece based on the Aesthetic Movement. The set will have to be full of peacock feathers and blue china, don't you know.'

'Well, I might be in it,' said Russell, not sure what to make of the doe eyes drinking him in.

'Ooh,' Henry touched Russell's cheek lightly with a varnished nail, 'you're a swarthy one.'

Russell grinned, 'I'm afraid I am spoken for.'

'Oh no, not still,' said Ellen. Russell heard disappointment in her voice. He hadn't realised Ellen liked him in that way before.

Someone had opened the curtains and Russell, finding himself alone as Ellen and Danny worked the room, drifted over to look at the moon. It was a perfect circle, brilliant white in a cold, black sky. He could feel the biting air through the half opened window. The sharp London frost was new to him, the cold had a different quality in Cornwall.

He thought of Flo and wondered how she was. He hadn't said goodbye and it haunted him. He knew he had moved so far away from her, it was as if he was in another country. He imagined what it would be like if he asked her to join him. What would she do with her day but wait quietly for him to return from the theatre? How could she live in his tiny room, there was barely enough space for himself. And the company? She would be an outsider, refused membership, not knowing the language and codes to gain entry.

Ellen was suddenly beside him.

'Are you pining, Russell? For home? It took me a year to settle in and I haven't seen my family for so long I've forgotten what they look like. It's the price I have to pay for the life I aspire to and however painful it is, I would do nothing to change it.' She pointed out of the window at the skyline cut out against the belts of drifting fog. 'There is so much opportunity here. London is the centre of the Empire. And there is such change coming. Can you feel it on the streets? I can. Oh it's going to be a good time. I know.'

Russell smiled at her enthusiasm and strength and then he said, 'I was thinking – when you lose something, can you ever find it again?'

'If I had a tattoo for every item I lost I'd look like the *Illustrated News*,' joked Ellen. She put a hand on his arm. It was close and comforting and Russell realised it was what he had been missing. He held Ellen's face and kissed her in a friendly way but she moved her tongue inside his mouth.

'Shall we go, Russell?'

They slipped out into the night and walked for miles before finding a Hansom cab. Ellen paid for it and they climbed the narrow stairs to his room. She took off her dress and lay down on the bed and Russell moved between her open thighs.

Florence woke suddenly and sat bolt upright. Something was wrong. The storm still roared outside and she could hear neighbours shouting to each other. She opened the curtains. Lemon Street was a river of water. At the back of her mind she vaguely remembered Angel calling for her outside the door. She put on her dressing gown and went to her sister's room. The bed was empty. She rushed down stairs to her father's study. In the dimming light of the oil lamp the bed was in shadows, but she saw him immediately sitting in his chair, a glass in his hand. He lifted his head and looked at her. His jowls hanging like pouches either side of his chin.

'Where is she?' Flo tried to keep the anxiety from her voice.

Her father nodded towards the bed. Half-hidden by a paisley, printed eiderdown she could see one of Angel's arms dangling over the side, her nightdress on the floor.

'What have you done to her?' cried Flo. She lifted her sister's naked body from the bed, her dead weight heavy in her arms. She carried her to a chair and lit another lamp. Angel's head lolled forward on her chest. Flo put her cheek to her nose and with relief heard her breathing.

'Have you harmed her, Father?'

'What do you mean? I just gave her a bit of medicine to help her sleep. She will wake in the morning.'

His fingers were twitching and Flo knew he was lying. Now and again he patted his hair over the thinning patch in the middle of his head. She waited for him to speak. When he did it was almost with relief as if she was a priest listening in a confessional box

'I do love her, Florence, more than is good for me. She is like your mother see. When I look at her, I think Isabella has come back to me in her daughter. Sometimes we don't know what wrongs we do.'

Flo felt the shock racing through her as her nightmare became real. Why hadn't she understood it before? She remembered now. Her father thrashing in the water calling her mother's name with his anguished face, the same face he had now, as he dived and broke the surface.

'I must tell you about your mother,' he said.

The wind pounded the rain against the window. In the garden the coup had broken up hours ago. Pieces of wood were floating in a lake of water among the dead chickens.

'You drowned her,' said Flo simply, 'I was there. I remember now. I came to find you. Angel had a baby sickness and I ran to fetch you home. I saw you pushing her under the water.'

'No, no, you don't understand cheild.' His eyes were burning with injustice.

'I know what I saw.'

Angel moved and Flo touched her forehead. It was hot, she could be running a fever. Her father began to mumble and she had to strain to hear him.

'She slipped, she...fell and her struggle was terrible to watch. I did everything I could to reach her. I saw her skirts wrap around her. I searched but she was gone and you were on the path and it was too late. I found a bundle in the mud, but it wasn't her, you saw no more than that, a bundle of old clothes. But you forgot, didn't you? And it was easy for me not to tell you. But now you know and...'

He drank from his glass and fixed her with his eyes, brandy dribbling from his chin.

'You are right, I killed her. It was my fault she slipped. I was vexed as fire and I pushed her away. In anger see, for I cannot describe the words she spoke. But I never meant her

251

to fall, didn't mean it you understand?' The tears rolled down his cheeks.

Flo held Angel in her arms. She didn't want her sister to witness her father's breakdown.

'Have you hurt her, Papa?'

No answer came from Mr Trevern. Whether his story was a delusion or the truth Flo would never know and at this moment she did not care. Angel was her priority. She carried her to the bedroom and laid her on the bed. She fetched a damp towel and put it on Angel's forehead. Downstairs she heard the front door open and slam shut. It was only the next morning she discovered the blood on her father's sheets.

He had to get to St Mary's, the house of God and redemption was the only answer. He prayed out loud as he tried to maintain his balance on the swamped path. It was raised above the road but the wash from the torrent of water covered his feet. Strangely, he had brought his umbrella. It was torn from his hand and in seconds his hair became stuck to his head. The noise of broken trees and objects banging against walls and cobbles was a deafening roar and a large branch almost sent him flying but he managed to save himself.

He never meant to hurt her. He felt her squashed body beneath him and sense had prevailed. He stopped. He rolled off her as if he had been hypnotised and Mesmer had suddenly snapped his fingers. But really he stopped because the fantasy had not lived up to his expectations. She was not Isabella. And afterwards, the guilt swarmed over him like insects on a piece of rotting fruit.

At the bottom of Lemon Street, a cargo boat torn from

its mooring was crashing into buildings. Gigs and barrels were floating window high, chairs and tables and parcels of books, desks with sodden pages of accounts, swimming costumes and shoes and boxes of sugar cane, islands of foliage supporting dead dogs. A man in a dingy was desperately trying to row out of Back Quay against the muddy current as an empty pram raced past him and floated into the maelstrom.

He knew there was no way he could cross the rising water. It was up to his waist. He looked back for a second to the house thinking of his two girls. They would be safe in the top room. Florence would have the brains to take Angel there. He wouldn't worry about them. He hardly registered the moment when he lost his balance. There was a small splash as he was pulled under and he was dragged into Lemon Quay bobbing about in the rubbish, a look of surprise on his face as if a shark had bitten him in half. And then he went under. He surfaced a few seconds later in the Truro River clinging to a log like Captain Ahab. But then he sank without trace.

Angel complained for weeks she felt sore. Flo held her close and gave her camomile baths. Somewhere in the back of her mind she knew she had to take responsibility for her father's abuse of her sister. She hadn't opened the door. She had turned her back on Angel and her father had neatly taken advantage. Her retreat into herself had been selfish and now she had to make amends. Angel remembered nothing of the night her father died and perhaps it was best for both of them if Flo never told her.

Angel's real suffering came from the sudden loss of her Papa. Flo grieved too. They were orphans. She put black curtains at the window and ordered their dresses for the funeral from Mrs Curnow's. Many people arrived to pay their respects, although there was no body. For weeks afterwards Mr Pasco paid for a boat to search the miles of river bank. Mr Trevern seemed to have vanished in the flood. But it was unusual. Bodies usually came ashore. The sea always gave up the dead for the living to bury.

Flo and Angel were in limbo until the funeral day, like phantoms drifting through the empty house. Sometimes Angel imagined she could hear him arriving home and she would run to the hall. Flo would find her patiently waiting by the front door. At other times she would forget and ask where he'd gone? It was a strange world for her without the attention.

As time passed, Flo felt more resigned. She realised it had been a merciful escape for all of them. She doubted he could have given up his love for Angel and inevitably, he would have driven them away again. It would have been tough to move to a strange city. This way they had their home and she had a skill. She was pragmatic. It would not be a bad life.

On the day of the funeral a grey mist travelled up from the sea, drenching the funeral cart in gossamer dew. There was a large turn out. The horse was black plumed and the coffin draped with the Truro coat of arms. In front of the procession, the clay pit brass band serenaded him as it led the mourners to the cemetery at the top of the city. Mr Trevern had bought his plot years ago. He was to be buried beside his wife. Flo and Angel looked down at the gaping hole and wept. They had often gone with their father to tend their mother's grave and now they had two to look after. The newspaper carried a long obituary which said Quentin Trevern was a respected owner of the China Clay Company, giving much attention to the well-being of his work force and an appreciable time to civic duties when required. Also he enjoyed a long relationship with the Truro Amateur Operatic Society, photographing many of their splendid productions. He was a photographer of great magnificence as exemplified by his photos of the new cathedral. His studio was light and comfortable and his speciality had been children. He had never failed to get a pleasing picture.

Flo and Angel came back to the dark house and opened all the windows. Angel practised her piano and Flo sorted through her father's room, putting clothes in a pile for the men in the workhouse. She took the bed linen off the bed and threw it away. By the time she'd finished, the room was empty except for a lingering smell of his cigar and cologne. She went downstairs to the study and began sorting through his papers. And that is where she found her mother's letter, tucked inside a copy of *Madame Bovary*, hidden in the desk.

> *My dearest daughters,*
>
> *I write not knowing when you will read this. Perhaps I am in the next room, an old woman returned home to see my grandchildren or maybe I will be in another country and yearning to see you. I hope that one day you can visit me. I have heard Havana is the most beautiful city. Full of houses like wedding cakes. It will be a long journey for you but I know Florence is sensible and will be responsible for my baby girl. The thought of her lying in her cradle upstairs brings me to tears. But what else can I do my sweetest things? When you are older you will understand what love can do to you. I want you to know how hard a decision it has been for me to leave. The truth is, and I cannot keep it from you any longer, it would be impossible for me to break free from your father without*

the support of the man I love.

If it is in your mind to do so, I would like you to meet him one day. He is very – how shall I say –. passionate! Not at all like any of us. He has a little girl too, just like Angel. Can you imagine! What a happy family we will be when you come and visit me.

Please, forgive me if you can. A heart that is exhausted with grief can never find peace. I will write you as soon as I arrive. I am proud of you my beautiful children.

Your ever loving Mama

Folded inside this letter was another letter in an envelope without a post mark, addressed to Juan. A. Perez, Ave de la Misiones, Habana Vieja, Cuba.

Dear darling one,

You have been gone for – I cannot remember how long, it seems like eternity – and how I suffer! You have no idea what missing you is like and I love you so completely that I pray you do not have such tears and wailing as I do. The ecstasy of your touch never leaves me. My dreams are only of you and sometimes I have to say, when I wake, I reach over to feel the empty pillow in the foolish hope you might appear. I have taken to sleeping in another room, (he makes a constant fuss about it!) But I cannot bear the thought of being in the same bed as him, it would be intolerable.

My sweetest one, I have finally decided I cannot live without you. I am in constant fear I might not see you again. Not even my girls can wrench this pain from me. Oh my love, if only you could only see Angel (It is the English version of the name I know you like so much.)

She is like me in face but I know she is you in nature. I know you would love her. And now we come to it. You see, my dearest, I must leave them in Truro as he has not agreed to let me bring them to you. The choice, as you may imagine, has been a trauma for me, I have been wracked with guilt. It seemed each way I moved I could not avoid some torture to my soul. For weeks I could see no exit from the hell. And then one day, I was walking past the little tavern in Penryn where we used to rent a room, remember? And a blinding light came upon me and I heard your words, 'Come to me Isabella, only action will give you the power to know your heart.' How wise!

My love, I burn for you, I feel intoxicated with our memories, they keep me alive. I feed off them as the roses in the garden feed off the sun and open their petals. Do not desert our love. Have faith. I will be beside you very soon and you can show me Cuba! Ah, what excitement! Be careful not to write again as I am afraid he will only open the letter and destroy it. I will let you know the time of my arrival when I start my journey. I am now putting on my shawl to go for a walk by the river to watch the sunset. You will be with me. My darling I love you, I kiss your kind face all over.

> *Ever yours,*
> *Isabella*

Flo put the letter in her pocket for safe keeping and started to cry. She cried for her mother's lost happiness with the exotic Cuban and she cried for the suffering she had endured. She cried for Angel's lack of maternal love and she cried for her father's stupidity. But mostly she cried at the selfishness of her parents.

31

F lo stood with Angel watching the girls in their aprons and boots, their hair neatly tied with ribbons, some of them huddled in giggling groups, or skipping, others playing hopscotch. Angel looked up at her sister a worried look on her face.

'Will they like me, Flo?'

Flo knelt beside her, 'Of course, you will make lots and lots of friends, and the learning you can do! Just imagine. Cornish girls are brave and stubborn. Come on with 'ee.'

They walked through the gate and the headmistress greeted them. She took hold of Angel's hand.

'I shall introduce you to your class, Miss Trevern. They've all been told of you.'

Angel glanced over her shoulder at Flo, a tear in her eye.

'I'll be here to pick you up, my darling,' called Flo.

At four o clock, Angel came running out of the school laughing, carrying a simple needlework sampler, full of her first day and the very special friend she had made, 'Mary Perkins from up to Trewithian Farm and she's got a pony she says I can ride.'

Flo felt calmed and responsible. She was even more of a mother now but a mother on her own. The quality of their lives depended on her. She had picked up the reins and carried on despite her lack of confidence. To begin with, it had seemed impossible but something inside her had changed, like the blinding light on Paul's Road to Damascus she realised she could be herself. There was no one there to edit her, no one to seek approval from and she hoped, no more lies to be discovered. Her father had gone and she could be her own woman. She needed to concentrate on the studio. Without an income they would have to let rooms or sell the house and that was not her plan.

A few weeks later she employed a housekeeper. Mrs Trevorrow was middle-aged and never stopped cooking. She took care of Angel giving Flo the freedom to build up her reputation as a photographer. This was her chance, the chance she had been waiting for, to make her own photographs in the way she wanted, to use her canny eye to find the elusive, unique moment that would single her out as an artist. And the joy when she saw it, when the unexpected detail happened, the turn of a client's head, the sadness or joy in their eyes, a hand caught touching the back of a roll of hair, a gull perched on a wall a fish head in its mouth, the silhouette of an old man his arm around a young child disappearing up a white road into the horizon, the excitement, the pleasure as she lost herself in the image, as she developed her prints. She needn't have worried, her portraiture was successful, she was considered modern. Her confidence grew. She bought new cameras and travelled the length of Cornwall, from Plymouth to Land's End, her pictures became well known. Sometimes the critical echo of her father would sound in her ears but when one of her photos was printed in the Royal Photographic Society's magazine she finally buried him.

In Newlyn she discovered new friends amongst the 'en plein air' artists who were forming a new community. The extraordinary light in the area had attracted them to St Ives too. They welcomed her when she arrived with her cameras and tripod. She took pictures of the seine boats moored side by side across St Ives harbour, so tightly packed and so many of them you could step off one quay and walk across the floating bridge to the quay on the opposite side. There was the photo of a horse cart loaded with pilchards, the sea lapping at its feet and the women with their baskets on their hips, their skirts caught at the waist as they waded out to unload the catch. The artistes wanted to use her photos, copy them to canvas and in turn she fed off what they were creating, standing behind their easels to understand what view was captivating them. Their painting was different from her father's, freer, more expressive. They loved to paint the slanting rain battering the women with their umbrellas, walking the promenade at Penzance. They felt as she did, that it was only when the artist was released from the studio, that he could be truly creative. She was invited to tea to listen to their ideas. They came from different backgrounds and the conversation was eclectic and wide-ranging. Flo sometimes found it difficult to keep up with them, but they liked her. She had purpose and discipline and a quiet concentration that kept her safe. Any man who thought to conquer her very quickly backed off realising she was untouchable.

One of them, Thomas Gotch was on a visit from London and fell deeply for her. They explored the cliffs together overlooking Porthmeor beach at Clodgy Point and stood side by side gazing at the roaring Atlantic. He held out his arms and inhaled the salty wind, 'Feel the power, Flo,' he said, 'it's infinite.' And she put down her cameras and closed her eyes and let the wet air blow in her face. When she opened them he was staring at the horizon, 'The other side of those waves is America. What bliss!'

He turned to look at her, his eyes glistening, hoping to kiss her. But she had become sad and was quickly picking up her equipment. She strode ahead, her mind elsewhere, and he realised she would never be his. Later in the hubbub of the Swordfish pub on Newlyn harbour, he talked to Walter Langley about her.

'She's been hurt badly,' Walter said, 'I dread to think what that girl has been through. I think it best you marry Caroline, Thomas, you have been engaged for a long time and she wants you. Come back and join us later. Our Miss Trevern is in love with someone else, although she never speaks of it.'

So Thomas went back to London and married his fiancée and Flo's reputation grew.

It was her secret love, nursed in its luscious place, which made her special at her craft. It gave her depth and understanding, an instinctive knowledge of when and where to point her lens. Russell fed into her photographs.

After her trips she would return exhausted to Lemon Street and Angel's boisterous greetings. She'd listen to her sister's school tales, discover a new pet she had found, a shrew she kept in a matchbox, cosy in cotton wool, a frog who leapt from the pond into her lap and finally a kitten who had crawled through a hole in the wall mewing for milk. So now they had Kitty. She slept arrogantly on Angel's bed and eventually found the shrew in the box and ate it.

A frequent visitor to the house was Mr Saunders. He came down from London to do business with Thomas, the carpet man at the top of Lemon Street. It was easy for him to drop in and Flo and Angel liked his jokes. They had many evenings playing parlour games before he returned to his hotel. Flo enjoyed his company but always kept him at a distance. Russell still walked beside her as if he was living a parallel life. Sometimes she could reach out and touch him.

One day Flo said, 'Take down the drapes, Mrs Trevorrow we will have light in this house. And order paint. Lots of it. I want white and I want blue.'

Mrs Trevorrow turned up her nose but wasn't in a position to question her employer's taste. So she arranged for her son to come and paint the house from top to bottom as Flo put her father's furniture and paintings up for auction. Every evening Angel came back from school to find another room changed. Mr Trevern's friends gossiped behind her back but Flo carried on with her home improvements until she had each wall painted white. She couldn't wait for summer to see it light up in the sun.

32

The steamship leaving Liverpool for America loomed massively above Russell as he waited on the gangway. A band was playing badly on the quayside and rows of flags strung along the different levels of the liner fluttered in the wind. People called and blew kisses to friends and relatives standing behind a barrier. A steward pushed past him ushering some of the company and their luggage to their cabins. It had been two years since he joined the D'Oyly Carte and he had a part in *Iolanthe* which was playing at the Standard Theatre on Broadway. Arthur Sullivan had written the music at Pencarrow House near Bodmin, he had to have a Cornishman in the cast. Danny was already aboard and unpacking in the second class shared cabin, but Ellen had decided not to come. Her involvement with the suffragette movement was taking up all her time and she decided to leave the D'Oyly Carte. William Morris was helping her with money and when she needed extra funds she gave recitals at dinner parties in aristocratic homes in Eaton Square. It was the perfect opportunity to convert the upper classes to socialism. She kissed Russell goodbye with her love, their affair had been over long ago and New York was beckoning. Arthur Sullivan had told him he could have a great career if he wanted it. He was a natural.

He squeezed past a group of chattering women dressed in their Sunday best and walked along the wide deck to the bow area. The band was now playing 'Slap bang, here we are again.' It sounded incongruous and wistful like a strange lament for an English way of life. A gull flew close, swooping in circles as it landed on the hand rail beside him. It looked up quizzically, a beady eye primed for food. He gazed out at the bleak Irish Sea so different from the blues of a Cornish cove and nostalgia hit him. He was back in Cornwall with Florence, innocent in the washlands, together in the long grass with a pillow of leaves making love in the warm, humid afternoon. A loud hooter made him jump. The massive ropes holding the iron ship on its mooring were untied, but the gangway was still there, ready for last minute boarders. Danny appeared on the second class deck and looked down at him.

'Come on Cornish, get your ass up here, we're having a sing song and we need a baritone.'

The ship heaved and creaked and unnoticed by the crowds on the shore, it gently pulled away.

As spring brought warm air threading through the streets, Truro seemed unchanged. The children played shove-half-penny on stone steps, the schooners sailed in, unloaded the wood and coal and drifted noiselessly up the river, neighbours engaged in never-ending gossip and feuds were continued

But much had changed in the house on Lemon Street. Children's laughter could be heard in the garden and music often played through the open windows. Inside, the furniture was lighter and simpler, some of it hand-painted in blues and pale pinks. On the white walls hung framed photos of Truro's well known characters, Ben Little the wassailer, holding a bowl of apple wood, white-bearded John Ogders, the town crier and old Mrs Peters in her white cap outside the almshouse in Pydar Street. Flo had captured a beat of the city that soon would be lost.

Angel had grown taller and become headstrong. There had been many times when her teacher tentatively knocked on the door to complain about her defiant moods.

'She's a proper wiz, I can't do a thing with her. She's clever mind and can do the learning, but she's got a way with her that is artful see, and I think she be too big for her shoulders.'

Florence listened politely and made assurances that things would change but inside she smiled. Her sister had a Latin temperament and there was nothing to be done about it. She was giving Angel the freedom she never had. She kicked off her shoes and ran wild. Florence could see the woman she would become and felt happy.

One morning Flo photographed Mrs Frith again. The old woman looked into the camera with a slight squint and the air of the elderly who have become forgetful.

'You're your father's daughter, I'll say that for 'ee. He'd be proper blawed to see you running the business, although he is very much missed, that's for sure. He didn't belong to go like that. 'Twas a terrible flood. I heard Mr Tonkin lost all his sheep.'

'I am ready to do the photo now. Is he asleep?'

Mrs Frith looked down at her grandchild on her lap and her face softened like a sponge cake.

'Now when I say yes, think about how you feel about baby David there. Yes.'

After Mrs Frith had left, Flo took the film into her dark room and tidied up the mess from her day's work. A cloth slipped from her hand and as she straightened she noticed for the first time the piles of boxes stacked against the wall. Why hadn't she moved her father's photos somewhere else? How could she have forgotten? This was the only room she had not cleared of his memory. Tucked away in a corner, underneath a black camera drape she found more boxes, each one marked 'private.' She heaved one of them to the middle of the room and untied the string. Some of the plates had collected a layer of dust but they were carefully stacked in rows for easy access. She took out a glass negative of Angel. The position was alluring. She sucked a sherbet dip, her large eyes made dewy and grown up by the angle of the camera. She wore a piece of muslin draped like a Grecian costume. It hung over one shoulder leaving the other one bare where her blonde curls tumbled. Carefully positioned against the light the outline of her body showed through the thin material and one of her legs was bent at the knee provocatively. Flo looked closer. There was rouge on her cheeks and her mouth glistened with lipstick.

She smashed the glass on the floor and searched through the rest of the boxes, breaking more plates as she went.

The next day she woke Angel early before breakfast and took her to the studio.

'We are going to do this together,' she said, 'I want you to be here because I want you to always remember this time.'

Angel was serious. She knew her sister was very upset and she needed to make it better for her.

'Of course, Flo, whatever you want me to do I shall do.'

They went out to the yard where their father's prints were piled high in a bonfire. His body of work. All of it. Not one remained.

'It has to go, Angel, and one day when you are a grown woman, perhaps I will tell you why, but for now, you see this match? I want you to light the paper, there. And stand back quickly mind, it will go up like tinder.'

Angel tentatively struck the match and stepped towards the pile. A picture of the half-built cathedral had dropped down and she picked it up and threw it on top with the rest.

They watched the flame catch and the smoke rise in the air over the granite walls. An image of Angel with the Duchess of Cornwall disappeared in a blue flame and rose twisting in the heat.

Flo held Angel's hand as they watched the fire. They were on the edge of their future and as long as the past remained buried, they were safe. Flo knew the bonfire was a ritual, a cleansing, a passing through the labyrinth from one side to the other. If the spirits understood the sacrifice perhaps their father might be saved. It was the least she could do for him.

Through the smoke Flo could see a shape coming towards her. Maybe it was Russell but she wasn't sure, her reasoning told her it couldn't be. She heard he was in America. Mr Saunders always told her about the Savoy Operas. The shape became clearer and more solid. He was getting off the train and carrying his bags down the hill, speaking to the boy selling fresh vegetables from his donkey cart. He was going to Lemon Street!

She rushed Angel away from the studio leaving Mr Trevern's legacy in smoking cinders. They turned the corner where shopkeepers were cleaning their awnings as they received their early morning deliveries. Russell had vanished from her mind and she prayed she wasn't wrong. Maybe the light was playing tricks? Surely he would have sent a letter or word he was coming?

But he wasn't there. Every day she waited and the weeks and months passed. Angel grew taller, her limbs were like young trees reaching high to find the light. Summer came and they watched the carnivals and went to the spring fairs and bought their brass pots from the market. They joined the new bicycle club and got lost wobbling through the narrow, hot shot lanes laden with pinks and ferns and then Nan gave birth to a baby girl. Flo and Angel went to the christening in a flower-strewn church and held a party afterwards at Lemon Street for all her relatives. Jack Peters came. He could hardly walk from his arthritic joints and had to be helped to a chair where he stayed all day, his glass of punch seemingly always full. When his new-born granddaughter was placed in his lap, his craggy face lit up and he cooed to her for hours until she fell asleep, a tiny, burping bundle cradled in his worn hands.

Flo stood by the new French windows that led out to the garden, watching the children of different ages dancing to a fiddler, while friends and neighbours clapped in time under the lanterns in the scented evening. If this was it, she thought if I only had this moment in my life to keep for ever. I would be content. I don't expect much more.

The letter arrived a few days later. It was postmarked New Orleans. Russell said his tour was coming to an end and so was his contract. He had travelled the length and breadth of America and it was a marvellous country. He would love to have the opportunity of telling her about it. He intended to come back to Cornwall before setting off for Milan, where he had an introduction to a company who performed Verdi. He hoped she might spend some time with him. If this was not possible, perhaps she could write to his rooms in London to let him know, so he could avoid disappointment. He said that in all the time he had been away, she was never far from his thoughts.

Flo ran out of the house and down through the town to the fields by the river. She stopped to catch her breath and make sure she was alone before she shouted at the top of her voice, the joy bubbling out of her. He was coming home.